Excerpt from Going to Another Place

"Where am I?" Michael asked.

"This is Delancy Manor. We are an estate outside the village of Darlington in county Durham, England," Mr. Delancy answered.

"What year is this?"

"1815, sir," an older woman said from the foot of his bed.

"1815 is impossible. I was born in 1980 and working a construction job. It's 2008."

Going to
Another Place

Lauren Marie

ISBN-13: 978-1491072257
ISBN-10: 1491072253

DEDICATION

This is dedicated to my family, Alison, Jim and Janet Hall.
I adore you and thank you for your continued support.

ACKNOWLEDGEMENTS:

Thanks go to Jennifer Conner and the folks at
Books to Go Now, for the opportunity.
They've been very patient with all my questions.
I appreciate your understanding.

A huge, back-breaking-hug thank you to my cousin, Chip
Davis, for giving me permission to use the title *Going to Another
Place*. Readers: if you're not familiar with Mannheim
Steamroller's Fresh Aire series of music, I highly recommend you
check it out. The piece Going to Another Place, and all the
albums, helped me wrangle through this story. Their music is
moving, joyous and heartwarming, and always takes me to
another place.
Thank you to my friends and extended
family for their support, too.
To Chris O'Byrne, thank you
for the hard workand kind words.
Gratitude, as always, to my readers, Caitlin Rettinghouse (SOA
unite) and Tiffany Wilde-Hinnenkamp (are the bells still
ringing?) and newbie Elizabeth Ainsley (you're hired). Your
feed back has been great and helpful.

If you have any comments after reading the story
please send them to:
LAURENMARIEBOOKS@HOTMAIL.COM

Chapter One

A bright flash of light exploded in the night sky.

Emma Wallace lay stretched out in the grass on the hillside above Delancy Manor and watched the stars. She often hoped and prayed on the stars that one day a dashing man would come to court her. He needed to be someone smart and strong enough to stand up to her benefactor, Mr. Clarence Delancy. Maybe the exploding star was a sign from the heavens.

She came out to the hillside most evenings to reflect upon her day's work and wonder about what possibly could be waiting for her in the future. It was a warm evening, and the sky looked clear. The bright yellow moon glowed off to the east, and the stars twinkled. The bed of grass she lay on felt cool and pillowed the ground beneath her. She did this same thing for so many evenings over the last ten years, watching the changes in the night and wishing on the stars.

On this evening, she saw one of the stars blaze in the sky. She sat up and watched with wonder as its shape stretched and glowed. Her brow creased as it became apparent the star was actually moving. She stood up, bending her neck to watch its progression. She clasped her hands in front of her and waited, almost breathless.

What unusual behavior for a star, she thought. As it came nearer, her heart began to race in her chest.

The area around the base of the hill became lighter and lighter, almost like daytime. Quite suddenly, a bright ball of flame flew over her head, and crashed into the trees.

"Oh, oh my," Emma whispered. Grasping her skirts, she pulled the hem of her dress up and ran toward the tree line. Several of the firs and cedars caught on fire as she made her way to the place where the star came down. She saw men who worked for Mr. Delancy run from the other side of the field, carrying torches and buckets of sand. There was no water source out in the trees and fields; Emma hoped the men wouldn't have to battle a huge forest fire. She continued toward the area that glowed. Smoke from the burning trees made her eyes burn, but she wanted to be the first to reach the spot in the woods where the star landed.

Although the moon shone bright, the cover of the trees made it very dark. Light swirled around, and she wasn't certain if it was from the fire or from the star. She squinted to see better through the smoke. She moved forward, and looked in all directions, trying to find the fallen object. A shower of sparks flew down from one of the tall trees, and the ground around her flamed. She danced away from the fire, patting the bottom of her dress where the sparks caught. She bunched the hem around her thighs to keep it from brushing against the ground.

Up ahead she saw something she couldn't identify. She quietly made her way to it, and stared. She had no idea what it could be. It was bright yellow and looked like a bowl, but it didn't resemble any china she had ever seen. She bent at the waist and picked it up. It felt light, but not like any kind of porcelain or glass. Tapping a finger on it, there was no ping, like with a glass. She flipped it around, and continued to examine it. She saw some kind of straps on the inside, with the name Drury written on them. She was very intrigued.

She heard a low moan come from the other side of some bushes. Mr. Delancy's workers weren't far behind her, and for a moment, she thought it might be wise to wait for them, but the moaning became louder. She moved toward the sound, around two trees twisted together. On the mossy ground by a row of bushes, lay a man. He was on his side, trying to push up on his arms, but kept falling back onto the ground. He wore the oddest clothing Emma had ever seen. He was very tall and his hair seemed nicely cut around his ears, but it was too dark for her to see the color. The sounds of voices shouting came up behind her.

"Sir, are you in need of assistance?" she asked, holding the yellow bowl tight in her hands.

The man looked over his shoulder and coughed. "I think I've broken my leg," he said, and passed out.

One Hour Earlier

Michael Drury looked out at the city of Seattle from his perch and heard the horn from a ferry as it approached the dock on Elliott Bay. It always made him smile to hear the city noises all the way from the top of a building.

It was a cold and rainy day, but from where he sat, the city scape looked gorgeous. He straddled a steel girder, forty-eight floors up from the ground. He'd been doing some minor repair welding, and after he turned off the torch, he listened to the noises around him. He loved the peace of just breathing. He looked out at Elliott Bay, watching the ferryboats and container ships come and go. It could be raining and pouring, but he didn't care. He loved being outside and watching life move around him.

He felt a hand tap his shoulder. He turned. Behind him, balanced in a squat on the beam, was his co-worker and friend, Jackson Davis. He was equal in height to Michael, which made them see eye-to-eye, easily. The guy had shaved his head and seemed to think he resembled Vin Diesel. Michael told Jack to grow up.

"Hey dude, you gonna sit up here staring off all day or what?" Jack grinned and stood up to his full height. "Are you coming out tonight to watch the baseball game?"

"Yep. Are we doing Parker's or Charlie's?" Michael brought his feet up and stood smoothly.

"The chicks at Parker's are hotter," Jack said, walking toward the building.

"I swear, Jack. Don't you have a girlfriend? If you're playing around, I hope you're practicing safe sex." Michael shook his head, following his friend onto the forty-eighth floor.

"You're kidding, right? I'm a stockholder in Trojan." He laughed, stepped onto the open floor and turned around. "Rachel and I are still getting acquainted."

"You've been with her for six months. How long can it take to get to know someone?"

"A lifetime, dude. She started talking about moving into a house together." Jack shivered. "That's a bit close for the first six months."

"Take it while you got it, man. Forget your divorce and go for it. She seems really nice and, if I remember right, she can cook. My mom would say that's a keeper quality." Michael walked the beam to the building with balance and grace, and caught up to his friend. "Are we going to get dinner first, or is it a nacho night?"

"Either's fine with me. I hope we can find you a babe. You've been a cranky ass lately. You need a woman." Jack continued to grin.

"I'm beginning to think the woman for me isn't in this country. Like maybe she's living over in Europe or South America. It could be time for a vacation to the South Pole. I need to get my mom to shut up. She's been on the grandmother march again."

Michael's friend tried for months to find him a date. He'd seen several women over the years, but hadn't found the one. He'd always felt he was a bit of a dreamer, and he'd never admit it to anyone, but he wanted the kind of relationship his mom and dad had built. They'd been married for twenty-five years, and there hadn't been a day that they didn't seem more in love than the last.

"Tell her your swimmers are in lock-down for now. Six o'clock at Parker's?" Jack asked.

"You're such an asshole. I'm not mentioning my anything to my mom. Is anyone else..." Michael heard shouting off to the left. He looked and saw a load of drywall swinging from a chain. "Shit, the main line snapped," he shouted, and sprinted toward the other end of the building.

The drywall was being brought up by a crane on top of the building on the fiftieth floor, two levels above them. Men pointed and yelled. One had a walkie-talkie and Michael heard him tell the crane driver to stop the haul; they had to get the pallet to stop swinging. If it hit the building it would break apart, damage the building, and could kill the people below.

Michael and Jack went around to the left and looked at the problem. "I can see the line," Michael said, inching to the edge of the building. "I'll go out on the beam. Have the driver lower the pallet slowly."

"Wait! Wait, dude, you need a harness," Jack said, moving back to where they'd originally been, to retrieve the safety gear.

Once Michael was hooked up, he inched his way out onto the steel beam. The pallet had slowed, swinging like a pendulum, but the wind made the thing move in circles. Michael got down on his stomach, making his way under 1500 pounds of drywall. When he got to the other side, he looked over his shoulder. He could see the loose rope hanging below the pallet. He pushed himself into a sitting position and turned around to face the swirling bulk. All he needed to do was grab the rope. They'd be able to get it under control if he could do that one thing. From where he sat, Michael realized his arm length wasn't going to reach far enough. He'd have to stand. He slowly got his feet under him and straightened up. He grabbed the rope and, with all his strength, got the pile of drywall stabilized.

He pulled the walkie-talkie out of the harness. "Tell the crane to move it to the building slowly." He put the receiver back into the holder and got ready to direct the pallet.

A gust of wind jarred the drywall, but Michael held it steady and kept it from swinging again. Before he realized what happened, the crane operator swung the pallet away from the building instead of toward it. The pallet hit Michael full-on and knocked him off the beam. He hung facedown and could hear yelling above him. The walkie-talkie slid out of the harness, and he watched it fly down forty-eight floors. He laughed; somehow he'd managed to keep the hard hat on his head.

Something moved on his back, making him think the men were pulling him up. It wasn't until he heard the snap that he realized the harness was pulling apart, and if he didn't get hold of something real quick ... Just then, the harness let loose, and he fell. He wasn't floating either, when he started his descent back to the ground.

He saw flashes of light that seemed to be traveling with him. It was cold, and the air blew so hard he couldn't open his eyes. And then, he passed out.

It was dark, wet, and mushy when Michael came to. His leg screamed at him. If he could push over onto his back, it would help immensely, but every time he pushed up he slipped back down. When he tried to move his leg, he ground his teeth together to keep from screaming.

He thought he heard an angel's voice ask if he needed help. He looked over his shoulder and found the face that belonged to the voice. She was beautiful in a clean and simple way. It was too dark to tell the color of her eyes, but he could see concern and wariness in them. He thought she was the most beautiful woman he'd ever seen.

Michael didn't know what to say. He mumbled, "I think I've broken my leg." Then he was floating again. He thought he was being carried somewhere and knew he drifted in and out of consciousness. He wished he'd settle and wake up in the hospital. He'd fallen forty-eight floors. How could he still be alive? He should be squashed like a bug on a windshield or road-kill. Maybe he was. He wondered if he was dead and going somewhere else. If he could just open his eyes and see what surrounded him.

When he finally stopped moving, someone was removing his clothes and he felt a searing pain in his leg, which made him want to shout out very loud.

The next thing he knew, he felt a cool cloth on his forehead. He could hear humming and opened his eyes.

Chapter Two

Emma attended to the stranger night and day, for the better part of a week. Mrs. Tharp helped Mr. Smithee get the man undressed and splint his leg.

Mr. Smithee is a pastor at the church in Darlington. He wasn't a physician but had taken care of many broken bones over the years. He put a splint made of two long sticks, on the man's leg to keep it from moving. Emma hadn't been allowed in the room then, but heard the stranger scream.

Mrs. Tharp came out of the room looking very pale and Emma could tell by the look on her face that things were very grave. She said she'd gotten the man into one of Mr. Delancy's nightshirts and he seemed settled.

As Mr. Smithee left, Emma heard him say to Mr. Delancy that he hoped he wouldn't have to take the leg. They would need to wait a few days and see how things progressed. If gangrene set in, the leg would have to be taken and likely the man would die. Emma felt horrified, and she became determined to do everything possible to keep it from happening.

Emma hummed and talked to the man as she cared for him. She told him about Delancy Manor and all the intriguing things going on around there. She tried to keep his brow cool, but could tell he had a fever. He dripped with sweat and moaned. He also said some very odd things. He'd said not to bother him since he was watching TV and needed someone called Harley Davidson. She found his voice odd, too. It was all too obvious he didn't come from Darlington or this part of the world; his accent sounded very different.

When Emma was twelve, she watched a fever take her parents. It ravaged the whole eastern part of England. She felt determined not to lose this man. If he was the one Helga, the seer, told her of, she would see to it he healed.

Mr. Delancy, her guardian, had been a business partner of her father's and was kind enough to take her in when the need arose. He'd provided a home for her and gave her much-needed guidance. Emma would be forever grateful to him for his kindnesses.

At eighteen years of age, Mr. Delancy began to make noises about a possible union between Emma and him. She could not think of a worse proposal. He was a man in his forties and to her seemed as a father would be--not a husband. She broached the issue with him gently, which he accepted, but he'd moved into a new role of matchmaker. He spent much time over the last four years trying to find her a proper suitor, bringing gentlemen from the city to visit. None of them were what she dreamed of, and she wouldn't agree to any proposals.

Mr. Delancy owned a large property with herds of sheep and fields of grains. His fortune had been made in the grain market, and he loved working the land. He enjoyed lambing season when the new little ones would bounce around the fields. She enjoyed that time, too. She loved to see Mr. Delancy smile.

In the spring, the Travelers came to till the fields and shear the wool from the sheep. There was a fortune teller amongst their tribe, an old woman named Helga who told Emma, just a year ago, that her man would come to her. He would travel from the stars on a bright, flaming light. The seer told her to be patient, and she would find happiness with a very good man.

Emma rinsed out the cloth and turned to put it over his forehead again, when she saw he had his eyes open. She smiled down at him. "Hello, sir."

He frowned and tried to say something, but started coughing. Emma got up and poured a glass of water from a pitcher on a cabinet. She helped him sit up, held the glass to his lips and he swallowed the water. He lay back down, put his hand over his eyes and rubbed them.

"Are you an angel? Am I dead?" he asked in a hoarse voice.

"An angel? Oh, heavens no, sir, and you are quite alive, I assure you. Although there have been moments over the last few days when we were not certain you would make it. Now I think you are going to be all right," she answered, smiled and wondered why he thought he was dead.

"Where am I?" he whispered.

She sat on the edge of the bed, and folded her hands on her lap. "You are in Delancy Manor, sir," she replied quietly.

The man took his hands off his eyes and frowned again. "Where?"

"Delancy Manor," Emma said more slowly.

"Is it some sort of rehab?"

Emma thought for a moment. "I am sorry, but I do not know. What is a rehab?"

"Is this a hospital or something?" He pushed himself up a little and looked around the room.

Emma stood and adjusted the pillows behind him. She poured him another glass of water ◯ Should continue ⊘and handed it to him. "I promise you, sir, this is not a hostel or a poor house. Mr. Delancy has guests from the city from time to time, but not regularly."

"No, I didn't say 'hostel,' I said 'hospital.'" He must have seen the confused look on her face. "What city is this? Am I still in Seattle? Where's my mom?"

"Well, we are outside Darlington by several miles. I do not know the name Seattle and who is your mother? We can get a message to her." She stopped again.

"You mean Darrington?"

"No, sir. I mean Darlington. I am sorry; I can see by the look on your face I am not being clear." Emma tried to figure out how to communicate with this gentleman. She smiled. "Sir, let us start over. May I ask your name?"

He looked at her strangely, and then nodded. "Yes, I'm sorry. I'm Michael Drury..."

"Ah, Drury. I know the name. It was written in the yellow bowl. Are you by chance related to the Drury's from Lincolnshire? Is that where we can find your family?" When he didn't answer, Emma continued. "My benefactor, Mr. Delancy will be able to help us. I am obviously muddling things up." She started to turn away from him. He reached out and grabbed her wrist.

"Wait, I'm sorry, this... I'm confused. I fell off of a building and should look like road kill." He frowned up at

14

her. "Your accent...where are you from? And, what did you mean about a yellow bowl?"

"I was born here in Darlington. My name is Emma Wallace. I noticed your accent, too." She smiled again. "I found the yellow bowl by you the night you fell from the stars." She stood up and retrieved his hard hat from the dresser.

Looking at it, he sat back and said, "I fell off the building in Seattle, but they brought me to Darrington to recover. This doesn't make any sense. I didn't even know there was a hospital in Darrington. Why didn't they take me Harborview or Swedish?"

to "No, no, Mr. Drury. It's not Darrington; it is...we are not Swedish. Oh dear, let me get Mr. Delancy. Hopefully he will be able to make things clearer."

* * * * *

Michael watched the woman leave the room and looked around again. On the bedside table was an oil-burning lamp, and he noticed two others around the room. Looking at the walls, he didn't see any light switches or plug-ins.

He frowned again. The bedcover was a sheet and quilt. He lifted it up and saw he wore a nightgown. It didn't look like the usual, fashionable, butt-exposing hospital gown.

No wonder I'm so uncomfortable, he thought, and then saw the splint on his leg. Two pieces of board followed the length of his leg. It looked as if a sheet had been torn into strips to secure it to his extremity. As he looked closer he saw black and blue from his thigh down to his toes.

15

He pulled the gown off and threw it on the floor. He put his hand back over his eyes, trying to think. Was this some sort of strange rehab? Why didn't he remember coming here? Where was his mom or the members of his crew? The questions stormed his brain, and made him tired. He started to drift off to sleep and found his dreams a puzzle.

When he was young, his father taught him wood crafting. They'd built bookcases and cabinets for their home and for friends. When he graduated from high school, Michael applied and was accepted as an apprentice on a construction crew. He'd spent the last ten years learning the trade. The construction market went up and down, but he worked with a good crew. No matter what they built, it always left him with a satisfied feeling when they completed a job.

His father passed away from a heart attack a couple of years back, and Michael missed him terribly. The elder Drury instilled in Michael an honor and dignity that, as the boy became a man, showed in all he accomplished. His father's standards were very high. Michael cherished the memories of the time they'd spent together in the shed behind their home, and he hoped to live up to those standards and make his father proud.

Michael's younger brother, Neil, was the complete opposite. He'd been born with a mind for science and mathematics and preferred sitting in front of his computer, rather than outside in the fresh air. Neil, a senior in high school, was one of the top students, and many colleges around the country approached him with scholarship offers. The brothers spent many years teasing one another, but were still very attached.

He heard a slight cough in the room, which caused Michael to open his eyes. A tall man with short, red hair and green eyes stood next to the bed. He was overweight around the middle, and Michael thought, *This guy needs some exercise.*

"Mr. Drury, I am pleased to see you awake. My name is Clarence Delancy. Your nurse, Miss Emma, tells me you are a bit confused about where you are and how you came to be with us. We, too, are confused by how you came to be in the back field, dressed as you were." Mr. Delancy picked up a straight back chair and moved it next to the bed. He sat down and adjusted his jacket, which looked to be made of crimson velvet.

Michael shook his head and looked at the woman who picked up the nightgown and stared at him with her mouth open. He felt his brows come together.

Another older woman with gray hair swept up in a bun, came into the room with a tray, and Mr. Delancy introduced her as Mrs. Tharp.

"I have brought you some tea and biscuits. I thought you might be a bit peckish," she said, and poured cups of brown liquid from a pot.

They all had accents, which reminded Michael of watching Masterpiece Theater on TV. He felt as though he'd entered an *Upstairs Downstairs* episode.

"Where am I?" he asked, as he accepted the cup from Mrs. Tharp.

"This is Delancy Manor. We are an estate outside the village of Darlington in county Durham, England," Mr. Delancy answered.

"England? That's not possible," Michael said, looking at the woman. It suddenly occurred to him that both women wore long dresses and their hair up in buns. He looked back at Delancy.

"Mr. Drury, where are you from?" the man asked.

"Seattle," Michael said, a bit wary. Mrs. Tharp put a plate of cookies in front of him. She kept calling them biscuits. He took one and shoved it in his mouth. He smiled at her, trying not to talk with his mouth full. His mom would kill him. "Thanks," he said, and spit some crumbs onto the sheets.

Mr. Delancy's brows came together as he thought about the name. "I am not familiar with the name. Where is this Seattle?"

He finished chewing the cookie and took a gulp of what turned out to be pretty good tea. "Washington, in the United States," Michael said.

"Ah yes, the colonies. You are a long way from home, sir. What brings you to England?"

Michael adjusted himself on the bed again and took another sip of the tea. "Mr. Delancy, I know I'm going completely nuts, but I'm not certain how I came to be here. I was welding a cross beam on the forty-eighth floor of a building in downtown Seattle when there was an accident. The last thing I remember...the ground came up really fast." He looked at the woman again who still stared at him.

Mr. Delancy followed his line of vision and turned to look at her. "Emma, please close your mouth. It is unseemly."

Her face flushed red and she smiled shyly. "I am sorry, sir. I have never heard an accent like his before."

"Miss Wallace, he is still a guest," Mr. Delancy said firmly.

"Of course. I apologize, sir." She turned and moved away from the bed.

"Mr. Delancy, if I could use a telephone, I'm sure we could get this sorted out," Michael said, and placed the empty teacup on the night stand.

"Sir, I am unsure of what you are saying. What is a telephone?" the older gentleman asked.

Michael started to laugh and then stopped when he looked at the three people watching him. "What year is this?"

"1815, sir," the older woman said from the foot of the bed.

Michael sat up too fast, and grabbed his leg in pain. The woman called Emma moved over to help him get comfortable again. Once he was settled, Michael looked up at Delancy. "1815 is impossible. I was born in 1980 and I'm twenty-nine years old."

The room became silent for a moment. Mr. Delancy stood up and straightened his jacket again. "Mr. Drury, it would seem you are still in need of rest. Miss Emma will continue to care for you diligently, I am sure. We will speak again when you are thinking more clearly." He turned and left the room, with Emma behind him.

Michael was completely flummoxed by what he was hearing from these people. 1815 was just absurd. What was this, H.G. Wells, *The Time Machine*?

Chapter Three

Mr. Delancy stopped suddenly in the hall and turned around. "That man is completely balmy. 1980, he says was his birth. That is almost 200 years from now."

"Sir, please," Emma implored him. "The gentleman still has quite a fever and could be delirious from that or the fear of possibly losing his leg. We must have patience, Mr. Delancy."

"Of course. You are correct, Emma. With you and Mrs. Tharp caring for him I am certain he will be recovered in no time. See if you can get him to stop talking nonsense."

"I will do my best, sir," Emma said, as Mr. Delancy walked down the hall.

She realized she still held the nightshirt. She wondered why it was on the floor, and then blushed. It came to her that he wore nothing else below the bed sheets, which made a strange warmth spread through her. She spent a moment trying to calm herself and then walked back into the room.

Mrs. Tharp poured the last of the tea and prepared to leave. Emma put the nightshirt on a cabinet by the door, and then moved to an overstuffed chair, picking up the embroidery she'd been working. She adjusted the oil-burning lamp to get better light and started to stitch.

21

"Your benefactor thinks I've lost my mind," Michael spoke to her from the bed.

"No, nothing of the sort, Mr. Drury. It is obvious you have been through a trauma and just need to get it worked out with yourself. I am sure it will be clearer in a day or two," Emma said, pulling the needle through the pillowcase she working on.

"What year do you think it is?"

"1815, to be sure. I do not think it; I know it for certain. I was born in 1793, so if it were really 2008, I would look very ancient by now." She smiled at him.

"Emma Wallace. Are you related to William Wallace?" he asked.

"William Wallace," Emma laughed. "Ach, no. You do mean the Scottish rebel from long ago?" She watched him nod his head. "Nay, not likely I would be related to him. How did you hear of him?" She set her stitching aside.

"I saw a movie called *Braveheart*. Four hours is a long time for someone my size to sit in a theater, but it was a really good film, and I hardly noticed the time passing," he told her.

"You have been to the theater?" She stood up and walked to the end of the bed. "How often do you get to attend?"

"I don't know. We go once every couple of months or so. I've taken dates there."

"On many occasions, I have tried to get Mr. Delancy to take me into the city to go to the theater, but he is too busy with his work. You said 'we' go. Are you married?" She tried being quite serious, but noted Michael was trying not to laugh.

"No, not married. I go with friends or take dates."

"Dates? What do you mean?"

"When men and women go out together it's called a 'date'. Surely you've been on a date before?" He chuckled.

She frowned and looked down at the bed. "There was a word you used a moment ago that I did not recognize. It was something about moving and film?"

"Do you mean movies?"

"Yes, that was it. What are movies?" she asked.

"Seriously, you've never been to the movies?" She shook her head 'no' and he put his hand to the side of his face. "What about moving pictures? No wait, that would be later. If it's really 1815, I don't believe movies have been invented yet."

Emma looked at him, and wanted more of an explanation. He spent the next half hour trying to explain and eventually talked himself to sleep.

Chapter Four

A couple of days passed quietly. Emma and Mrs. Tharp did their best to keep Mr. Drury entertained. It was difficult though. He allowed them to read to him, but after a while he'd fall asleep. They brought him several books from the manor's library, and as long as it wasn't in Latin, he could read it. One evening, they asked if he'd like to play a game of whist, or perhaps chess. Mr. Drury taught them card games called Texas Hold 'Em and Screw Your Neighbor. Neither of the ladies could quite figure out what the names meant, but laughed and enjoyed themselves very much. He showed Emma, Go Fish and Crazy Eight's when they were alone.

Mr. Smithee came to check on Mr. Drury's leg at the end of the second week. He announced that it looked much better and he didn't think he'd have to remove it. He recommended Michael stay in bed for a couple more weeks at least.

The patient wasn't having any of that. He asked Emma if she knew where he could get a set of crutches. When she looked at him blankly, Michael described them to her. Finally, he saw her smile, and nod her head.

"Of course, those would be walking sticks. I will go find Bailey. I am certain he will know exactly what you are describing." She left the room and came back with a man whom she introduced as Mr. Bailey. He worked for Mr. Delancy and, was apparently very good with woodwork.

Michael explained what he wanted and even made a drawing for Mr. Bailey. The man scratched his chin and looked at the drawing.

"Yer 'bout eighteen hands, yes? I would say if we make 'em 'bout fifteen hands, it might work for you. I think I might be able to find some sticks long enough," Mr. Bailey told him.

"I'm not sure what you mean by hands, but thank you. I'm six-foot, four inches if that would be of any help."

"I am not sure what you mean, sir, but I will do my best."

Michael noticed a small grin and twinkle appear in the workman's eyes. He relaxed back onto the bed, but wondered what the man found so humorous. The two men shook hands, and Mr. Bailey left the room.

"Mr. Drury, why are you in such a hurry to get away from the Manor?" Emma asked.

"It's not that. No, I'm just not used to being inside and lying around so much. I love being outside in the fresh air as much as possible. I'm one of the few who actually likes to work," Michael answered.

"Do you work outside all the time?"

"Pretty much, yes. I'm a construction worker. I mostly do welding, but I can do just about anything except electrical and plumbing. I stay away from those jobs."

"So, you work outside a lot?" she asked again.

"And camp and fish. I used to hunt, but I shot an elk once and that was enough. Too much blood, and the thing was covered with ticks. It had the biggest, brown eyes I'd ever seen, and I felt guilty for weeks after I took its life." Michael shook his head with the memory.

"When you first woke up you said you were working on the forty-eighth floor of a building. Mr. Drury, really, how is that possible?" Emma looked at him, as she stood at the end of the bed. "I have seen tall belfries and towers in churches, I have even heard some cathedrals are very impressive, but forty-eight floors just does not make any sense."

Michael sat and smiled at her. "Why doesn't it make sense to you?"

He saw her brows come together as she appeared to think about it. "Something that tall would surely fall over with nothing holding it up."

"In my time there are buildings well over one hundred floors, and they don't fall over." Michael smiled, arching his brow.

"You are teasing me, sir, and it is not appreciated."

As he watched her turn to get his breakfast plates back on the tray, she spoke about plans for his day. She told him that she wanted to neaten up the room. He may not like it, but he was going to have a bath today. He'd developed a terrible aroma. Although it wasn't the worst thing she'd ever smelled, it was a manly scent, and she knew Mr. Delancy wouldn't approve. Michael kept his eyes on her with a grin and listened to her every word.

"Bailey and a couple of his men will bring the tub up from the kitchen and help you take a bath today, Mr. Drury."

He sniffed around his under arm and then glanced back up at her. "I guess I am getting a bit ripe," he said, with a laugh.

Emma laughed with him, and pinched her nose with her fingers. "You do say the strangest things, sir."

Michael watched her move about the room. "You are so pretty, Miss Wallace. How come you aren't married?"

"I have not found the right match. Mr. Delancy has been very kind and invited many prospective suitors, but I have not met one who could steal my heart," she answered, and pulled a set of sheets out of a cabinet. "I am going to change your bed today."

"Would it be possible to get a razor? I'd like to shave. I probably look like a bear at this point," he said, and scratched his jaw and cheeks.

"I am sure it would not be a problem. Mr. Delancy has several." She lifted the tray and left the room.

* * * * *

In the middle of the morning, Bailey and some of his men came in carrying a large metal tub. After several trips, the men had the tub filled with hot water. Michael felt amazed at the strength of the guys that brought the water up the stairs.

Bailey explained to Michael that he thought Miss Emma was pressing the point about the need to be cleaned up a bit much, but when he helped Michael up from the bed and into the tub, the smell had caused the estate managers eyes to water.

27

"I would say a pig-pen smells better than you sir. Here is some soap," Bailey said, throwing a bar into the water with a splash. "I will wait in the hall. Give me a shout when you are ready to get out."

"No, don't leave, Mr. Bailey." He was curious about the man and wanted to get some information from him. "Tell me about life here at Delancy. What brought you here? What is it you and your men do in a day? " Michael ran the bar of soap around his shoulders.

"I met Mr. Delancy in London. It poured down rain, and I had taken shelter in a pub. He did pretty much the same when his carriage broke a wheel. We talked for a long while, and he said he would give me a good pay and a roof over my head. I could not think of anything better to do, so I came to Delancy."

Bailey told him about the daily work he and his men did around the estate. Besides working the fields, they tended a heard of sheep and a few head of Black Angus cattle. He talked for a bit, and then brought up the walking sticks. "There is one thing though which bothers me. Those pieces which are to hold you up, they could rub some mighty raw spots under your arms, sir."

"Ah, yes, I forgot about that. We'll need to wrap some cloth around them several times. It will give them some cushioning, but I've done crutches before. You're not supposed to bear down on them when you're walking."

"Very good, sir. I will see it is done." Bailey nodded his head.

"How long have you worked here at Delancy Manor, Mr. Bailey?" Michael ducked his head under the water, getting the soap out of his hair.

"Near fifteen years now. I did not 'spec to stay so long, but I cannot think of a place I would rather be." Bailey smiled.

"Is Mr. Delancy a good boss?"

"If you mean does he treat his workers good, aye, he does that."

"Miss Wallace? Does he treat her well?"

Bailey grinned and nodded. "Yes, he does treat her well. I would say he spoils her a bit much. There was a time, a few years ago, we all thought Mr. Delancy was going to wed the girl, but something stopped his courting her, and we know not what happened."

"How did Miss Wallace come to be here?" Michael leaned against the back of the tub.

"Her da owned the estate next to Delancy. Back when she was one and ten, I believe, her folks caught a grave fever. It took them within a fortnight. Mr. Delancy was very good friends with Mr. and Mrs. Wallace and made arrangements for Miss Emma to come live here when they passed. He has kept a watchful eye on her since."

"I see," Michael said, thinking about what Emma must have gone through, losing her parents. It reminded him of the emptiness he'd felt when his own father died so suddenly. "Bailey, I just realized the wood in the splint is soaking up the water."

"No need to worry yourself, sir. Miss Wallace worked it out, and we made you a new splint. I will help ye with it when you are out of the tub. Leave the old one alone for now."

Bailey helped him out of the water. Michael balanced on one foot, drying himself with a linen towel.

"Miss Wallace adjusted some of Mr. Delancy's slacks and a shirt. She believes they will fit you nicely. Would you like to get dressed, sir?" Bailey asked, holding up the slacks.

"Please, call me Michael, and yes, I think it would be great to wear clothes again. I've been naked for almost two weeks now," he answered and laughed.

They changed the splint, and while the men scooped up and emptied buckets of water from the tub out the window, Bailey helped Michael get dressed. The left leg of the pants had been let out a little so that it would fit over the splint. They were made of wool and a bit short in length. It took Michael a minute to figure out the button fly. The shirt was made of linen and collarless. Bailey said there would be a collar and jacket to follow. If Mr. Drury planned on eating his meals in the dining room downstairs with Mr. Delancy, he would be expected to wear a jacket

When Emma came back into the room, Mr. Drury sat in a chair by a window looking out at the front of the manor. When he heard her approach, he turned and saw she was carried a bowl of water, soap, and a razor.

"Does that not feel better, Mr. Drury?" she asked, smiling.

He looked up at her and smiled back. "As a matter of fact, it does. Thank you for making me understand that not bathing for two weeks is a travesty."

"I brought the things I believe you will need to shave. Once finished, I think you will be back in high spirits."

With her help, Michael got his whiskers shaved off. He'd never used a single blade razor before and missed his Gillette steel triple blade. After he'd dried his face, he smiled at her again.

"Not too shabby, Miss Wallace. I think I only nicked myself twice," he said, and looked at the towel for blood.

"Would you like to try coming downstairs for the afternoon and evening? I could ask Bailey to assist you down," she said.

"Well first of all, I'd need my shoes and socks...well, at least for one foot; maybe just a sock on my left foot." Michael looked down at his feet. Even though the break was in his thigh, his foot was swollen, but the black and blue was fading and there were a few patches of pale yellow and green. "I don't think I can get my other shoe on," he said, and looked back up at her, Michael smiled. "Yes, once I have my shoe, I'd love to get out of this room for a bit. Is it warm enough to sit outside?"

"Oh yes. There is a lovely area behind the house, and the sun is shining very brightly today," Emma said. She opened a cabinet and pulled out the shoes he'd arrived in.

Michael felt relieved to see his work boots. It made him feel as though he hadn't lost his mind completely, that at least his shoes were real.

Emma knelt down and helped put his white sock on his good foot. "I do not believe I have ever seen stockings such as these. Are they from Scandinavia?" she asked.

"No, they're from a company called Jockey." Michael saw a frown appear on her face. "A jockey is somebody who rides a horse in races," he said, and suddenly felt as though it could be the dumbest thing he'd ever uttered.

"Races like the Royal Ascot? I have heard of that. I did not know they made stockings." She smiled up at him, arching her brow.

Michael laughed. "Now who's doing the teasing, Miss Wallace?" He watched her shake her head as she picked up his boot and helped him put it on. "You are very good with the laces, ma'am."

"Laces are not very difficult, sir," she said.

"You could make it a little tighter." Michael leaned over to help and realized he had a perfect view of the top of her breasts. They were beautiful and looked very firm in the bodice of her dress. His mouth went dry and he sat up, and clasped his hands together to keep from reaching down.

Emma finished tying the bootlace and looked up at him. He thought she knew he wasn't looking at her, but seemed to be entranced with her chest. As she glanced down and discovered what he saw, he felt the room grow warm and his breath caught in his throat.

Michael's eyes moved up to her face and saw the innocent knowing in her gaze. He unhooked his hands and reached to touch her bottom lip.

"I...I should get Bailey to help you," she stammered as he continued touching her lips.

"Miss Wallace, if you're trying to distract me, it's working." He moved his hand around her neck and pulled her up between his legs.

Emma put her hands on his chest, and applied pressure to push away, but he realized she grabbed the linen shirt, and he felt her hands on his hard chest underneath. He heard her breaths come out in puffs, and when he put his hands on her cheeks, she sighed.

"Miss Wallace, I'd like to kiss you, if I may?"

"I have never been kissed by any man, Mr. Drury," she whispered, looking at him shyly.

"I'll be gentle, I promise." He leaned toward her and brushed her lips with his. "Part your lips slightly."

She did as he said and he moved to her, placing his mouth gently on hers. He slipped his tongue past her teeth, and the room grew much warmer. One of his hands moved down her neck, lightly touching the skin at the top of her dress. His palm moved over her breast, cupping and pressing on it.

Emma's breath caught, and she pulled back. "Mr. Drury," she squeaked, looking at him. "You are causing me a bit of excitement, sir."

"Only a bit? May I try for a little more?" He grinned.

"No sir, really." She moved to stand up quickly and stumbled over his foot.

Michael put his hands on her waist, in an attempt to keep her from falling. "Miss Wallace, I'm sorry. I didn't mean to frighten you." He frowned, and wondered if he really was in 1815.

"I am not frightened, sir. Just shocked," she said, pushing his hands away. She backed up a couple of steps and straightened her dress.

"I did ask permission."

"To kiss me, yes, but not to fondle my..." Her face turned red. "I will get Bailey now to bring you down stairs." She turned and he watched her make way out of the room.

Chapter Five

The air in the hallway felt much cooler, and Emma stopped to catch her breath. She fanned her face with her hand, trying to cool off the heat boiling in her like a pot on the fire.

After she oversaw Mr. Drury's move down into the garden and made certain he was settled in the sun light, Emma excused herself and went for a walk along the hillsides. She passed the tree line where Mr. Drury was found two weeks ago. Her heart still raced; and every time she thought it calmed, she'd remember the feeling of his tongue in her mouth or his hand touching her, and her heart picked up speed again. She felt warm and a strange excitement tickled her insides. She had never known such feelings, and although she liked the warmth, she was frightened by it.

She tried to settle her thoughts, and made her way along the stream but stayed away from the tree line. She sat under a willow and threw rocks into the water. She wanted to make sense of what she felt, and found no way of knowing if her feelings were correct or if she was turning into a harlot.

She thought about what the fortune teller, Helga, had said to her a year ago. A man would come to her from the stars. Could Mr. Drury be the man? There had been a

35

very bright light that evening. It could be possible that he was the one.

Emma put her hands in her hair, and held her head tightly. She felt confused and didn't know what to think. Mr. Drury was very attractive and seemed a gentleman, but today he let his hand wander to her bosom. He could be a rogue and might want to use her in an unseemly manner.

She stood up quickly, and patted down her skirts. She knew who she needed to talk to about the subject. She walked quickly back toward the manor house, hoping she would find Mrs. Tharp available to have a private discussion. The woman was once married and would surely know about these kinds of feelings.

As she made her way through the kitchen area, she grabbed a green apple from a bowl on the counter and took a bite. She wasn't really hungry but needed to do something other than think about Mr. Drury.

"Where have you been, child?" Emma turned quickly, when she heard Mrs. Tharp's voice in the corner of the room. "The hem of your dress is quite muddy."

Emma bit into the apple and looked down at her dress. "I walked along the stream and went much farther than I intended."

"Mr. Delancy was very concerned, and you missed dinner. He thought to send Bailey and the men to look for you, but since you have done this before, he decided not to wait and they have already eaten."

Emma sat down at the table where Mrs. Tharp held a book and a cup of tea. "May I ask a question?" She looked at the older woman.

"You may, but first, do you want something more than an apple for dinner?" Mrs. Tharp closed her book and started to stand up.

"No, I am not very hungry," Emma said quietly, and stared at the piece of fruit. The older woman was as close to a mother as Emma had ever known. "Mrs. Tharp, when Mr. Tharp courted you, when did... I mean, was he...?" She looked away as she blushed bright red.

"Miss Emma, are you being courted?" Mrs. Tharp asked, sitting back down.

"No," she answered flatly. "Most definitely not." Emma thought a moment and put the apple on the table. "Mrs. Tharp, if I tell you something, you must swear you will not tell another soul."

"Of course, I will keep your secret close. What has you so up in arms?" the older woman asked and sounded concerned.

Emma sat back in the chair and looked at her hands. "This morning I helped Mr. Drury put on his socks and shoes and --" she looked across the table at Mrs. Tharp -- "he kissed me," she whispered, and felt the heat rise in her face again. Her eyes were opened so wide, she thought they were going to pop right out of her head.

Mrs. Tharp let out a sigh and chuckled. "Did you enjoy it? Did it make you feel a little wanton?"

Emma stood up and looked down at her with shock. "I felt no such thing, Mrs. Tharp. I should have known he was no gentleman when he threw the dressing gown on the floor and insisted on being dressed in nothing but his..." She stumbled over her words again.

"My dear, if it was so upsetting, perhaps we can delicately tell Mr. Delancy and have him make arrangements for Mr. Drury to convalesce somewhere else. Please, sit back down and calm yourself." The older woman smiled at Emma.

She sat down in her chair very hard. "No. Mr. Delancy would react very ill and would most likely kill Mr. Drury."

"For one kiss? That is very unlikely. Emma, you are being silly." Mrs. Tharp shook her head. "Child you act like you are a puritan."

"Mrs. Tharp, I have never done the likes of this before," Emma said, suddenly afraid. "Oh my, Mr. Delancy can never know. He will think me loose with my morals."

"Emma, kissing a man does not make your morals run away from you. There are some intimate things between men and women that are best to experience after marriage, but to hold hands and kiss is not likely to steal your virginity."

Emma blushed again. "It was truly my first ever, Mrs. Tharp."

"And did you like it?"

She sat back in her chair and thought. "I have nothing to compare it to. It did make me feel rather warm, and my heart raced and thumped in my chest."

"It sounds as though Mr. Drury is practiced at kissing. Did he drool all over you?"

"No," Emma said quietly, and felt at ease with the discussion. "Did Mr. Tharp drool?"

"Oh, my heavens, no, but there was another boy before Mr. Tharp came into my life." Mrs. Tharp raised her eyes to look at the ceiling. "I did not find his kisses to be very attractive."

Emma nodded and became uneasy for not telling when the man touched her bosom. Certainly that action would put her morals into question.

"Mr. Drury did ask about you this evening," Mrs. Tharp said. "He seemed a little sad not to see you at the dinner table and was very quiet."

"He was sad?" Emma asked.

"Yes, dear. I believe you have caught his attention." The older woman smiled.

"Where is Mr. Drury now?"

"Bailey helped him back upstairs and assisted with his getting ready for bed. The walking sticks are being worked on, and Bailey said they should be ready by the end of the week. I think Mr. Drury will be happier to walk on his own."

"I will check on him on my way to bed." Emma smiled at the older woman. "Thank you for your kindness, Mrs. Tharp."

"You are welcome, child. You should stop by the library before you retire and let Mr. Delancy know you have returned."

"Yes, I will." Emma got up and left the kitchen.

She walked down a hallway going to the door of the library, which had been left open. She found Mr. Delancy reading by the fireplace.

"Good evening, sir. I am sorry if I caused you concern," she said. She walked into the library and sat across from him. "The afternoon was so beautiful, and I walked farther than I had planned."

Mr. Delancy put his book on the table next to him and sat forward in his chair. "Miss Wallace, thank you for your apology. I became concerned you might have wandered off of the estate and were taken by bandits."

"No such thing occurred, sir." She smiled at him.

"This Mr. Drury...does he still act strange? He seemed very courteous this evening and only had one glass of port with dinner." Mr. Delancy clasped his hands and looked up at Emma. "He said very little and did not bring up all of the nonsense he was speaking of when he first awoke; when he was falling from a building in ... what year was it?"

"Two-Thousand and Eight."

"Yes, 2008. How silly is that? Is his mind still in a muddle?" Mr. Delancy asked.

"He does still say he is from the future, sir. Mr. Smithee said he seems a healthy man and thinks he may have been through a terrible trauma that caused his mind to be somewhat addled. Mr. Smithee believes with rest, Mr. Drury should come to his senses soon," Emma said, and twisted her hands in her lap.

"Well, if that is what Smithee says, then I guess we should be patient. However, perhaps it would be a good idea for you to limit the time you spend with Mr. Drury. This evening he seemed very one-minded on your whereabouts. I would not want him to have any designs in his head about you," he said.

"Mr. Delancy, whatever do you mean?" Emma asked, astonished.

"Emma, it is known throughout the county that you are going to be quite wealthy in a couple of years. I am sure there are those unsavory types out there who would love to have control of your wealth. They could use you most unsuitably, and as your guardian, I could not stand for it." He looked at her frankly, and then turned to pick up his book.

"I do not believe Mr. Drury is that type of man, sir." She briefly thought about the kiss that afternoon but shook her head. "No, I think he is a gentleman. If he should decide to court me, then I would give him the opportunity to prove himself worthy, sir."

"I see. It is of interest you should feel that way. We shall speak of this again. I think for now you should get up to your room and rest. You have had a long day in the fresh air," he said, opening his book.

"Mr. Delancy, really ..." she started.

"Emma, that will be enough for this evening. We will speak no more of it tonight. Go get some rest," he said, and waved his hand as he would to dismiss one of the staff.

She stood up and said good night. As she walked out of the room, she thought about Mr.Delancy's behavior and wondered if he had really gotten over her refusal to take his hand in marriage.

She made her way up the stairs. Quietly, she opened the door to Mr. Drury's room, she leaned around the door just slightly and looked in. He sat up in bed with a book in his hands. The candle on his night stand had burned half-way down. She tried to close the door silently but heard it squeak.

"Miss Wallace, is that you?" he called from inside the room.

She opened the door all the way and stepped in. "Yes, Mr. Drury. I did not want to disturb you while you read. I just wanted to make sure you were comfortable," she said, as she stood in the doorway.

"Miss Wallace, please come in. I must apologize to you for the way I acted earlier. I shouldn't have been so forward. Will you forgive me please?" he asked.

She took a couple more steps into the room but stood back from the bed. "You are forgiven, sir. Are you comfortable?" She frowned. "Why is your forehead so red?" she asked, as she looked at him.

"It's the weirdest thing. My face feels really itchy. I must have some sort of allergy. Come and talk to me. I missed you this afternoon and would like to just talk to you for a while." Michael set the book aside and patted the bed. "Please."

Emma advanced into the room. She moved a straight back chair from the table and set it by the foot of the bed. "What would you like to discuss, Mr. Drury?"

* * * * *

He watched her movements as she sat in the chair, and folded her hands in her lap. She looked so beautiful, her blue eyes and face calm. For a moment, he wondered what her hair would look like if it flowed down around her shoulders instead of up in that bun, but he stopped himself from letting his mind wander.

"First of all, would you please call me Michael or Mike? All this Mr. Drury stuff makes me uncomfortable," he said, and kept his eyes on her. "I know England prefers more formality, but really I'm not so stuffy."

"All right, you may call me Emma, except when Mr. Delancy is present. He is a stickler for manners," she answered primly.

"Okay, I think I can remember to call you Miss Emma or Miss Wallace when he's around. Now, tell me, are you guys Amish or something?" he asked.

She frowned and sat back in her chair. "What is that?"

"Amish?" He watched her nod her head. "It's a religion. They choose to live simple lives without modern amenities."

"Such as?"

"Well, they don't have electricity or telephones. They don't drive cars or watch TV-- that kind of stuff. I noticed today that you guys don't even have a radio downstairs."

Emma's mouth tried to form words. "You speak such a strange language sometimes," she said, and shook her head. "We are not Amish. We attend the Church of England in Darlington. Are you still feverish?"

"No, I think this is the clearest I've felt in days."

"Mr. Smithee gave you some morphine to help with the pain when you first arrived, but that was almost two weeks ago. It would have worn off by now," she said. "Your words are confusing."

"Morphine? No wonder I felt so weird. I don't react too well to morphine; it tends to make me barf. What do you mean my words are confusing?" he said, almost to himself.

43

"Well, just now you said barf. I have no idea what such a word means."

"I see. It's another way of saying throwing up. You know vomiting?"

"Oh yes, I know this word." She looked at her hands. "How does your leg feel?" she asked.

"Oh, a bit achy. Do you have any aspirin or ibuprofen?" He looked at her hopefully.

"I do not know what those are, sir ... I mean Michael." She smiled.

They became quiet, and Michael could tell Emma was thinking about leaving him to rest. He saw her lean forward to stand and say good night, but he interrupted.

"Okay, so you're not Amish. I have a vague memory of Mr. Delancy saying the year was 1815," Michael said quickly, and noticed she was startled by his statement. She sat back down. He didn't want her to leave.

"That is correct, yes," she answered.

"I must be in a coma in my own time and having a really strange dream." He leaned back into his pillow.

"You said you were from 2008. How is that possible? I mean really, unless God brought you here for some particular purpose, I just do not see how it would be possible to come from a time that has not happened yet. I am sorry, Michael, but it does seem rather delusional," Emma said.

"Yeah, I suppose I could have hit my head and lost my marbles, but I don't think so," he said. "I remember what happened too well." He looked at Emma and could see she waited to hear more about his fall. He told her what happened with the drywall. He saw confusion in her eyes, and after he asked what she didn't understand, he spent a few minutes explaining drywall. He reached up and touched the wall behind the headboard. "This feels like plaster. I think drywall was invented after World War II," he said, and brought his arm down.

He looked at her and saw her cheeks had flushed a bright red. He looked down at himself and found his sheet and blanket had slid down. His groin area showed itself. He grabbed the covers and pulled them back up to his waist. "Emma I'm sorry, I didn't ..."

"No, no," she said, putting her hand up. "You were not aware. It makes me wonder, though why you do not wear a nightshirt?" she whispered. "Sir, you are bleeding." She stood up from her chair and moved to get something to place on his head.

He put his hand up to his head and felt a wet spot in his hair above his ear. He looked at his fingers. They were red. Emma handed him a cloth, which he put on his head. "I must have scratched myself. This is strange."

"You were going to explain why you do not wear a nightshirt." She took the cloth from him and looked at his head, then placed the towel over the spot.

"I have a tendency to sleep pretty warm at night. If I'm wearing pj's, I roast. It gets too hot."

"What are pj's?" she asked seriously.

He felt her pull the cloth away from his head. "Pajamas." He looked at her. "They're similar to a nightshirt, only they have pants."

"Ah, I see." She nodded her head, turned, and moved the chair back to the table by the window. "Mr. Drury, you are a mystery and some of what you say is a different

language to me. With that, I shall bid you a good night."
She smiled, and held the towel as she moved to the door.

"Emma?" he said, looking at her.

"Yes?" She stopped halfway to the door and turned to face him.

"I-I..." he stuttered, and it was his turn to blush. "I find you very attractive. That's why I kissed you this morning."

He watched her smile fade a little as she looked at him. Her cheeks turned red again, and he wondered if she felt the same warmth he did.

"You think me attractive?" she asked.

"I do, yes, very much." He watched the information sink into her brain. "May I kiss you again?"

Emma put her hands around her middle and looked at him. "Michael, this is not appropriate while I am standing in a gentleman's room. Although, Mrs. Tharp said there is nothing wrong with kissing or holding hands, I have a notion of what you are thinking. You did not see me this morning, you saw my bosom and..." She stopped. "I have never kissed a man before..." She clasped her hands in front of her, and twisted her fingers. "I must leave now. Good night," she said, moved quickly through the doorway.

* * * * *

She closed the door loudly behind her and walked down the hallway to the other wing of the house.

Emma went into her own room, and shut the door behind her. She leaned against it feeling her heart pound again. She thought he had cast a spell over her. She was completely taken with this man. She hugged herself and looked at the mirror on her vanity. She sat down, and took the pins out of her hair. Picking up her brush, she looked in the mirror and smiled.

* * * * *

Michael put his arms behind his head and smiled at the ceiling. He still didn't believe he was in 1815, but if it happened that way, he could be happy. Emma Wallace was the most beautiful, wonderful woman he'd ever met. She was simple in her appearance, and didn't need a bunch of makeup or hair spray to add to her attractiveness. Her blue eyes were bright and alert. She could tease him and laugh when he teased her. She was unlike any other woman he'd ever dated, and he found the change refreshing.

He heard the door open and looked up in time to see Emma lean over him. He felt her hair brush his cheek. He put his hands on either side of her face and pulled her lips to his.

She put her fingers over his mouth and looked into his eyes. "You will tell me if I am doing this wrong, please?"

Michael smiled behind her fingers. "You didn't do it wrong this morning."

"Oh," she sighed as he pulled her to him.

Michael pressed his lips to hers. He lightly nibbled her bottom lip and chin. It caused her to open her mouth, and he moved in feeling her warmth. When her tongue shyly touched the roof of his mouth, he wrapped his arms around her and pulled her into a sitting position. She balanced on the edge of the bed next to him. Michael moved his hands up her back and to her shoulders. He pressed his lips against hers more tightly. Their tongues danced, and he found Emma became more passionate, slowly moving her hands around his naked upper body. He felt her fingers smooth along his spine.

He gave her several soft pecks on her chin, cheeks, and eyes. "Emma, I'm so glad you came back," he whispered, and continued the kisses. He put his hands in her hair and felt the soft curls. "I'm glad your hair is down. It's beautiful."

Emma took in a breath, and he watched as she opened her eyes, looking innocently at him. "This does not make me a harlot, does it?"

"No, baby, no way." Michael looked at her seriously.

"I am in a gentleman's room ... a naked gentleman's room. Are you sure I am not a woman of ill repute?"

Michael smiled down at her and ran a finger over her lips. "No ma'am. You are one of the most upstanding citizens I know," he said, and kissed her chin again. "However, if we continue this, with me having no clothes on, your reputation could be damaged. I want you, Emma, but this isn't right. I want it to be right." He hugged her against his chest. "I can feel you shake, and I want you to come to me comfortable and not afraid. Okay?"

Emma sat up and laced their fingers together. She smiled at him. "Get a good-night's sleep."

"You, too." He released one hand and cupped her cheek. "Dream of me, okay?"

They kissed once more. Emma stood and walked to the door. He watched her leave and grinned. Could it possible he'd found the girl of his dreams?

Chapter Six

Several days went by. Bailey finished the crutches, and Michael was pleased to get up and move around again. His leg still hurt, and he was careful not to put too much pressure on it, but the swelling finally lessened and the color changed to a lovely yellow. Mr. Smithee came by and said Michael should keep the splint on for at least another week, preferably two.

Emma and Michael grew closer as the days progressed. They sat in the shade of the trees in the garden and talked about their different lives and worlds. Emma told him she thought he weaved a fancy tale for her. When he spoke quietly of missing his family and friends, he started to feel she believed him a little. He told her about his mom and dad, and that his father died a few years before and how it affected everyone in his family. He said his dad provided something called a life insurance policy from his work that made things easy for his mother. The woman worked hard at keeping her two sons on the correct path. Emma said she wondered if it might be possible he'd done exactly as he said, falling from 2008, and it was a mystery to her, but she was ever so grateful to whomever it was that brought him to her.

Mr. Delancy kept a close eye on the pair. Michael thought the benefactor disapproved of any relations

49

developing between them, but the man, so far, said nothing to him about Emma. The older man was always cordial at dinner or if they met somewhere on the estate. When Emma and Michael walked around the outside of the house, he saw Mr. Delancy watch them from the library windows.

They'd walked to the border of the back field and the tree line. Sitting under a giant oak tree, they enjoyed a peaceful afternoon. Michael looked up at the hillside where he'd apparently been found and wondered.

"Emma, what happened the night you found me?" he asked, holding her hand.

She glanced at him and then looked up at the hill. "I was up on the hillside, lying in the grass and watching the stars. I like the quiet out in the fields, and up on this hillside at night. When the crickets are not chirping, it can be so serene." She looked up at the sky. "There was a very bright star that appeared up there. I could tell it was not any usual star; it moved and came this way very fast. I stood up to watch, and it flew over my head and smashed into the trees about half-way up. I ran as fast as I could to see what it was and there you were." She leaned her head against his shoulder. "Bailey and some of the men were down by the barn when it happened, and it caught their attention, too. They came over here and helped me get you to the house." Emma continued to tell him of her memories of the night. "We were all very excited. We very rarely have men fall out of the sky here at the manor." She looked up at him and smiled. "What do you remember about that night?"

"The accident, I can recall very well, and falling, but after that everything is a blur. When I opened my eyes again, I heard an angel ask if I needed assistance, and I saw you." He smiled. "I've been thinking, maybe we were destined to meet."

"Do you believe in destiny?"

"It's either that or it wasn't my time and God's people screwed up. Maybe he decided to send me back pronto." He laughed a little.

He saw Emma frown. "What does this screwed up mean? I have heard you say it before."

"It's another way of saying someone made a big mistake." Michael leaned his head back against the tree and closed his eyes. "Except I'm glad there was a mistake. I'm so happy I got to meet you."

She smiled into his chest. "Me, too," she said, quietly.

Off in the distance, Michael heard Emma's name called. It sounded like Mrs. Tharp was looking for her. He watched as she stood up and brushed off her skirt.

"It seems our peaceful respite is over." She leaned over and held out her hands to help Michael get back on his feet.

He grasped her hands and bent his good leg to push himself up. He hopped on one foot until Emma got the crutches under his arms. They slowly moved toward the field and could see Mrs. Tharp waiting patiently on the other side.

When Mrs. Tharp saw the pair was moving slowly, she picked up her skirts and started to run quickly toward them.

"Mr. Delancy is looking for you Emma. I will assist Mr. Drury back to the house. You go on. Mr. Delancy is waiting for you in the library," the older woman said and moved up alongside Michael.

"What does he want?" Emma asked.

"How would I know, dear? Go on with you now." Mrs. Tharp pointed toward the house.

Emma smiled at Michael and then ran to the manor.

* * * * *

Emma wanted this taken care of quickly so she could get back to her time with Michael. She became more attached to him than she'd ever been with anyone. She found it difficult to leave him anytime during the day. It was even worse at night. She wanted to be with him always. His smile seemed easy and he told stories she found of interest. She also thought he had a very good heart.

Moving through the back of the house, Emma went down a hallway to the library door. She knocked lightly and heard the usual "come". She walked into the room, and felt it stuffy and warm.

"Mr. Delancy, why do have you the windows closed up so tight? It is a beautiful day outside, and the air is very fresh," she said, and moved to a window to open it.

He sat in a leather high back chair with his hands tented in front of his chin. "I had not noticed it really. Where have you been all day, Miss Emma?"

Her brows creased when he said Miss Emma. The sound of his voice made her think he might be upset with her.

"Outside walking with Mr. Drury, as I am certain you were aware. I saw you at the window. You should be outside exercising; it is very good and healthy for a body," she said and sat on the piano bench.

"Where did the walk take you? To Darlington, perhaps?" he asked.

"No, not to Darlington, that would be too far. We walked through the fields and up to the hillside," she answered and smiled.

Mr. Delancy stood up from his chair. He turned to her and put his hands behind his back. "Emma, I hope you have not become attached to this young man," he said.

"Why should I not? He is a good man."

"We know nothing about his character. I asked him if I could send a message to his family, and he said they were too far away. What kind of answer is that? He could be a rogue of a most scandalous nature, and we would never know it," he said with concern in his voice.

Emma stood up. "Sir, Mr. Drury is no rogue. He is a bit confused about his appearance here, but he is not of a bad nature. Surely you know this; you have spoken with him many times and know he has a good heart."

"Have you spoken to him about his intentions toward you?" Mr. Delancy looked at her very seriously.

"We have not, sir. It might surprise you to learn he misses his family very much. His mother and brother are in this town called Seattle. His father worked in industry but died very suddenly, several years ago, when his heart gave out. Since they are so far away, Mr. Drury prefers not to dwell on them at present. What is wrong with this?" She crossed her arms and felt anger begin to rise in her.

"Emma, please consider, I have nothing but the best intentions for you. This young man says he is some sort of mason or builder. It is not acceptable for you. You deserve so very much more..."

"What?" she cut him off. "I deserve a man who considers me a pretty thing? Mr. Drury treats me as though I have a brain. He likes to hear my opinions," she said and moved back to the door. "Unlike some men who feel pretty things should not be heard. Sir, you have made me very angry, and it is too beautiful a day outside to be inside having upsetting discussions," she said and slammed the door behind her as she left the library.

Emma walked toward the back of the house. She knew Mr. Delancy had only kindness in his heart and wanted the best for her. She wondered, though, about his intentions.

Two years past, Mr. Delancy expressed to her the idea of them being married. She was only nineteen at the time, and Mr. Delancy being twenty years her senior seemed much too old for her. She hadn't come right out and said this, but told him she thought of him more as a father.

Mr. Delancy took it well and said he would help her find a proper suitor. He then brought to the manor several candidates from the city. They were mostly acquaintances from Mr. Delancy's business dealings and all were quite dull. She supposed he would continue this until someone caught her fancy.

Emma looked out at the field and couldn't see Mrs. Tharp and Michael anywhere. She glanced at a path leading out to the barn and saw their backs slowly going in that direction. Hurrying her steps, she caught up to them.

"I am back, Mrs. Tharp. Thank you for giving Michael your attention." She smiled at the older woman.

"That was quick," Mrs. Tharp said, and looked at Emma with a question in her eyes.

"Mr. Delancy's subject was not time-consuming, nor of any interest to me," she said. She smiled at Michael. "You have walked very far today. How is your leg feeling?"

"I'm still stiff, but it does feel better to move around. I think I'm getting stronger and better at working these walking sticks." He smiled back at her.

"Are you ready to go back inside?" she asked.

"No, I think I'd like to go a bit farther if it would be all right with you?" he answered and looked at her hopefully.

"Well, you two continue your walk. I have got things to do in the kitchen." Mrs. Tharp turned up the path and made her way back to house.

"Lead the way, milady." He smiled, following her to another path.

They went into the trees and walked slowly enjoying the shadows and coolness around them. For several bends in the path, they remained silent, but Emma wondered if Michael was curious about her latest conversation.

"Have you enjoyed our stroll today, Michael?" she asked.

"Yes. What did Mr. Delancy want, Emma?"

"It was nothing of importance," she said. She picked a wild flower and smelled its sweet aroma. She held it up to Michael's nose and let him sniff.

"You had quite a frown on your face when you caught up to us." Michael stopped in the middle of the path and balanced on his good foot.

"Yes, I suppose I did. Mr. Delancy is concerned about our growing admiration for each other. I told him not to worry himself so," she said and watched Michael with the flower under her nose.

He took a couple of steps. "I guess I can see why he'd be concerned for you. I'm a stranger. I show up out of nowhere and say I'm from a different century. He must think I'm completely nuts."

"Completely nuts? What does this mean?" she asked and walked along with him.

"Crazy."

"Ah, I see. I do not think he believes you to be completely nuts," Emma said, smiling.

"Then what is his issue?"

She stopped and thought for a moment. "I think he is mainly concerned about your work as a mason. I think he fears it could be a problem with your leg, and you would have no way to support yourself."

"Sweetheart, I'm a welder not a mason. I don't do brick work," Michael said quietly.

"Yes, I remember you telling me about welding." She smiled at him. Her brows creased together as she seemed to be listening to a noise on the road below the manor walls. She grinned ear to ear and clapped her hands together. "The Travelers have returned," she said excitedly.

"Who are the Travelers?" Michael asked.

"You will see. Follow me." She moved slowly enough for him to follow.

They walked along the path, which ended at the road. They had gotten ahead of the noise, which seemed to be coming toward them.

As they watched, a team of horses came around a bend, pulling a huge wagon, which could have been a motor home; its size was so great. Emma saw Michael's mouth gape in awe as it approached. There was a man and a woman sitting in the front seat. Emma smiled and waved, shouting greetings. Several more passed while Emma continued saying hello. She knew Michael watched her, and loved the animation in his face as wagon's continued on the road. Everyone returned her greetings and waves. She walked into the road, and approached one of the wagons.

"Mrs. Martinov, hello, how are you?" she said, and walked along with the wagon.

"Fine, dear girl. We are all doing very well," a dark-haired woman said.

"Where is Estrella?" Emma asked.

"She is several wagons back, Miss Emma. She married several months ago."

Emma laughed and bounced on her feet. "She and Spiro, yes?"

"Of course. Who else do you think she would have or would put up with her? She is also quite pregnant, too."

The woman motioned to her own belly. "Who was that man you were standing with under the trees?"

"His name is Michael Drury. I will bring him and introduce you. I would love for you to meet him." She looked back and could no longer see him. "I have to go back. You are going to set up your camp in the back field, yes?"

"Yes, Miss Emma."

"Good. We will come by tomorrow. I am so glad you are back." She waved and ran away from the wagons, back to Michael.

She found him leaning against a tree, watching the parade of wagons. His face looked pale. "Michael, what is the matter?" She touched his forehead to see if the fever had returned, as he continued to watch the wagons pass.

"It just really hit me." He looked down at Emma and she saw confusion on his face. "This is really 1815, isn't it?"

"Yes it is," she said above the noise from the road.

"Emma, how will I ever get home?"

Chapter Seven

They returned to the manor. Michael seemed exhausted and deep in thought to Emma. He said his leg ached, and he wished he had something called Ibuprofen to kill the pain. She didn't know what these medications were, but wished she could help him more. He mumbled something about trying to wrap his head around the fact that he somehow time-traveled back to 1815, but couldn't find any answers. While still out on the path, he'd gotten very weak. Emma said she'd run back and get one of the men to help, but he asked her to stay with him. He didn't want to be alone.

After she settled him comfortably back into his room, Emma went down to the kitchen and prepared them tea and a plate of biscuits and cheese. She thought about the afternoon spent with Michael, and the interruption from Mr. Delancy. It annoyed her very much.

Mrs. Tharp entered the kitchen while Emma waited for the water to boil. "There you are, child. I wanted to speak with you without Mr. Drury stealing your attention," she said. "Did Mr. Delancy tell you a guest is arriving in a fortnight, and he has arranged a dinner to be here at the manor? He is preparing invitations to the upper class sort in Darlington and spoke with Cook about the dinner to be served."

"No, he said nothing of the sort," Emma replied.

"Ah, he said someone of great importance will arrive. Perhaps, I am overstepping my boundaries and should let him tell you about his arrangements." Mrs. Tharp turned toward the doorway.

"Mrs. Tharp, please, wait a moment," Emma said and reached for the older woman's arm. "May I ask, did Mr. Delancy say who it is of great importance that will come to dine with us?"

The older woman glanced around the room to ensure their privacy. She took Emma's hand and led her to the table. "Mr. Delancy invited that snobbish man who visited us last summer, Lord Simonton. I dare say the only thing that man has which shows any kind of good regard, is his name. The rest of his persona is very rude." Mrs. Tharp stopped and looked Emma in the eye. "My dear, Mr. Delancy received word from the Lord that he thinks you suitable as a wife. I cannot believe Mr. Delancy would agree to such a proposal, but he just this afternoon explained to me about the upcoming visit." Mrs. Tharp folded her hands at her waist and pressed her lips together.

"I am appalled. There is no likelihood I would ever agree to any terms Lord Simonton might propose." Emma felt hot stings in her eyes. "How could Mr. Delancy agree to such a visit without discussing it with me first?" she whispered.

"I have no idea, my dear." Mrs. Tharp shrugged her shoulders. "Perhaps Mr. Delancy feels Mr. Drury will sweep you away and take you to that far away city he is from."

"I suppose that could be his thoughts on the matter. I will have to devote some time to Lord Simonton when he is here, but I wish to be with Mr. Drury and devote myself to his needs," Emma said.

"You know, my dear, I may have an idea of a way you could get out of this dilemma. Your water is boiling. We will discuss this more after dinner." Mrs. Tharp patted Emma's arm and left the kitchen.

Emma went to the stove and took the pot off the fire. She poured water into a teapot and placed it on a tray. She couldn't be angrier with Mr. Delancy at this moment. She realized she couldn't come right out and say she was beginning to fancy Mr. Drury. Her benefactor shouldn't have picked this time to have one of his dinners.

She carried the tray up to Michael's room, and found him leaning against the wall and staring out the window. She put the tray down, walked up behind him, and put her hand on the small of his back. She expected him to turn, but he only continued to stare out the window.

* * * * *

Michael put his hand behind him and brought her hand around to his stomach. He pulled her to his back and wrapped her other arm around his waist. He felt her put her head between his shoulder blades.

He held her hands tightly. "Emma, I'm growing very fond of you."

"I find I have feelings for you, too, Michael," she said quietly.

He released her hands and turned around slowly on one foot. When he finally faced her, he sat on the windowsill and put his hands on her waist. "Sweetheart,

61

this is not fair to you," he said. He put his fingers over her lips as she started to protest. "Wait, wait, and hear me out. This isn't my time, Emma. I don't know why I'm here. I'm not sure I'll ever understand why this happened. My brother could probably explain it to me." He saw confusion enter her eyes and prayed he didn't break her heart. "I have to find a way back. My mom's probably worried sick about me and that's not fair to her."

Emma let go of his hands and moved away from him. She went to the table, and turned her back to him. He saw her look down at the teapot and clasped it with her hands. Her eyes were closed and he thought she might begin to cry.

"From the talks I've had with Mr. Delancy, it's obvious he doesn't approve of us being together. I'm a builder and in this time period I have nothing to give you. I have no job or money to provide for you." Michael pulled himself up on one crutch and maneuvered his body behind hers. He put his free hand on her shoulder, looked over and saw her tight grip on the porcelain teapot. Her knuckles were turning white. He reached around her, and tried to get her to release it.

She turned quickly, and put her hands around his neck. "Michael, I do not want you to leave. Never, ever," Emma whispered.

He felt her press her cheek to his chest. Her eyes were closed tightly, and he could tell she tried to be strong.

"I know, sweetheart. If we could figure out how to get me back to my own time, maybe you could come with me," he said and held her tightly.

She slowly looked up and he saw a stunned expression on her face. "Go with you? To 2008?"

"Sure, why not? You could make it there. Of course, I'd support and help you every step of the way."

"Oh Michael, that is very frightening. I would have a whole different world to learn about," she said, frowning.

"Well, it's not something to worry about yet. My leg is still a week away from the splint coming off, and I don't really have any idea how to go back. I doubt you have any science geeks hanging around." Looking down at her, Michael saw a tear roll down her cheek. "Emma, don't cry. It's all going to be all right. I promise." He pulled her back into his arms and held her.

"If you were to leave, I would miss you very much," she said. "I know it could be some time until you find your way back, and I understand your reasons, but it will be hard."

He watched her eyes close again, as the tears continued. "Why would it be hard, Emma?"

"It is neither here nor there, Michael."

"You wouldn't have brought it up if it wasn't important." He smoothed his hand over her hair and rested it on her neck. "Tell me."

"Why do we not sit for some tea before it gets too cool, and I will try to explain?"

Michael agreed, and they both sat down at the table. Emma poured a cup of tea for each of them and set Michael's before him.

"Several years ago," Emma began, "Mr. Delancy asked if I might be interested in an engagement to him, and we would eventually wed. I thought about if for many weeks and finally found the only way to decline the offer without hurting his confidences was to say I loved him more as a father and would only ever see him as such. Mr. Delancy has tried to find a perfect suitor for me since then." She looked at Michael and he noticed she did not smile. "It is most annoying, and I have asked him to stop, but he continues to bring men from the city here to the manor so I can make their acquaintance."

"I think he should continue, Emma," Michael said. The thought of any other man touching her was not something he wanted to contemplate. It caused his gut to tighten, and he felt his blood pressure pump in his neck and temples. If he didn't stay here in 1815 though, she would need to find someone to love and protect her. He couldn't stand the thought of Emma being alone or, worse yet, with Delancy.

He looked up at her and Emma stared at him with color flaring in her cheeks. "Michael, there is a thing Mr. Delancy does not know about. I fear to tell him lest he think I have gone mad." Emma looked across the table at him again and he felt her fear.

He sat back in his chair and crossed his arms over his chest. "What is the thing, Emma?"

She let out a puff of air and stood up from the table. Pacing back and forth, she twisted a napkin in her fingers.

"Sweetheart, you're acting like a caged animal. Why does this thing make you so nervous?" Michael asked, and watched her closely.

She stopped in her tracks and laughed behind her hand. Using the napkin, she wiped her eyes dry. "I am afraid you may also think me mad."

"I wouldn't think it, ever, but I do think you're acting silly for thinking it. Please, sit down and tell me the thing," he said a bit more forcefully.

She sat and put her napkin on the table, but didn't look at him. "A year ago or so, I had a seer tell me about you coming to the manor," she said quietly.

"A seer? Do you mean a fortune teller?"

He saw her brow crease and she was silent. She then nodded. "I believe that is another name for a seer, yes." She still didn't look at him.

"What did the seer tell you?" he asked.

She glanced at him. "I hope you are not disappointed with me. It is the most curious thing. She said in thirteen months time the one I am waiting for, my heart's desire, would arrive from the stars. Helga saw a bright flash of light in the night sky and said he would steal my breath; I would hear no other voice. She called him a traveler, and I always thought she meant he would be from Mr. Martinov's group, but now I think she truly saw you in a vision."

Michael reached over to her and loosened her fingers from their death grip on the napkin. "Do I do that? Steal your breath?"

She looked at him and touched his hand. "Yes," she answered in a low whisper, "Right now you have caused my heart to pump very hard in my chest."

Michael continued to play with her fingers. "You take mine, too, Emma." He watched her eyes turn to him. They were no longer fearful. "I'm not certain I fully believe what the seer told you. Now don't frown, it's not that I'm not open to your beliefs. It's just that in my time a lot of these fortune tellers are rip-off artists. They convince people they're somehow connected to the other world and steal money from them. They give people nothing but lies."

"Oh, no Michael. This seer is real. I swear it. She has never told me anything that did not come true. She is very accurate. She said your appearance would be bright like fire, and it was. When you flew down out of the sky it was very bright. The flame of it set some of the trees on fire, and it was like daytime."

Michael looked at Emma with wonder. She truly believed in this urban myth or folk-tale. She was so innocent, and it seemed to him that she understood what he'd been telling her all along. He pushed himself up on his good foot and hopped to her, using the table for balance. When he got to her chair, she turned to look at him. He put his fingers on her cheek and traced her lips.

"Miss Wallace, you have stolen my heart," he whispered and leaned over to lightly touch her lips with his. He placed his warm hand on the back of her head, and tangled his fingers in her bun. He felt her lips part and gently ran his tongue around her mouth. He became warm when hers shyly reached in, slightly brushed along his teeth. He could love kissing this woman; she hadn't let herself go yet with passion and force. She was gentle and tender. He hoped she would feel completely at ease with him one day.

He felt the warmth run down his body. He continued to mess with her hair, which was coming out of the pins. He pulled away from her lips and put his forehead against hers. The fingers on their hands laced together. He kissed her forehead and whispered, "God, I want you, Emma." He felt her head move away to look up at him.

"I am right here, Michael. You are holding my hand," she whispered.

He stared down at her blue eyes and smiled. "Not that kind of want, baby." He let her hand go and circled his fingers around her wrist. Directing her palm to the front of his trousers, he moved it along his enlarging shaft. It jumped with her touch.

He saw her mouth drop open as she watched him move her hand over the buttons. She blew out another puff of air and seemed to him hypnotized by his movement. Her eyes slowly moved up to his. "Oh," she said, out of breath.

Michael watched as she slowly licked her lips, which caused his hardened member to move once more under her fingers. He saw her fingers shake, and he realized she shook all over. He stopped her and kissed her hand. His inner guilt kicked in, and he looked at her innocent face. He realized this was the wrong time and place. If he were to take her innocence and then go back to his own time, he would leave her in a terrible situation. He just couldn't bring himself to do that to Emma. She was too sweet.

He felt her take his hand off her wrist, and move it to her breast. He could feel its shape and firmness through the fabric of her dress, and when he put his thumb over her nipple, pressing down, she lightly squeaked.

Closing her eyes, Emma said quietly, "I have never done this before, Michael. I do not want to disappoint you or turn into a harlot."

"Sweetheart, you could never disappoint me and, today, it's not going to happen. I don't want to ruin you and ..." He stopped when he felt her start to shake. His breathing was tightened in his lungs and made it difficult to speak. "Emma, I won't steal your virginity. It would be mean to do that to you and then leave. Besides, Bailey's supposed to come up in a bit to adjust the crutches. Damn, I want to taste you."

She stared at her hand and moved it back to the front of his trousers. She caressed him. "You do say the strangest things at times, Michael. What do you mean 'taste me'?" When he didn't answer, she stopped her hand over the bulge in his trousers and looked up at him. "Mrs. Tharp explained to me about relations between men and women. She did say it would be on the marriage night. Wait one moment." She stood up and he watched as she walked to a dresser in the room. Opening a drawer, she pulled out a skeleton key. She continued to the door and locked it. "I hope you do not mind. I would hate for Mrs. Tharp or Mr. Bailey to walk in at this moment."

"Emma, you are a darling woman, but we can't do anything that would tarnish your reputation," he said. Michael hopped to where she stood and took the key from her hand. He unlocked the door and put the key on top of the chest. "On another day maybe we can explore a little further, but not today. Let's sit down and have tea." Michael smiled back at her.

"Thank you for the compliment, but are you sure you would not like to try? I could remove my dress, if you like?"

"Things are so different these days." He hopped back to the table and sat down. "You're playing the temptress very well. I don't know what's wrong and what's right."

"Michael, are not relationships between men and women the same in your time as they are now? What is this difference you speak of?" She sat down across from him.

He looked at her and thought seriously about how to say what ran through his mind. He had no idea what relationships were really like in 1815. He only had a movie or two he'd seen on TV to go by.

"No, I don't think they're really the same," was all he could sputter.

"How are they different?" She asked, and sipped her tea.

Michael swallowed and tried to figure out how he could explain the twenty-first century to her and still speak English. "Things are much more open and free in my time."

"How?"

"How what?" He turned his attention to his cup of tea.

"How is it more 'open'? What does that mean?" She set her cup down and leaned toward him with her arms folded on the table.

Michael sat back in his chair and looked at her dress. "Well, women dress differently. Sometimes they wear pants or shorts. Their skirts are shorter, and I know the underwear is different."

"The skirts are shorter? How short?"

His mouth dropped open, he stuttered, and then became quiet.

"A skirt above the ankle is unseemly. I am almost afraid to hear the answer." She adjusted her napkin. "And, really, what does clothing have to do with relationships between men and women?"

He looked away from her. "They're shorter than that," he mumbled. "See, things are more progressive in 2008. Women work and support themselves. They make their own choices and they vote." He turned back to her and smiled.

"Again, I ask, what does that have to do with relationships?"

"Man, this isn't easy." He rested his elbow on the table, put his chin in his hand and rubbed his cheek. "See, men and women sleep together all the time, whether they're married or not. There's a thing called 'a one night stand'. They'll spend one night together and never see each other again. Sometimes men and women just live together and don't get married." He glanced at her. "And I can tell by the look on your face I'm not making any sense. Don't get me wrong, sweetheart, I want you. I'm sure you felt how much I want to make love to you, but I want it to be right between us." He saw her frown. "Emma, you were shaking so much. I don't want you to be afraid of me. If we make love, I want you to be completely certain it's what you want."

"But, Michael, it *is* what I want. I do not want to end up living my life as a spinster." She put her hand across the table to him. "Is it not normal to be frightened the first time?"

"I don't know. I only know I want it to be perfect for you." He kissed the back of her hand. "I don't think I know the right way to explain the twenty-first century to you." He tried to smile.

"Michael, I do not understand. Did I do something wrong?" She looked at him and seemed to be pleading.

His heart pounded in his chest, but it wasn't excitement that caused this. He worried that she was afraid she'd done something to make him want to turn away from her. "No, you did everything perfect. I just won't feel right being with you if you're afraid of my touch. My leg hurts from hopping around the room and I don't think I would be a very good partner for you. Don't worry. If I stay, there will be no way of keeping me from you. *That*, I will guarantee."

He saw her sit back in her chair and frown. After she finished her tea, she excused herself and said she should go to her own room to straighten her hair.

* * * * *

As she sat and brushed her blonde locks, Emma thought about the discussion she'd just had with Michael. She thought he wanted to make love to her, but she'd felt very nervous. She understood why he wouldn't find such behavior very attractive. Perhaps, now he thought of her as a wanton or whore.

She felt slightly disappointed but also relieved they hadn't continued. Caring for him as she did, she found that her admiration had grown even more. Michael cared for her feelings enough to slow things down, which would make the anticipation for when they did become intimate even better. She hoped he wasn't too disappointed with her.

Sitting back in her chair, she looked at the back of her brush. She shivered slightly as she remembered the feel of Michael's warm manhood as it jumped under her fingers. She felt the warmth return to her lower body and wondered what it would have felt like if they'd continued. He was very large, and she tried to figure out a lady-like way she could ask Mrs. Tharp about a man's size.

Chapter Eight

After she daydreamed for several minutes, Emma sighed and sat up to finish her hair. Once it was neatly in place, she went back to Michael's room and knocked on the door. She heard a low "come in", opened the door and poked in her head.

"Are you ready for dinner, Michael?" she asked. It surprised her to see he wore a dinner jacket. It looked a little short in the sleeves but seemed long enough in the body. Michael certainly was built differently from Mr. Delancy.

Bailey sat on a chair, and wrapped the arm pieces on the walking sticks with some thick lamb's wool. He looked closely at his work and smiled. "There you are, sir. I think this will make the travel a wee bit better on your arms."

Michael took the crutches and leaned on them. "Yep, that does the trick. Thank you, Bailey."

"Nothing to it, sir." He stood and moved to the door. "Good evening, miss."

"Get some dinner, Bailey." Emma looked at Michael and raised an eyebrow.

"Why are you smiling at me, Miss Wallace?"

"I have never seen you wear a dinner jacket before. You look very handsome," she said.

He nodded his head and then grimaced. "I had to cover up," he said, and then pulled the jacket up so she could see his crotch area. "I'm still hard in the nether regions, babe. Every time I think about you it gets harder."

"Is there not a way for you...ah, to calm it?" she asked and blushed.

Michael raised his eyebrows. "Well, yes there is, but we haven't time, do we? No, no wait, I'd start sweating like a pig and would have to get cleaned up again."

"I am sure Mr. Delancy is already waiting downstairs for us," she started, then stopped.

"And he shouldn't be made to wait." Michael smoothed the jacket down. "I'll be all right."

"Does it hurt very much?" She looked up at him as he moved toward her on the crutches.

He smiled at her and scratched his jaw. "It's not a painful kind of hurt, honey. It's more of a 'makes me catch my breath if I move wrong and try very hard not to explode' sort of sensation. I believe I will excuse myself early tonight."

"I meant the crutches, Michael. I hoped, after dinner, we could continue our discussion about how things differ between your time and mine. I still have many questions that I do not feel we touched upon earlier." She smiled at him.

Michael adjusted the crutches under his arms, and they started to move out the door. He mumbled something about how the walking sticks were fine and how he'd just love to continue their conversation.

When they arrived downstairs they found Mr. Delancy in the dining room. He looked out a window with his hands behind his back.

"Sir, I am sorry we are so late," Emma started.

"It's entirely my fault, Mr. Delancy. I convinced Miss Wallace to walk farther than I really could," Michael said, interrupting her. "My apologies."

"No apologies necessary, Mr. Drury," Mr. Delancy said, and raised his chin. "I am aware, though, you both returned in the mid-afternoon. I do certainly wonder what could have caused the delay." He arched his eyebrow.

Emma looked at Michael and then back at Mr. Delancy. She felt heat move into her cheeks and knew she was blushing.

"Come along, you two. Sit down and eat before it gets too cold to enjoy." Mr. Delancy took his place at the head of the table.

The discussion around the table during dinner was quiet. Mr. Delancy continually looked at both of them, and Emma was sure he knew her guilt.

"I assume you are aware the Travelers have returned?" Mr. Delancy asked.

"Yes, we watched the wagons come along the road during our walk today. I saw the Martinov's. Estrella and Spiro married and are expecting a child. Mr. Delancy, if I may ask permission to have a carriage and horse prepared in the morning, I would like to take Mr. Drury over to the camp tomorrow," she asked and set her fork down.

"Perhaps the next day we could arrange for this, my dear. I cannot spare Bailey tomorrow," he answered.

"Mr. Delancy, you know I do not need Bailey's assistance to drive a two-seat carriage." Emma crossed her arms and tried to look stubborn.

Michael's head moved from Mr. Delancy to Emma as though he were at a tennis tournament. The discussion went back and forth between the two.

"Emma, I know you are more than capable. My only concern is for Mr. Drury. He is not able to defend himself from a highwayman. I am certain harm would come to you both," Mr. Delancy said, equally as immovable.

"Mr. Delancy, we have not had highwaymen in this area for years. Besides, we will be on the manor's property the whole ride out," she said. She felt ready to continue her argument.

"Fine, fine. I will have the two-seater prepared for you in the morning. Please, just be careful, all right?" Mr. Delancy finished the conversation.

"Will the shearing start soon?" she asked, changing the subject.

"No, not for another fortnight, perhaps longer. The wool is not quite ready yet." He put his napkin on the table. "I will be leaving early in the morning to ride into Darlington. I expect I will not be back until late." Mr. Delancy stood up. "Mr. Drury, my ward can be extremely stubborn at times. Please keep an eye on her tomorrow."

"Certainly, sir," Michael nodded.

"Mr. Delancy, the Travelers are no threat to us. You have known them forever and often say you do not know any other workers as reliable and trustworthy," Emma said.

"Another thing, Drury. She has a very long memory," he said and moved from the table. "I will see you in two days. Oh, we are going to be having guests in two weeks time. Mrs. Tharp will see to the arrangements. Please plan on staying around the manor, Emma. She may need your assistance."

"Who is coming, sir?"

"Later, my dear. We will discuss it further." His voice faded as he moved to the doorway.

Emma sat back in her chair, and watched Mr. Delancy leave the room. She looked at Michael and saw him laugh into his hand. "What do you find so funny, sir?"

"Nothing, nothing at all." He grinned at her. "What was that all about?"

She looked back at the door and smirked. "I will tell you later. I have to speak with Mrs. Tharp."

* * * * *

Michael and Emma said good night at the door of his room. He shed his clothes and crawled onto the bed. He was able to relieve himself using his hand. All he had to think about was Emma's soft, luscious lips and shapely body to bring about a climax. He wasn't completely fulfilled, but it helped with the discomfort he'd felt through most of the evening.

Mr. Smithee would return sometime in the next week and, hopefully, remove the splint from his leg permanently. This afternoon, for the first time in a couple of weeks, he'd had serious pain. He didn't think it came from his leg, but from the splint. When he'd put some weight down on his foot in the last couple of days he'd felt little or no pain. He thought they walked too far today.

Once he was free from the splint, Michael had to find a way home. He knew his family and friends probably wondered what had become of him. How was it being explained that he'd fallen from the forth-eighth floor of a building and disappeared? Michael could only wonder.

Emma was a wonderful woman and he'd fallen in love with her, but they almost went too far this afternoon. If he found a way home, it would be unfair to take one of her many virtuous assets and then leave. He would never respect himself again.

Sometime during the night, Michael felt the bed move. He lay on his back, and became alert. He opened his eyes and found Emma lying beside him. She put her finger over his lips and whispered to go back to sleep.

He turned on his side and looked at her. She wore a dressing gown, buttoned all the way up her neck. "Sweetheart, what are you doing?" he asked quietly.

"I am sorry. I know it is wrong of me since we are not man and wife, but I just wanted to be near you. I wanted you to hold me and keep me warm."

"Would you care to tell me what was going on at the dinner table?" Michael propped his head on his hand.

"It was nothing really. Mr. Delancy is angry with me. I am not being very receptive to the guest he has invited to the manor," Emma said.

"Is there a problem with the guest?"

"It is one of Mr. Delancy's suitors for me. The gentleman is not someone I would consider being acceptable, but my benefactor is determined once again. This one can be very difficult."

"Why?"

"He is a lord and is quite snobbish. I would be better seen than heard in this man's opinion, and I just do not find it acceptable. I want to marry for love, not position."

"Does Mr. Delancy think it would be better for you to have a fancy family name?" Michael asked, somewhat shocked to find out this information about her benefactor.

"No, I think he wishes for me to be safe and well cared for, but Lord Simonton ..." She looked up at him. "Well, you will meet him at the end of next week, and you can gather your own thoughts about him." She snuggled closer. "Now, perhaps we could continue our discussion from earlier today. Just what did you mean when you said you wished to taste me?"

Michael wrapped his arms around her and held her tight. "Ah sweetheart, let's discuss this tomorrow. I'm pooped."

Emma giggled. "You do say the strangest things, Mr. Drury."

Chapter Nine

When he woke up the next morning, Michael found Emma gone. She must have gotten up sometime during the night and tip-toed back to her room.

He lay in bed for a time, and tried to figure out a way they could be together. He found his brain didn't come up with anything.

He knew he had to get back to his own time but didn't want to leave her. She had become very important to him. He loved the sound of her voice and her laughter. The way her eyes looked at him innocently, tugged at his heart. He could see her as she tried to decipher what he said about things from his time. He wanted to be completely honest with her and not lead her astray.

Michael moved gingerly off the bed. He hopped over to the table and prepared to shave. He'd adjusted to the straight razor quickly, but found if he didn't go slow he cut himself up pretty bad.

* * * * *

Emma woke up very early. She listened to Michael breathe deeply. Her head rested on his shoulder, and he lightly held her hand on his chest. She'd wanted to laugh and weep at the same time, she felt so much in her heart for him.

When she moved away, the sun was rising. She'd quietly gone back to her own room, dressed and prepared for their outing.

She couldn't wait to introduce Michael to the Martinov's and catch up with her long-time friend Estrella. The Travelers had come to Delancy Manor for many years. They always arrived in the spring, helped with sheep shearing and worked the fields. They stayed through the summer into the fall, and then departed. They never announced their arrival and never said good-bye.

Emma and Estrella grew up together. They spent their childhood's running through the fields and learning from each other. Emma taught Estrella how to read and write; Estrella taught her about people.

Now Emma felt a little jealous. Estrella was only eighteen-years-old and already married with a baby on the way. Emma worried she might become a spinster at the age of twenty-two.

As they rode in the carriage toward the back fields, Emma explained to Michael about the Travelers. She mentioned they preferred to stay away from cities and towns and kept pretty much to themselves. There were other groups who stole and caused trouble in those places. The Martinov group always dealt honestly with Mr. Delancy. She wasn't certain how the relationship began but felt grateful.

"Michael, may I ask a question?" She looked at him, holding the reins of the two horses tight in her hands.

"Yes, of course."

"Do you wish to have children of your own one day?"

"Yes, yes I do." He moved his arm around her shoulder.

"Good," she said and nodded.

"What about you? Do you want kids?"

"I do, yes, very much one day." She smiled at him.

"I'm glad we think alike, Miss Wallace," he said and squeezed her shoulder.

She continued to smile the rest of the way to the camp. It was almost 11:00 in the morning when she pulled the horses up to the edge. There were thirty families in the back valley. It always amazed Emma how quickly they managed to get things set up. Tents were pitched and wagons were lined up along the path.

As Emma slowly made her way through the camp, people came out of their domains, and waved a greeting. They could hear children playing and smell the aroma of all sorts of foods cooking.

Emma halted the horse in front of the Martinov's wagon. Mr. Martinov came around from the back, holding up his hand and laughing.

"Ah, Miss Emma, how very nice it is to see you." He helped her down, and then they both helped Michael.

"Mr. Martinov, I would like for you to meet Mr. Drury," Emma said, introducing the two men.

"Is this the one Miss Helga mentioned?" he asked.

"I believe so," Emma answered and saw a confused look on Michael's face. "Miss Helga is the seer I told you about yesterday," she explained.

The two men shook hands and greeted each other cordially. Suddenly, there was a loud, high-pitched squeal, and a very pregnant young lady could be seen hurrying toward them.

Turning, Emma saw her friend Estrella almost running to her parent's wagon, her arms outstretched.

"Emma, Emma, Emma," she said, almost dancing a jig.

Emma put her hand over her mouth, and tried to hold back her surprise at the size of the woman's belly. They hugged as best they could, and both giggled uncontrollably.

Stepping back from her friend, Emma grinned. "Just look at you, Estrella. You look absolutely radiant."

"I've never been so happy, Emma. Spiro is a good husband and treats me very well. He never beats me. There are the times when he wants to be master, and I let him think he is, just until we are between the sheets. Then I am the master." The woman's dark eyes twinkled. "Who is this handsome man you have with you?" she asked, indicating Michael.

The introductions continued for a while. Michael met the whole Martinov clan and even Spiro came over from another wagon and joined the group. Mrs. Martinov came out of the wagon and got a fire started to warm water for tea.

Estrella managed to move Emma away from the group of people. They walked arm in arm around the camp, and then came to a downed tree trunk where they sat, and enjoyed the warmth that came from the sun.

"Emma, are you going to marry this man?" Estrella asked, and held her friend's hand.

"I do not know," she answered. "It is a little complicated."

"Complicated? Love isn't complicated. Helga saw him by the road and said he isn't from this time. Is he the one she spoke of? The one who was to fall from the stars?" Estrella asked.

Emma frowned a little. "What else did Helga say?" The old woman, Helga, lived with the Martinov group for a long time and was deeply in touch with other-world connections.

"Not too much else, really. She did say she couldn't see the outcome, only you torn between two different worlds. She says you will have a foot in both places."

"Torn is correct. Michael wants to find a way back to his own time. He has a mother and brother and does not want them to worry," Emma said.

"Will you go with him?"

Emma went silent and stared at Estrella. "I do not know. I mean, could I go with him?"

"We'd have to ask Helga. She would know what to do."

"Oh but, Estrella, I could not leave Mr. Delancy. He is so good to me."

"Silly, silly girl. Mr. Delancy is a grown man. He needs to find a woman his own age and let you find your way," Estrella grumbled.

"You know I am his ward until I am twenty-five. So, in three years I will be able to make my own decisions, but I do not know what to do," Emma said.

"Does this Michael know about your trust left by your parents?"

"No, I do not think so. We have never discussed it."

"Good, he's not after your money. This is good," Estrella said and nodded her head.

"Lord, I never even thought about it," Emma said quietly. "At first I thought he might be a scoundrel, but since I have come to know him, I have changed my mind."

"Has he kissed you?" When Emma's face turned red, her friend got an answer. "Has he made love to you?" Estrella stared at her and waited for an answer.

Emma had an attack of discomfort. She crossed her arms. "I wanted him to, very much, but I was afraid, and he seemed to sense it. Michael stopped us. He said he did not want me to be afraid and...well, he stopped us," she said, her voice fading.

Estrella's mouth hung open. "Did you touch him?" Emma nodded. "And he stopped things? Was he hard?"

"Estrella, really." Emma's hands went to her cheeks and she giggled.

"All I have to say, my friend, is he must be a very good, strong man to stop like he did. My Spiro is a good man, but he cannot stop. Go, go, go...always. I love it." She pulled Emma's hands down. "Tell me, why are you afraid? He's a handsome man, very good body. Why?"

"We are not married or even engaged. If we were caught, it would be scandal for Mr. Delancy, and I cannot abide that."

"Emma, the only way Mr. Delancy finds out is if you say to him about it," Estrella said.

"I had not thought of that," Emma answered.

Estrella stood and took Emma's hand. "Come, let's walk some more. Momma says the more I move and exercise, the better for baby. Maybe I can convince it to come out sooner than later."

"When is the baby due?"

"Next week, next month, who knows? I'm ready to meet this one though. He runs around my belly too much." Estrella moved her hand over her large bump. "Ah, see?" She put Emma's had on an active spot.

"Oh, my goodness," Emma giggled. "Do you really think it is a boy?"

"So active, this one ...it can only be a boy."

* * * * *

They walked around the camp several more times, and stopped to talk to others along the way. When they arrived back at the Martinov's camp, Emma found Michael seated on a stump, with piles of wood chips around his feet and on his trousers. Mr. Martinov and Spiro had propped up the wagon, and prepared to take one of the wheels off. All three men had taken off their shirts since the day turned warm.

Emma walked up to Michael with her hands on her hips. "Just what are you doing, Mr. Drury?" she asked.

Michael looked up and smiled. "Mr. Martinov had a couple of cracked spokes in the wagon's wheels. I'm helping fix them," he said, and ran a sharp knife over the wood.

"Your man is very good to the wood, Miss Emma. He treats it with respect," Mr. Martinov said, as he and Spiro lifted the wheel off of the wagon.

Michael smiled at her again, arching a brow. "Your man," he whispered.

Emma clasped her hands in front of her. "I think I like the sound of that." She nodded and turned toward the tree where Mrs. Martinov and Estrella worked on stitching and making clothes for the upcoming baby.

"There's tea if you would like, Miss Emma." Mrs. Martinov looked toward a pewter tea pot.

It was a relaxed afternoon as the men replaced the spokes. The ladies brought tea to them and water as they needed it and Mrs. Martinov prepared lunch.

At one point, Emma heard a whistle and her name called. When she looked over at the men, Michael was beckoning her over. She got up and smoothed her skirt down. She saw his eyes watch her as she walked to him. His gaze made her feel warmer.

"What do you need, Michael?" she asked as she stood next to him.

She felt him take her hand and put the handle of the knife in the palm. "I need you to do me a favor," he said. He pulled the leg of his slacks up and uncovered the splint. "This thing needs to come off. It's driving me nuts and," he looked around them, "when it's warm, the blasted thing smells. I think the wood is rotting. It itches like crazy," he whispered.

"Are you sure? Mr. Smithee will be by this week and..." She saw the look on his face and could tell he was very serious about getting it off. She knelt down by his leg and smelled the odor he commented about. Pushing the pant leg the rest of the way up, Emma cut the strips of sheet Bailey used to secure the splint after Michael's first bath.

Mrs. Martinov watched them and got up, bringing over a pan of warm water and a cloth. Michael thanked her and watched Emma work at the strips.

She carefully cut the last one and pulled it off. The wood fell off, and landed on the ground under his feet. She saw the swelling was down and Michael's leg returned to its normal pink color in areas. She picked up the pan and towel, and cleaned off his leg. When she finished, before lowering the pants leg, she kissed his knee.

"Better?" she asked.

"Yes ma'am, it is. I may still have to use the crutches, but I'm glad to get that thing off." He slowly bent his knee a couple of times and tried to work out the stiffness.

"I will have to adjust those trousers again. The legs make you look off-balance." She crinkled her nose.

He kissed her cheek. "I'm not too worried about what I look like at this point. I'm just so glad to be rid of the splint."

Spiro broke up the wood from the splint and threw the pieces into the fire. Emma did the same with the strips of sheet.

When Emma sat back down with the other ladies, Mrs. Martinov chuckled. "Now you have to run, Miss Emma. He's going to chase you."

Chapter Ten

The ladies got dinner ready for the men-folk. Michael, and the other men, got the spokes of the wheel fixed and put back on the wagon. Later that afternoon, Michael asked Emma when they were going to head back to the manor. She said they could go after dinner unless he wanted to leave sooner. She looked at him, and asked if he was very tired.

"No." His shoulders straightened. "I just thought we shouldn't worry anyone."

"Mr. Delancy probably will not return from Darlington tonight, and Mrs. Tharp knows where we are." She set a plate in front of him and smiled.

After dinner, the whole community gathered around the fire-pit in the center of the camp. They sat and drank homemade wine, which Michael found extremely strong. Several people pulled out fiddles and guitars, and there was music and storytelling.

Michael sat and held Emma's hand and then put his arm around her shoulders. She leaned into him, and he felt warmth come from her. They listened to the stories, and he was quite taken with a tale Miss Helga told about a man who travelled through holes in the stars. The old woman sat across the fire from them and weaved an intricate web which turned the whole group quiet and attentive.

After she finished, a fiddler began a quiet tune. Michael put his lips up to Emma's ear and whispered, "Would my woman care to dance with her man?"

"Do you feel up to it, Michael?" she asked. He nodded his head and smiled. "Then yes, she would."

Michael got up onto his good foot and slowly put pressure onto the other leg. He held his hand out to help her up.

"Are you sure your leg is all right?" she asked, again.

"My leg feels great. It's happy to have that skanky splint off. It wants to dance," he said, and pulled her away from the group to a clear spot under the trees.

He pulled Emma tight into his arms and moved a hand around her waist. He felt her put a hand on his shoulder, slightly surprised by how close she let him hold her.

"Do you know how to waltz, Michael?" she asked, looking up at him.

"Nope, I can't waltz. I do a basic two-step thing."

They moved side to side and around. Michael held her securely, and felt her warmth wrap around him.

Michael looked down at her, and noticed the gold from her cross reflected in the light from the fire. It had an unusual glow about it.

"Do you think Miss Helga's story was about me?" he asked. He touched the gold chain at the back of her neck.

"It is possible she was speaking of your arrival. She mentioned a yellow hat, and I wanted to laugh."

"Why?"

"I found your yellow hat, but I did not know what it was. It is in a drawer back at that manor. Do you remember I showed it to you?" She looked up at him.

"I remember that, yes." He turned them slowly in time with the music. "I have to tell you something," he said, whispering into her ear and kissing the lobe.

"Yes?"

"I love you. You've stolen my heart completely, Miss Wallace," he said, and felt her pull back.

She looked up at him with those beautiful blue eyes. His heart skipped a beat and excitement burned in his veins.

"Michael, are you certain?" she asked.

"As certain as I am the sun will rise tomorrow."

"I love you, too." She moved closer to him as they continued to dance.

* * * * *

They stayed at the camp until well after dark. When they finally got in the two-seated carriage to go back to the manor, the night air felt chilly. Mrs. Martinov gave them a wool blanket to put over their legs.

They rode in silence for ten minutes until Emma stopped the horses in the middle of the dirt road. Turning to Michael, she put her hands on either side of his face and put her lips on his. She was quite forceful, which Michael found extremely agreeable. After they'd kissed a few minutes and both their hearts pumped wildly, Emma urged the horses to move on again.

Michael leaned back, and put his arm around her. "Miss Wallace, I'm very shocked by your behavior this evening."

She looked at him, and smirked. "I dare say, sir, I was very hurt not to receive a kiss for hours. First, I helped free you from that smelly splint. Then, you held me close while we danced and still no kiss. I suppose it will shock you further to learn I removed my undergarments before leaving the Travelers' camp."

Michael sat up and looked at her. "What?"

"I see you are shocked, sir. Do you think I am acting wanton and that my behavior will create a scandal?"

Michael laughed. "Shocked? No. But Emma ..."

"I know what you are going to say, and I can assure you I no longer care to hold onto my innocence. I am twenty-two years old, and what I do is no one else's business. Estrella is only eighteen and see what she has accomplished?" She pulled the carriage off the road and moved into a circle of trees.

"Emma, what are you doing?" Michael asked, as she tied off the reins.

He watched her pick up the wool blanket and get down from the carriage. "I am finding a nice, quiet, private spot to be alone with my man." She placed the blanket under the trees and turned back around to him. As he watched, she began to unbutton the top of her dress.

Michael saw the front of her dress slowly opened. It quickly became apparent that she had told the truth about her under things. He saw the curve of her breasts.

She looked up at him. "Michael, I need you to come down here. I am cold and could use a bit of your warmth."

"Emma, wait a minute," he said and maneuvered himself down from the carriage. Once down, he limped over to her. His leg stiffened up on the ride back and now throbbed. He walked up and stopped her from slipping her dress off of her shoulders.

"My friend Estrella, who is married, told me the best way to convince you to make love to me. She said once we make love, you will stay and never want to leave." Emma explained as he re-buttoned her dress. He saw a frown on her beautiful face. "Michael, you say you love me. Does love mean something different in your time?"

"No, sweetheart. It means the same thing, and I do love you very much," he said, as he finished the buttons. "Let's sit down and talk." He pulled her down onto the blanket.

"Michael, I want you to stay. I know you are concerned for your family..." She stopped. "Why is your brow creased so? Do you not want to stay?"

"If I were to stay, I might begin to hate you and resent the fact that you'd kept me here. I'd always wonder what I'd put my mom through, and it wouldn't make for a very happy life. Emma," he said, taking her hand and kissing the palm. "I will love you for a very long time. I don't want to make any room for bad feelings." He looked at her and saw tears start down her cheeks. "I spoke with the woman you mentioned -- the seer."

"You spoke with Helga?" she asked, sniffling.

Michael nodded. "Yep, after I explained to her what happened to bring me here, she told me how I could get back. I asked her if you could go with me."

Emma's eyes seemed to clear. "What did she say?"

"She didn't know for certain. There is apparently, from time to time, some weird rip that occurs. It creates a hole between the different times in history. Helga said this current rip is lasting longer than usual. She doesn't understand but thinks it will last until the fall or even into the winter. She wasn't sure."

"So is it some sort of doorway where you walk into another time?" Emma asked.

"Something like that, yes. When I asked Helga why I came here to this time, she called me a stupid boy and asked if she looked like she knew everything about a person's destiny. She said she doesn't get told these things by God. Anyway, if you were to try to go through, there's no guarantee you'd end up in the same place and time as me. Helga said since I'd already come through, there's something that will draw me back -- sort of like a beacon -- when I step in."

He watched Emma put her head in her hands. "What do you have to do? We have no buildings forty-eight floors high."

He smiled at her. "Emma, please don't be angry with me, but I'm not going to tell you. I don't want to frighten you."

She extracted her hand from his and stood back up. She crossed her arms and walked to a tree, leaning against the trunk. "Thank you for being concerned about my emotions," she said, with a slight sarcasm in her voice. "You are concerned about causing me fear but do not seem all too worried about my heart." She pinched her bottom lip between her fingers.

"That is not true, Emma. It's killing me to know I'm hurting you," Michael said calmly, as he pushed himself back up.

"I have been so stupid. To think I fell for it. Mr. Delancy said men would try to trick me. I guess he was right."

She attempted to move past him, but he grabbed her arm. He felt her try to tug it away from him. "Emma, what are you talking about? What did you fall for?" he asked and pulled her around to face him.

"It is nothing. We should get back to the manor," she said not looking at him. "Please, let me go."

"We need to discuss something. I'm not sure what, but why do I get the feeling you've lost your trust in me?"

"You have not enough trust in me to tell what you are planning. You expect me to trust you?" He saw her get very angry, but couldn't tell if she was mad at him or with herself. "It is strange. I never would have thought it of you, but I see I was wrong."

Michael let her go and watched as she folded the blanket. She held it to her chest and frowned at him.

"Emma, sweetheart, I'm confused." He shook his head.

"You have acted the part very well, Michael. Is that your real name? Michael Drury? Mr. Delancy will compensate you to keep your mouth closed about my unspeakable behavior. I will see to that. I should think you would be able to leave the manor by week's end." She moved quickly to the carriage and climbed back in, throwing the blanket under her feet. "We should return now," she said, and waited for Michael to return.

He slowly got into the seat next to her. She turned the horses back toward the road and got the carriage moving.

"Emma, my name is Michael Drury, and I'm at a loss. I've obviously said or done something to upset you, but other than not telling you what I have to do to get back to my own time, I can't for the life of me think of what it is. What do you mean by compensation?"

"It is not important. I will have to tell Helga she does not know everything." Emma urged the horses to move faster and cracked a whip.

The carriage bumped over the roadway causing Michael to grab the seat. "This isn't the nice, leisurely ride we had this morning. Slow down Emma."

She gave him no response and kept the horses trotting at a fast clip. Michael decided not to say anything further and held onto his seat. He kept his eyes on the road and on Emma, who stared straight ahead.

When the carriage pulled up in front of the house, one of the men who worked for Delancy ran out from the barn to take care of the horse. Emma picked up Mrs. Martinov's blanket, jumped off the rig, and moved quickly into the house.

Michael wasn't able to keep up with her and gave up. He saw Mrs. Tharp come to the door and look out at the drive. He used the crutches to get up the steps.

"Mr. Drury, Miss Emma was very curt with me just now. Was there a problem today?" she asked, stepping out to help him up the final steps.

Before Michael could answer, there was a slam upstairs and he looked up to the top of the stairwell.

"Mrs. Tharp, I spoke to the seer in the Travelers' camp today. She told me how I could get back to my own time. Emma wanted to know what I'd been told, but I chose not to say anything. I didn't want to cause her fear. She went off like a firecracker and I think she believes I've been conning her," Michael finally said.

"What does 'conning' mean?"

"She thinks I've been telling stories or lying to her about my being here. I think. I'm not sure what I did," he finished, exhausted.

"Mr. Drury, you should go on up and retire for the night. You can deal with Miss Emma in the morning. Everything will be better after a good night's rest."

"Ma'am, I don't like going to bed angry. Although, I'm not angry. I'm just worried about what I've done that's got her so riled up."

"I will check on her, sir. There is no need to worry. Emma can be very headstrong at times." She squeezed Michael's arm. "Do you need any assistance getting up the stairs?"

"No, I can make it. If she speaks to you, tell her I'll be awake and reading for a while if she wants to talk." Michael turned and made his way up the stairs. "We had such a good day," he mumbled.

* * * * *

When Emma got to her room, she stripped off her dress, shoes, and stockings. Putting on her dressing gown, she climbed under her sheet and quilt, buried her head under the pillow, and cried. She was very angry but not certain who she was mad at -- herself or Michael?

When he wouldn't tell her how he could to return to his own time, she knew, in her head, he only wanted to protect her, but she felt he'd treated her as though she was merely a child. It caused her heart to hurt and pound. He'd also refused her. Couldn't he see she was willing?

This thinking brought more tears as she convinced herself that he wasn't attracted to her at all. When she had a moment of clarity, she realized that wasn't right. He was attracted to her. When they danced, she'd felt his excitement grow through her dress.

Someone knocked on the door, but Emma ignored it. She didn't want to see anyone. She heard the door open and could see a candlestick put down on the night stand.

"Emma?" Mrs. Tharp asked. "I know you are awake, my dear." The side of the bed sagged a little and shook as Mrs. Tharp sat. She pulled on the case enveloping Emma's head. "Now you are acting like a child. Tell me what disturbs you so."

Emma came out from under the pillows and knew her eyes were red and still tearing. "Mrs. Tharp, did you and Mr. Tharp have disagreements?" She found her handkerchief bunched under the pillow and dried her eyes.

"Oh yes, we disagreed at times. It is a normal thing, Emma."

"Michael spoke with Helga who said he could return to his own time, and how to do it. He will not give me the details, and I must assume he no longer cares for me or perhaps wants only my parents' estate and not me." She looked anxiously at the woman.

"Did you accuse him of this?" Mrs. Tharp asked, frowning.

Emma thought for a moment. "I believe so... yes... perhaps. I am not certain what I said. He turned me away.

I offered myself to him and he said no. Twice he said no and ..." She stopped when she saw the horrified look on Mrs. Tharp's face. Emma blushed and because the light in the room was so dim she wasn't sure if Mrs. Tharp could see her embarrassment.

"Emma, child, have you gone mad? What were you thinking?"

"Estrella said if I gave myself to him, Michael would stay and we could marry. Mr. Delancy would no longer have to bring home those dolts from the city," Emma replied and hugged her pillow.

"That explains everything. Emma, because the Travelers are loose with their morals, does not mean it is something you should follow," Mrs. Tharp admonished her.

"They do not have loose morals. They love each other and swear fealty to one another for life. They may not wed in a church before witnesses, but it is before God."

Mrs. Tharp looked at her sternly. "That may be, but to offer your body to a man to try and trick him into staying with you is morally incorrect, and it is no wonder Mr. Drury is so confused," she said, and frowned. She shook her head. "The fact that Mr. Drury said no to you has increased his standing in my eyes. Emma, he said an interesting thing. He said he did not like going to bed with anger. I think this is good, and if you are going to get any sleep tonight, I advise you to get this sorted out." Mrs. Tharp stood. "He said he would be in his room, reading, if you would like to talk. I believe, young lady, you should speak with him and clear him of any guilt. He has a good heart, even if his thinking is a bit addled."

Emma looked up. "I said such terrible things to him."

"Just tell him the truth; you had gone out of your mind for a moment." Mrs. Tharp raised her eyebrows.

"Thank you, I will. Maybe I could say it was the moon," Emma said.

"I think not. That is superstitious mumbo jumbo. Good night, Emma," the elderly woman said and left the room.

Emma popped off the bed and went to her mirror. She lit a candle and looked at her reflection. Her eyes were puffy, and her hair a mess.

After running her brush through her hair, she decided to leave it down. She put on a robe and slippers. Picking up the candlestick, she moved into the hallway and went to Michael's door. She stood outside and felt anxious. She did not know what to say to him. She finally became impatient with herself and knocked.

"Come in," Michael's voice came through the wood to her.

She opened it slowly and saw first that his bed was empty. Looking into the room, she saw Michael stood by the window. He was without his shirt and shoes, and for a moment she admired the muscles in his chest.

Leaning on the doorjamb, Emma began to feel unsure again. "I wanted to apologize for the way I treated you earlier. I am sorry." She put her head down and started to leave the room. As she gripped the doorknob, she heard his footsteps behind her and his hand covered hers, stopping the door from closing.

"Emma, wait," Michael said. He took her hand off the knob and swung the door shut. He took her hand and led her back into the room

She wanted him to wrap his arms around her and keep her warm and safe, other than hold her hand. He moved no closer. She stepped away from him and sat at the table where she'd had her senses awakened the day before.

Sitting up straight, she folded her hands in her lap, but couldn't bring herself to look at him. The last thing she wanted to do was cry, again.

Michael walked to the other side of the table and sat down. "Just for the record, Emma, my name is really Michael James Drury. I was born in Seattle Washington, in the United States of America, June 1, 1978. In my time, I'll be thirty in a month or two. My father's name was James, and he passed away several years ago from a heart attack. My mother's name is Elizabeth. I have a younger brother who is seventeen-years-old. His name is Neil, although I have always called him 'geek' and he calls me 'loser'. Where I'm an out-of-doors type of guy, my brother is not. He prefers to stay inside, tinkering around on a device called a computer. What else can I tell you to convince you I am telling you the truth?" he asked quietly.

"Nothing. You need not say anything further. I was being irrational. I am sorry if it caused you discomfort." She looked up at him, and saw the man she wanted to spend the rest of her life with. Her eyes burned. "Since you are leaving soon, perhaps it would be best..." She had to stop and swallow the lump that formed in her throat.

"Perhaps we should spend little time together. It will make parting from you easier."

"Is that what you really want, Emma? Do you not wish to spend any more time with me?" he asked. His voice so low that she could barely hear him.

She looked down at her hands and twisted her fingers together. She bit her bottom lip.

"No, no, no," Michael said. He stood, squatted down in front of her and put his hands on her thighs. "I want you to look me in the eye and tell me you don't want me around you before I leave." He moved her chin up and couldn't see her eyes through the tears. She shook, put her hand over her mouth, and let out a muffled sob. "Babe, don't cry," he said and pulled her into his arms.

Emma lost the battle and cried for ten minutes. She held tight to his shoulders and watched her tears run down his shoulder.

When she calmed down, she found she was on the floor, tangled around Michael. He held her in his strong arms and rocked her. He smoothed her hair with his fingers.

"I am sorry, Michael," she whispered.

"I know," he said, not letting her go.

"Deep in my heart I know you have to go. I do not want to say goodbye though. I really do want for you to stay."

"I won't say goodbye then. On the carriage ride back to the manor this evening, you said Mr. Delancy would compensate me, and I'd keep my mouth shut. What was that all about?"

Emma groaned and straightened her back. "It was nothing. I rambled, and I was angry with myself, and you, and this situation." She did not want to go into the trust and how wealthy she'd be in three years. "How much longer have we? When must you go?" she asked, and looked up at him. She traced her finger over his lips, and felt the stubble that grew from his chin.

"Helga said she wasn't sure when the doorway would close, but didn't think I needed to rush right off."

"Good, then there is still some time." She wrapped her arm around his neck.

"Emma, let's go for a picnic sometime soon when the weather is good -- just you and me." He continued rocking her and held her against his chest. He moved his hand down the curve of her back causing her to shiver.

"I would like that very much." She looked up at him again. "Michael, may I stay with you again tonight?"

"Are you sure it's a good idea?"

"I know you will leave. I will cry and feel sorrow no matter when you go. I know Mrs. Tharp probably has her ear pressed to her door to be sure I return to my room. When the house settles, I shall quietly come back to you." She sat up and brushed her lips over his, and then quickly looked away.

Michael helped her to her feet and walked her to the door. He held her in a tight embrace and kissed her face. "I care for you very much Emma Wallace. Never doubt that."

Emma nodded her head a little and left the room.

Chapter Eleven

Two weeks passed by and Michael's strength got better. With the walking sticks, he was able to get around the mansion on his own and on a number of occasions Mr. Delancy found him in the library, looking through the bookshelves or relaxing with a novel.

Delancy thought he should discuss Michael's situation, but didn't know the best way to approach the subject. He also wanted to discuss Emma. Delancy was concerned for his ward. She seemed quite taken with their strange guest, but if Delancy had his way it wouldn't last for long. Lord Simonton would arrive on the weekend, and if his letter gave a true indication of his sentiments, Emma would be engaged by the turn of the week.

Emma and Mrs. Tharp continued to give attention to Michael. They made certain his every need was met. If they couldn't provide for him, they spoke with Bailey, who privately spoke to Michael and helped where he could.

Mr. Delancy planned a private dinner on the lord's first night, and then guests were invited for the next weekend. He hoped they'd have an engagement to announce at that time.

* * * * *

On Friday afternoon, their quiet world turned upside down. Lord Simonton arranged for his assistant, butler, dresser and footman, several maids, and a dog walker all to arrive ahead of him to prepare the manor. The maids practically took over the kitchen, and Mrs. Tharp exchanged a few hard edged words with Nigel, the lord's butler. He was upset that his master's suite of rooms weren't up to their usual standards.

Emma and Michael didn't find any chance to talk. The house was in an uproar to prepare for visitor's, and Emma kept very busy helping the butlers and maids find their way around the house.

Michael watched the entire hubbub from the window in his room. He found a fascination with the number of wagons that pulled up to the front of Delancy Manor and the amazing assortment of items unloaded. The biggest surprise was a cart that held a four-poster bed and a set of furniture to complement it. Michael shook his head and couldn't fathom bringing a bed along on a journey. It just seemed nuts.

Bailey and the other men made several trips back and forth into the manor. Michael could hear bangs and footsteps on the floor below him and up and down the stairs. He wished he could go down and help. He wished they had a crane or even an electric trolley to move the stuff. It would have made things so much easier for the men.

He felt a hand on his shoulder and glanced up to find Emma behind him, looking out the window.

"Is Mr. Delancy going to rearrange all the furniture, Miss Emma?" he asked.

She laughed. "No. All that you see belongs to Lord Simonton. You would think he was moving in for a long stay."

"How long will he be here?"

"Only a fortnight or so, which is several days longer than the house staff would like. Mr. Delancy received a note from him several weeks ago. Apparently, Lord Reginald has some interest in me as a wife."

Michael turned in his seat, and looked at her with his mouth open. "What?"

"Yes. Mr. Delancy continues his endeavor to find me a husband. I often feel guilty that I am disappointing him with my decisions, but I have not found any of his choices acceptable, yet. I do have concerns of becoming a spinster if this continues, but who knows?" She smiled at Michael. "Perhaps Lord Reginald holds a hidden quality I will find attractive, but I doubt it." She moved to the chair next to Michael's and sat down. "Mrs. Tharp told me that perhaps I should play harder to catch with him. If he believes I might find someone else of interest, he might be more inclined to be less of a snob and more of a gentleman, but, as I said, I doubt it."

"Why do you doubt it?"

"He is from a family in London, which once had quite the standing. I have recently discovered his coffers are very low on funds."

"Why would he find you of interest then?" Michael looked back out the window.

He saw her frown, and her brows creased. "I am not certain."

Michael heard her voice falter and glanced at her. "Emma, you are an extremely attractive woman. Surely, Mr. Delancy has provided well for you."

"Indeed, he has. My marriage dowry is well stocked, but, unlike Lord Reginald, I could never marry for station. It makes me all the more curious as to why he should find me so attractive. I have nothing, really."

Michael sat back in his chair and felt as though Emma had lied to him. He wasn't sure how he knew it or what the lie was, but he knew it happened all the same. He thought this might be a good time for him to leave. If this Lord Simonton turned out to be a good match for Emma, Michael could return to his own time with a clear conscience.

"So, when does Lord Reggie arrive?" he asked.

Emma laughed again. "Michael, I do not believe it would be wise to call him by that name. He would be most insulted. He and the rest of his entourage will arrive tomorrow. Dinner should be quite good since he provided all the pheasants and geese we could eat in a year."

"Pheasant? Does he hunt?" Michael shook his head.

"I doubt it. He did not seem the type to shoot animals."

"I could make it a topic of dinner conversation. So, I shouldn't call him Reggie. What about Jughead or Archie?"

Emma put her hand over her mouth and laughed very hard. At one point, she snorted, which caused her to laugh even harder. When she settled, she tilted her head and smiled at him. "Mr. Drury, your words are very sly.

Could you explain to me where the name Jughead originated from? Is it German?"

They spent until mid-afternoon discussing the origins of names and other sundry items. Michael spoke quite highly about the Archie comic books as very good reading for children.

Chapter Twelve

Mr. Delancy arranged for the best wines in his cellar to be served with dinner the first night of Lord Simonton's visit. He was very pleased with the selection and wanted to thank Mrs. Tharp for her outstanding choices.

Several days before, Emma borrowed a pair of dress slacks from one of the ladies from church in Darlington. She tailored them nicely for Michael. They fit him quite well and looked a better sight than those he'd borrowed from Mr. Delancy. They were at least the proper length.

The day of the big dinner, Bailey assisted Michael to get dressed. The time traveler found it difficult to get the tie Emma gave him arranged around his neck. Bailey explained it was called a 'cravat' and helped get it fastened on Michael.

"This thing looks really prissy," Michael said, as he looked at his reflection in a mirror.

"It is what gentlemen be wearin' these days, sir," Bailey answered, and slipped the dinner jacket onto Michael's arm. "It is what Miss Wallace provided."

"Then I suppose I'll have to put up with it. Does it have to be so tight?" He put his fingers around the knot and tried to loosen it.

109

"Sir, if you continue to pull on it such, it won't be centered proper." Mr. Bailey frowned.

He assisted Michael down the stairs to the living area. No one else had put in an appearance, so Michael took a book off a shelf and sat by the window. He found he had chosen a goofy book of sermons from the church in Darlington. They were interesting but he was not a religious man. He did appreciate their sentiment about the treatment of others, but in no time he began to yawn.

Michael heard footsteps come into the room and a saw a strangely dressed man look around. The man put his hand on his lapel and straightened it.

"If you would excuse me, sir, has Mr. Delancy come down yet?" the man asked and looked serious.

"Not yet." Michael smiled.

The man stiffly turned and left. A few minutes later, Mrs. Tharp walked in and carried a tray. Emma came in behind her.

"Good evening, Mr. Drury," Mrs. Tharp said.

"Hello ladies."

"The others will be down shortly. Would you like some refreshment to start off the evening?" Mrs. Tharp set the tray down and smiled at him.

"Whatever Miss Wallace has is fine."

"I will get it, Mrs. Tharp. You need not wait on us." Emma walked to the tray and turned two glasses up.

Michael was generally a beer man, if he drank, but felt he should participate as close as possible with the times. After a minute, Emma handed him a glass.

"It is a bitters and gin, Mr. Drury. I hope you find it suitable." She sat on a couch across from him, and held her own glass.

Michael took a sip and worked very hard to not make a face and spit it back into the glass. The drink tasted very tart and heavy on the gin. He thought if he drank two or three of them, he'd be out before the dinner even got started. *Better take it slow,* he thought.

"So, Miss Wallace, since we're being formal, how are you this evening?"

"Quite fine. Thank you for asking." She smiled at him but wouldn't look him in the eye.

"Are you nervous, Emma?" he asked.

She finally looked at him. "Nervous? Whatever do you mean?"

"You know, meeting a suitor, someone who could possibly be spouse material?"

"Yes, I see, and no, I am not at all nervous. I have met Lord Simonton before so I feel there is no reason to be uneasy. After some quiet reflection, I feel I may have misjudged him. He may be the perfect match for me."

Michael couldn't believe the words that came from her luscious lips. He thought for a moment and realized it was what he wanted all along. However, right now, he felt his jealous streak come to life. He sat up straighter in his chair and touched the weird tie at his neck. He needed to make the move to get home before the situation drove him crazy.

"So, you're going to give him a chance?"

"I think I should. He did come all this way. I do not believe he has changed much from our last meeting, but there is always a possibility of such an occurrence." Emma sipped her drink.

"Miss Wallace, are you being a tease?" Michael grinned at her.

Before she could answer, they heard voices. Mr. Delancy and Lord Simonton made their way in, and laughed, slapping each other's backs. They said good evening to Emma and Michael, and then the lord's footman went to the makeshift bar and poured two drinks for the gentlemen.

The lord sat next to Emma on the couch and accepted his drink from the servant.

"Mr. Drury, I understand you are from the America's. What brings you to England?" he asked. When Michael didn't immediately answer, Lord Simonton continued. "Are you here on business or just a leisurely trip?"

"It was a bit of an unexpected excursion," Michael said, and watched the lord very closely.

"Mr. Drury has relatives over in Cardiff, Lord Simonton. He was on his way for a visit when he fell and broke his leg," Emma commented quickly.

Michael looked at her and frowned, knowing that she lied again. The Drury's in Cardiff were unknown to him and they may not be relations of his. He could tell from the way she presented herself, she danced a thin line. He would talk to her about it later.

"I imagine, then, you are quite anxious to get down to Cardiff," Lord Simonton said.

"Not really. Mr. Delancy and his house staff are very gracious and I don't want to over stay my welcome. I'm not in a big hurry, though," Michael said and sat back in his chair.

The conversation turned to the lord's business in London and Paris, but it was mostly between Simonton and Mr. Delancy. Michael found he stared at Emma, bored beyond belief. His mind wandered, and at one point he found himself daydreaming about unbuttoning the back of her dress.

* * * * *

Dinner was not really what Michael liked to eat. The lord provided fresh pheasant, prepared by his own cooks. The meat was dry and tasted gamey. Michael sat in his chair and looked at the plate. He wondered if there might be lead balls or buck shot in the beast. The potatoes were under-cooked, and the green beans didn't seem cooked at all. He played with his food and wished for one of his mom's juicy sirloin burgers with Swiss cheese and mushrooms.

"Lord Simonton, would you consider an estate out in the country? There are several desirable mansions available north of Darlington?"

Michael heard Emma's voice and paid closer attention to the conversation.

"No, I have not looked at all, Miss Wallace. The country life is not of my taste. I do not mind brief visits now and again but do not care to be away from London. The company is much more genteel."

He saw the look on Emma's face change, as what Simonton said hit home. The lord apparently noticed it, too. Michael marked a scorecard in his head. He was ahead, so far that night.

"My apologies, Miss Wallace. I did not mean to say that the present company is not genteel enough to associate with." The lord smiled at her.

Emma glanced at Michael, and he saw a tight smile appear on her lips. "No apologies are necessary, sir. We are a bit relaxed out here in the country."

The dinner continued on and on. Late in the evening, Emma excused herself from the men's presence.

Michael followed Delancy and Simonton into the library where the lord's footman served them brandy. He prepared cigars for all three of the men. Between the gin, the wine with dinner, and now the after-dinner drink with cigars, Michael thought he would become sick if he didn't find some real food. He brushed aside the footman's offer of a cigar and stood up from the chair he'd taken.

"Gentlemen, if you'll excuse me." He set the brandy snifter down and limped to the door, wanting out of the room.

"Mr. Drury, are you feeling unwell?" Mr. Delancy asked through a cloud of smoke.

Michael turned to the men, and straightened his shoulders. "Yes, a bit. I don't smoke, sir, and I'm afraid the smell has upset my stomach. Please, excuse me.

He made his way to the kitchen, and found Mrs. Tharp at a table.

"Dear lady, I need your assistance," he said, and took her hand.

"Whatever is the matter, Mr. Drury?" She stood up from the table and touched his arm.

"I'm in desperate need of real food -- something without botulism or lead." He saw her questioning look.

"The dinner was awful, and I didn't eat much, but drank more than I'm used to. Is there some bread and butter around or something like it?"

"I see. You sit yourself down, Mr. Drury, and let me see what I can find. I will not be but a tick."

Michael sat down at the table and rubbed his temples. He loosened the tie around his neck and pulled it off, stuffing it into his pocket. A plate appeared in front of him with a pile of fresh bread and butter. It looked heavenly.

"Mrs. Tharp, you are an angel." He stuffed the bread into his mouth and chewed with relish. "This is so good. Thank you, thank you," he said through the doughy mouthful.

"You are quite welcome, Mr. Drury. I gather Lord Simonton's pheasant was not to your liking?" She sat across from him and raised an eyebrow. He saw a sly look on her face.

"Pheasant can be good, but these must have been the grandfathers in the flock. They were pretty dry and over-cooked."

"Unfortunately, Lord Simonton insisted his cook prepare the birds. Mr. Delancy's cook would do a much better job," Mrs. Tharp said quietly. She glanced at the doorway, as though to make sure no one listened. "Mr. Drury, do you have a cook in your own time?"

"No, no cook for me." He smiled.

"Heavens, do you prepare food for yourself?"

Michael laughed and tried not to choke on the bread. "I get a lot of fast food. When that gets boring, I go over to my mom's. There are usually some good leftovers in the fridge."

Mrs. Tharp sat back in her chair. "Miss Emma told me you say strange things sometimes. I do believe she is right. Tell me about fast food. What makes it fast?" She looked at him expectantly.

"Well, it's food ready in five minutes or less. Sometimes it takes a little longer, but you order the food and it's ready to eat. They put it in a bag and off you go." Michael set a slice of bread down on the plate.

"A meal cooked in such a short time cannot be very good." She frowned.

"It's not good for a person to eat that kind of food all the time, but on the fly, it's acceptable." He saw a look come across her face that he'd see on Emma's when he spoke modern day language. "Where are you from originally? I notice your accent is a bit different from Mr. Delancy's and Miss Emma's."

"I am originally from Scotland. We definitely sound different, but I have tried to accustom myself to the King's English. It is the proper way of speaking in a manor of this size, sir."

"I see, I think." Michael sat forward in his chair and frowned. "Mrs. Tharp, I'm going to leave soon."

"Miss Emma is quite fond of you, sir. She will be very upset at hearing this."

"I'm going to leave and not say goodbye or anything to her. I can't ..." He stopped. He folded his hands above the plate and looked at his fingers. "I won't say goodbye to her. I don't want to break her heart."

"I am afraid that will be a problem, sir."

Michael nodded his head. "Promise me you'll watch over her. Don't let her become a spinster or do anything dumb."

"I will do my best, sir. I promise."

Chapter Thirteen

The next day, Emma spent the morning in the kitchen. She prepared a lunch basket for a picnic outing with Michael. She hadn't slept much the night before and was tired. She snuck back to Michael's room after midnight; she lay next to him not wanting to forget a single moment of the night. He had kept her warm in his arms.

They talked long into the night. Michael asked her so many questions she could only remember half of them. He stated his concern that she found it so easy to lie to Lord Simonton about Michael's supposed family in Cardiff. She laughed and explained that she was only trying to ease the conversation. It wasn't really a bad deceit.

He'd asked why she told him that she thought she had misjudged the lord and how he could possibly be a catch for her. She'd laughed, again, and said she thought to tease. She felt there were more meaningful questions, but Michael did not bring up anything further and they fell asleep.

Looking up from the basket, she realized she could hear Lord Simonton's voice out in the hallway. He spoke to his butler and the voices approached the kitchen. She closed the basket and quickly turned to the back door.

She took the steps down to the lawn and walked toward the gardens. She heard a voice beckon her.

"Miss Wallace?"

Emma stopped and looked over her shoulder. Lord Simonton came toward her. He grinned and took jaunty steps.

"Good morning, Lord Reginald. Is there something you need?" Emma clasped her hands in front of her rib cage.

"No, no, Miss Wallace. I am fine. I do not wish to disturb your stroll, but may I join you for a turn about the garden?"

"If you wish, sir." Emma turned and made her way toward the garden path.

"It is a lovely morning. Would you agree?" he asked. "Perhaps we could make a day of it and take the carriage up into the hills or over to Darlington?"

"Indeed it is a beautiful day, sir. I am afraid I have a prior engagement to attend to, though." Emma looked around her. The blue sky and bright sunshine made the lawn greener and the trees shimmered. "The flowers should be in bloom soon, now that the warmer days are here more regular." She did not wish to spend the day with Lord Reginald. There was only one man she wanted to spend any time with and felt there should be no further discussion about this subject.

Emma continued on silently but felt her discomfort growing. The fine hairs on the back of her neck felt sensitive, and it caused her to turn to look at the manor. In one of the windows on the ground floor she could see Michael watching them. She pressed her lips together, and when Lord Simonton was along side of her, she took his arm.

"So tell me, sir, are you enjoying your stay?" she asked and looked up at him.

"Yes, I am. Mr. Delancy is a very good host and tolerates the intrusion very well."

"Oh, it is no intrusion, sir."

"Miss Wallace." He stopped the stroll and took her hand in his. "I must be honest. The sole reason for my visit is to determine if you would consider taking our knowledge of one another to the next level?"

"Whatever do you mean?"

"I am certain Mr. Delancy told you of my interests. I have spoken with him and received his permission to discuss extending our relations. Of course, the distance between us makes any kind of courtship impossible." Emma turned, and slowly began to walk again. She felt his eyes follow her. "It does not mean we do not know each other well enough to forgo some formalities and decide if we are suited for marriage."

"I see," she said. She let go of his arm and continued to walk. She clasped her hands and felt her brows come together. "I do not believe we would be well suited, sir. You made it quite clear at dinner last evening that country life does not interest you. I am certain I would not like city living. It would be much too busy for me."

"Miss Wallace, how can you say such a thing? The society alone is so intriguing and intelligent. Not to mention the access to the theaters and playhouses. I assure you, it is never dull in London."

Emma stopped. "And do you find the company here at the manor dull, Lord Simonton?"

"I did not intend to sound that way, my dear. The company here is quite enchanting. I just fear I would become bored out here...ah, forgive me, Miss Wallace. I have become tongue-tied. I do believe, though, that we should be speaking of our compatibility," he said. "I find you very attractive and think we would make a very handsome couple."

"Lord Simonton, I appreciate your attentions, but I do not believe it is a wise match. I have no desire to live in London or any other large city. I was born and raised here in this area, and it is my home. I have no wish to give it up, and I doubt you would give up your position in London. I do not believe there is anything further to discuss."

Lord Reginald took in a breath and frowned. "Mr. Delancy said you are a headstrong woman. Perhaps it would be wise to ask his counsel on the subject, and he could help you see how advantageous it would be for you to consider my proposal."

"I am sorry, sir, but there is no need to trouble Mr. Delancy's mind with this subject. I do not love you and do not believe it would be possible to have any feelings other than friendship for you. I have every intention -- if I marry -- to do so for love and only love. I hope you will understand in time." Emma turned and walked away from him.

"Miss Wallace, really, your lifestyle out here has caused you to be carefree and stalled in your growth."

Emma almost lost herself in a burst of laughter. When she realized Lord Reginald was serious, she contained herself. "Sir, I assure you, I have had an outstanding education provided by Mr. Delancy. I thank you for the feelings you have expressed, but I cannot accept your proposal. I do not wish to leave the country, and you prefer the city. We would never be happy." She turned to walk back down the garden path to the manor.

The lord followed her and continued his argument as gently as possible. "Miss Wallace, how can you say such things? You have never experienced London. I do not understand why this one particular thing is of such importance to you."

"And it is a thing I am not wanting desperately. Lord Reginald, I do not mean to be rude, but it recently was brought to my attention that you may have another objective in mind regarding a betrothal to me."

"Whatever do you mean, my dear?" He moved ahead of her to open the door that lead to a back hallway and held it as she passed.

"Please, do not play coy." She quickly walked down the hall, and turned into the library.

Mr. Delancy put down the local newspaper he was reading when Emma and Lord Simonton entered the room.

"Mr. Delancy, please talk some sense into your ward. She is being very difficult," Lord Reginald said and sat on a lounge chair across from him.

"I assure you, sir, I am not being difficult. I am trying to be level-headed about the aspects of Lord Simonton's proposal. He believes I would be happy in London, which I doubt very much." She walked to a teapot on a sideboard and poured a cup.

"Yes, and you accused me of ulterior motives but will not explain. How am I supposed to understand the meaning?"

Emma took a sip of tea and looked over the rim of the cup at Mr. Delancy. He frowned at her. She thought about bringing up her dowry but realized from the look on her benefactor's face that she should not broach that domain. "Lord Reginald, let us just leave it there. I refuse to accept your proposal. As I previously stated, I do not love you, and there is nothing that could sway me to those feelings. I am sorry if this causes you to feel upset, but I just cannot accept any proposal at this time."

Mr. Delancy huffed from his chair. "Well, there you have it, sir. I am sorry if it is not the outcome you had wished for and hope it will not make your trip to the country uncomfortable."

"Mr. Delancy, I do not believe this is the end of the subject. Perhaps if Miss Wallace would like to go rest for a bit, you and I could discuss the situation further."

"Simonton, my ward has made herself very clear on the subject of your proposal. I do not believe I would have anything further to offer." He looked at Emma and smiled. "She has a very good head on her shoulders and knows what is best. If these are her feelings, then I will not try to sway her."

Emma set her cup down and walked to Mr. Delancy. She kissed his check and whispered, "Thank you, sir," in his ear. "Good day to you both. I have an engagement to keep."

* * * * *

Michael watched Emma and Lord Simonton stroll around the back yard. At one point it looked as though they were having a very serious discussion; the topic he didn't have to guess. The lord was probably proposing to Emma. Michael felt jealousy stab his heart.

He'd gotten the information from the seer on how to get home, but the old woman said he'd need to talk to Bailey about the details, which seemed strange. Michael didn't understand why the estate manager would know anything. He walked out of the back door of the manor house and followed a path to the barn. Bailey had a small room set up in the attic, but Michael found him sitting quietly outside the barn door, smoking a pipe and drinking a cup of tea.

"Good morning to ye, Mr. Drury."

"Good morning," Michael said, and sat down on a stump across from the man. "Would you have a minute?" The grounds-keeper nodded his head. "I'm not sure you remember, but when I woke up, when I first arrived, I claimed to be from another time," he said, putting his hands together and crossing his legs.

Bailey's brows came together. "I remember, yes."

Michael looked away from him. "I spoke with Helga from the Travelers and for some reason she said I needed to talk to you. She thinks you know how I can return to my own time." He stopped and let out a breath. "My own time. It still seems weird to think this is 1815. Part of me doesn't want to believe. Everything here is strange ... the language and the way people are to one another."

"Contractions."

"What?" Michael asked, somewhat confused.

"Contractions are a part of grammar. You know, like can't, won't and doesn't. It took me a while to figure out what was wrong, but I soon realized Mr. Delancy, Miss Emma and the rest of the workers around the manor don't use contractions, ever. Or if they do, it's a slip up. It was a hard adjustment." Bailey continued to watch Michael. He took another draw on his pipe and tapped the stem against his teeth. "Mr. Drury, I'm going to be saying something to you that I ask you not to repeat." Bailey stood up and looked around the yard to ensure their privacy. "I was born in 1965 in San Jose, California." Bailey's accent faded, and he sounded very west coast.

Michael stood up, and his mouth hung open.

"I was rock climbing with some friends at Yosemite. I'm still not sure how far up we were, but I lost my grip and woke up here in England, in this time," Bailey said.

"Is your name really Bailey?"

"Joseph Bailey, sir."

"You knew this whole time and said nothing," Michael said, pointing his finger at the other man.

"Mr. Drury, what good would it have done for you to know sooner? You broke your leg and weren't going anywhere. Let me ask you a question. How certain are you about wanting to go back?" Bailey knocked the contents of his pipe out on the heel of his shoe and pulled a bag of tobacco out of his pocket. Michael watched as he refilled the pipe, and then Bailey looked over at him. "The reason I ask is I went back to my own time, and I couldn't shake the feeling I was in the wrong place."

"Why do you say that? Wrong place?"

Bailey looked around him again. "The first thing you'll notice is it always seems noisy. It never quiets down. I can tell, since you're nodding your head, there is some understanding of what I'm talking about, and you haven't even been back yet."

"Yeah, when I first arrived it seemed too quiet. Now, it's just peaceful and relaxing."

"I also didn't care for the way things raced around. I know with automobiles we could get to Darlington in no time. But unless you like the faster lifestyles, it's hard to go back."

Michael looked away from him. "To get back here, did you have to jump off a mountain again?"

"No, let me explain. Helga should have told you, but obviously she withheld some information. For some reason -- and believe me, I'll never understand how it works -- the way you came through to this place is only open to you. I had a path for me, but these doorways are only open for so long. When I went back to my time, I wondered why I didn't arrive back at Yosemite. I woke up in a field above San Jose. It was strange, but the doorways seem to know where we belong. But, as I said, they're only open a short time."

"Helga said it was good until the fall equinox," Michael said, sitting back down on the stump and rubbing his leg.

Bailey raised his eyebrows. "Hmmm ... that's good. It gives you time to really think about what move you want to make. We would need to get you back to the hillside where you landed. That's where your portal is located, I think. If you want to come back here, you repeat the process."

"You mean I have to jump off the building again?" Michael asked incredulously. As he watched Bailey shake his head no, Michael threw up his hands. "This is all so weird."

The caretaker relit his pipe. "No, you would return to where the doorway spits you out. My one concern, Mr. Drury, is for Miss Wallace. It's obvious to all around her, that feelings have developed between the two of you. Your leaving will break her heart."

"Bailey, she is a strong woman. She will bounce back," Michael said. "We're going for a picnic today. After dinner this evening, would you take me to the hillside?" Bailey stared at him in silence. Michael was suddenly focused on Emma and how she would react. "I think the sooner I go, Bailey, the better. Emma will get over her feelings and be able to move on. Maybe she'll even consider Lord Simonton a good catch." He saw Bailey frown. "The longer I stay will only make it harder for her, and I don't want to do that." Michael stood. "After dinner, come and think of an excuse for me to leave. Tell me you want me to look at something in the barn."

"You should probably give Mr. Delancy a heads-up. He could run some interference," Bailey said.

"Michael, are you out here?" He heard Emma's voice and footsteps come toward him from the path.

"Bailey, would you mind very much talking to Delancy? It would seem it's time for the picnic." Michael stood up. "Emma, I'm here."

"I'll speak to him for you. I think you should see him before you go, and thank him for all he's done for you," Bailey said quickly as Emma came around a corner and approached them. "Good morning, Miss Wallace." Bailey tipped his hat and took on his English accent again.

"Gentlemen," she curtsied. "Mr. Bailey, I hope I am not interrupting an important discussion, but Mr. Drury and I do have a picnic planned. He will need to take his leave of you now."

"Ah ma'am, no, 'tis not a problem. We were not saying anything of matter," Bailey smiled. "We can pick it up later."

She turned to Michael. "We could walk to the river or if your leg is not up to it, I could have horses saddled," she said.

"No, I think the exercise will do me good," Michael said. He noticed she stood away from him.

"Good, let us go up to the kitchen to get the hamper, and we can set off." She smiled at him.

Michael could see a shadow in her eyes and knew she was trying to be cheerful. It tore at him what he was doing to her. He thought about making the break with her now and have Bailey show him the hillside straight away but he wanted to give her a relaxed, and beautiful afternoon. Something he could take back with him to his own time and, hopefully, something she would cherish.

Chapter Fourteen

Michael and Emma walked in silence across a field of tall grass and carried the basket between them. The sun shone brightly, which caused the tops of their heads to turn warm. Michael wished he had his Seattle Mariners' baseball cap.

They walked to the trees - elms, oaks and willows - which surrounded the field. Michael thought they would go up the hillside, but Emma turned and walked along the tree line, where it felt cooler under the canopy of trees.

Emma wandered around the tall oaks and willows, and picked wild flowers. She didn't say much on their walk from the manor. Michael sat down under a tree, and watched her bend at the waist and gently snap the colorful blooms, creating a lively bouquet. He could tell she was deep in thought and didn't want to interrupt this time for her. She needed to think. He spread out the blanket, closed the basket, and relaxed back against the tree trunk.

After a time, he decided it would be best to have a talk. "Emma, are you going to pick all the flowers on the hillside?" he asked.

She smiled at him and walked toward the blanket. "No, I wanted only to pick the yellow buttercups and sweet peas. They smell heavenly." She held the bouquet down for him to sniff.

"Mmm. I see what you mean. They are very pretty," he said, and looked up at her. "How was your stroll with Lord Simonton this morning?"

"I saw you watch us from the window. Oh, Lord Simonton," she sighed and sat on the blanket a couple of feet away from Michael. "He did propose marriage this morning."

"And?"

"I am afraid I said no. He wants to live in London, and I just cannot stomach that thought. He said the country had made me too carefree, and I suppose he is right. I just do not want to live in the city. I have never been to any place but Darlington, which is not really a city. There are other reasons why it would not be a very good match." She looked at her flowers.

"Why are you so far away from me, Emma?" he asked quietly.

She glanced at him quickly, and then turned her back to him. "The only thing I can really think about at present is your leaving and ... I do not want to cry again."

Michael moved up behind her and put his hands on her shoulders. She tensed and moved away from his touch.

"We probably should not do anymore of that, Michael."

"Emma." Michael was unsure of what to say. "You're not going to make this easy for me, are you?"

"I know I am only trying to protect my heart. Honestly, I want your hands and mouth all over me." Emma stood up and backed another step away from him. She looked at him with sad eyes. "I want to feel your warm breath flow across my cheeks and neck, but it is torture now. The memory of those moments will torment me for the rest of my life. So, no, I guess I will not make it easier for you."

Michael pushed himself up, and watched her. He frowned slightly. "Damn, I wanted this to be a terrific day for us. One we'd both remember forever. The weather is so perfect. The sky is so blue, and I have the company of a beautiful woman ..." he said, and moved toward her. He put his fingers over her lips, then touched down her throat. His eyebrows came together. "Emma, where is your cross?"

"I took it off this morning," she answered, and kissed his hand. She looked up into his eyes. "Say no more, Michael. It only adds to the torture, and I find it difficult enough." Her voice begged, and cracked with emotion.

He put his hands around her waist, and pulled her into his arms. She put her head on his chest and moved her hands around to his back, and held him tight.

"Emma, I'm so sorry. I don't want to hurt you," Michael whispered.

"I know it is hard, and I am trying to be strong," she said. "I know the reason you will not make love to me is you want to leave me pure and innocent. Michael, I could care less about my purity. I will never marry anyone but you, so there is no need ..."

"Emma," Michael said harshly. He pushed her away and held her arms in a tight grip. He shook her slightly. "You must promise me you will take every opportunity to meet a gentleman. One who will love you as you deserve to be loved. Marry him and have lots of children; you will soon forget about me."

"I am sorry, but I will make no such promise," she said, with tears running down her cheeks. She pulled out of his grip. "Why did you say you wanted this to be a special day for us?"

Michael looked at her, and realized he needed to watch his words. "I want all days to be special and magic for you, babe. Promise me you will keep your heart open to other men," he said, and hoped to move the subject back to marriage proprosals.

She stepped away from him and leaned against a tree. "I will not promise anything of the sort, Michael. When you leave, I shall become a spinster and grow old alone."

"Sweetheart, don't do this." Michael crossed his arms over his chest.

"I want no other man than you. None will be able to satisfy me, or make me laugh, or think the way you do." She shook her head and bit her lip. Wiping her face, she looked up at the trees. "It is a beautiful day, do you not think?"

They strolled under the trees and along the river. Michael wanted to fish the river, and told Emma about fly fishing and shadow casting. He sensed she was only half-listening to him.

As the sun shifted to the west in the sky, they decided to head back to the manor. They were to meet Mr. Delancy and Lord Simonton for dinner in the main hall.

After dropping off the hamper in the kitchen, they walked up the stairs together. Michael wanted desperately to touch her, hold her hand, sweep her into his arms, and never let her go, but knew he shouldn't take such liberties.

When they reached her door, she turned to face him and said, "Thank you for an almost perfect day."

"Emma." He reached up and touched her soft lips. "May I kiss you?" he asked softly.

She looked up at him and gave a slight nod of her head. He gently lowered his lips to hers, and felt her tightly clench her mouth closed. He put the palm of his hand on the back of her neck and his other arm around her waist, and pushed her back against the door. He pressed his lips to hers and traced her lips with his tongue. He wanted her to allow him passage into her warm mouth one more time. Her lips slowly parted and she relaxed into his arms. He found his way, caressing her tongue and teeth.

Her hand came up to his cheek, and she moved her lips away from his. When he opened his eyes, he found her staring at him. Tears again rolled down her cheeks, and flooded her beautiful blue eyes.

"I cannot do this, Michael," she whispered, and pushed him back. She opened her door and closed it in his face.

He could hear her crying in her room and wanted to go to her to give her comfort but knew it would only make matters worse.

He slowly walked back to his room and made a decision. He changed into his T-shirt and work boots, but his pants were cut off when he'd first arrived. It surprised him to find his yellow hard hat in the dresser drawer just where Emma said it would be. He needed to find Bailey and have the manager take him to the place where he'd find his doorway to go home. The sooner he left, the sooner Emma could start the healing process.

After getting his work boots tied up, he tucked in his long-sleeved T-shirt and flannel shirt into the pants Emma had tailored for him. He put the hard hat under his arm and opened the door to his room, checking the hallway to see if it was clear.

As he came down the stairs and turned to go toward the back hallway, he saw Mr. Delancy sitting in the front room, reading a book. Michael walked into the room and shut the door behind him.

"Mr. Delancy, I want to thank you for allowing me to stay here and for all my care. I'll never be able to repay you."

Mr. Delancy set the book aside and stood up. "I assume, since you are wearing your very strange clothing, you are taking your leave of us?" he asked.

"Yes, sir. I just wanted to thank you and ask ... would you please watch after Emma?"

"We will, of course."

"Sir, she doesn't know I'm going. I think it would be for the best not to say goodbye. It will only upset her." Michael turned back to the door. "Please tell Mrs. Tharp thank you, too. She's been very kind."

"Of course, we will keep an eye on things. I see my judgment of you was incorrect, sir. I believed you were here only to steal from Miss Emma. Please forgive me," he said, and moved toward Michael. He held out his hand. "Good luck to you Mr. Drury. Journey safely." They shook hands.

Michael wanted to say more but didn't feel he had the time. He was afraid Mr. Delancy thought he might steal Emma's virginity and wanted to assure him it was left intact, but it was time for him to go. If he stayed any longer he'd never want to give up Emma or the peace and solitude he'd found in the manor.

He turned away from Mr. Delancy and headed through the back hallway, exiting the house from the kitchen.

He found Bailey in the barn. The manager nodded his head, gave instructions to a couple of the men, and directed Michael to a path which lead to the back fields. They silently walked toward a hillside covered with tall trees and bushes.

Bailey veered onto another path and then up an incline. Michael's thigh burned slightly, and he hoped he wouldn't re-break the bone on this excursion. His heart thudded in his chest, and he found himself riddled with guilt for not telling Emma his plan.

They reached the area where Michael had first arrived. He could see a black scorched spot and some of the trees were singed. Although he didn't recognize it, he felt a strong pull, hitting him from the area where the ground was black. There seemed to be an energy crackling around him, which got stronger and caused his body to tingle.

"This is where we found you," Bailey said.

"What do I do?" Michael looked around and thought he could see a pattern in the grass.

"Just walk into the area. You should feel an electrical current around you. As you get closer to the area, the feeling gets stronger. You may want to keep your eyes closed. If you watch the motion it will upset your stomach," Bailey said, and leaned against a tree.

Michael shook his head, trying to stop the dizziness that began to swim in his brain. He took a step forward. "Thank you for your help, Bailey." He turned and looked at the foreman. "Keep an eye on her. She's will be angry with me."

"Will do, and I'll let Mrs. Tharp know. She'll keep Miss Emma busy. Good luck, Mr. Drury," Bailey said.

Michael moved toward the spot of his arrival. He felt the air pull at him and it seemed to direct him to the proper spot. He kept his eyes open as long as he could and watched the trees begin to spin around him.

* * * * *

Bailey watched, the area around Michael began to flash and brighten. The air around the trees became heavy, and Bailey found himself stepping back. He put his hand up to block the bright glare. He saw Michael put on his hard hat and stretch his arms out to his sides. There was a final flash of light, which blinded Bailey for a moment. As his eyes adjusted, he saw Michael was gone.

Bailey turned to the path back to the manor and thought, *This is going to be a difficult evening.*

Chapter Fifteen

Neil Drury stared at the items in the vending machine. He was hungry but knew his mom would kill him if he got something trashy. He looked back and forth at a regular bag of peanuts, to the M&M's with peanuts. Either way, he'd get some protein and could use that as an argument if his mom protested. He didn't think she would argue much; she was so worried about Michael.

They'd kept a constant vigil over Michael for three months. The only time Neil got a break was when he went to his classes. At first, he'd found it hard to concentrate, but as the routine got into place, he was able to focus more on his studies. When they'd done the brain biopsy and EEG, Neil had nightmares. Fortunately, those tests hadn't shown anything abnormal, so he'd been able to sleep better.

He saw a reflection in the glass on the vending machine and realized someone else was waiting. He put his quarters and dime in and picked the M&M's.

"You know, Mom would hate you eating that crap."

He heard a voice behind him and turned around quickly. Standing there, like nothing else in the world was happening, was his brother, Michael. His hair had gone gray, and he'd aged a lot, but Neil knew who he saw.

"How-how are you here?" he stuttered.

"Just remember to tell me to hang on tight. I almost let go, but didn't because you told me to hang on tight.

137

It's very important." The man turned away and disappeared.

Neil forgot all about his treat and headed back to his brother's room. His heart raced as he thought his brother must have died and he'd just seen a ghost. He turned the corner and moved to the foot of the bed. Staring at the heart monitor, he saw it beat a steady rhythm.

"Neil, are you okay? You've gone white as a sheet," his mom said from the chair by the bed.

He looked over his shoulder to the hallway and then back at his mom. "The weirdest thing just happened." He looked back at his brother. "I was out by the vending machines and -" he stopped. He suddenly didn't want to give his mom anymore to worry about, and if he told her what he'd just seen, she'd have a stroke or think he'd gone nuts. "It's not important. I'll tell you later. Why don't you go get something to eat and maybe rest a while?"

"Thank you, I do want to head home and check the mail. You are sure you're all right?"

"Yeah, I have a lot of studying to do." He tried to smile.

"Okay, I'll be back by ten." Mrs. Drury got up and picked up her purse. "Love you, son."

"Love you, too, Mom."

* * * * *

Michael kept his eyes closed tightly. He sensed his body moving and heard crashing and popping noises around him.

When things quieted down, he felt the air cool, and his body became tight and painful. He tried to move but found any notion of movement caused pain to scream in him.

He finally managed to open his eyes. They were out of focus and dry. He blinked several times, and tried to clear his vision. He could hear something beeping but couldn't see what made the noise. Looking straight up, all he saw was something shiny and gray. He blinked a couple more times and moved his eyes. He tried to see what was around him. Fear suddenly grabbed his heart, and he thought he might be dead.

Trying to speak, he found his voice didn't work, and all he managed was a squeak and cough. Something moved in the room to his right, and he saw his younger brother frown over him.

"Loser, are you in there?" Neil said, his eyes open wide. "Are you awake?" Michael blinked at him a couple of times. "Shit," the teenager cursed, and pulled his cell phone out of his shirt pocket. "Hey, mom," he said into the phone. "I think you need to come back. I think Michael's awake . . . well, yeah, he's staring at me and blinking. He even made a weird noise." Neil snapped the phone closed and watched his brother.

Michael tried to whisper something, but Neil didn't seem to be able to hear him. He leaned nearer to Michael.

"You look like shit, geek," Michael said in a scratchy voice.

Neil smiled. "Slacker, it's about time you woke up. Mom hadn't said it, but I know she's been worrying like crazy about you not waking up." He heard his brother whisper again and leaned over.

"You still look like shit, geek,." Michael said, and tried to smile.

"Yeah, you think I look bad? You should see yourself, Mr. I'm-Going-To-Save-The-Dry- Wall-All-By-Myself. The film will be out in the fall. Your bruises have faded, but, dude, bathe sometime. You stink." Neil grinned. "Mom's going to be relieved you're back."

"How long was I out?"

Neil looked up at the ceiling, as though trying to remember. "You fell at the beginning of April and it's mid-July now ... "

"What?" Michael felt a jolt in his guts.

"Yeah, it's been a little over three months. I don't think I'll ever understand how you survived the fall. Don't get me wrong, loser, I'm glad you survived, but really, forty-eight floors? A scientist is doing research into up-draft. I can't wait to see his findings."

Michael frowned. "You are really turning into a science freak, you know?" he whispered.

And then all hell broke loose as Michael's mom flew into the room, thanking God she'd only been in the parking lot and not on the freeway. She would have wrecked her car. When she learned Neil hadn't gotten a nurse or doctor to check on Michael, she went into her 'what were you thinking' mode and left the room, searching for someone to help.

Things moved pretty quickly for a while. Michael found a cast on his leg from his hip down to his ankle. Apparently, some surgeon had repaired the break in his thigh with a metal rod and screws. The doctor said the cast was supposed to come off in a week, so he didn't see why Michael couldn't start rehabilitation first thing in the morning.

One of the nurses said she understood why he was so stiff and sore. Lying in bed for three months, with minimal movement to keep him from getting bedsores, meant his muscles got lazy. It wouldn't take long to get them back into shape, but since he'd been unconscious for three months, they'd have to be careful not to overdo any strenuous activity.

His mom came in every day to help with the rehab. In a way, Michael felt embarrassed for her to be there. He barked at her a couple of times to go away; he was almost thirty-years-old and didn't need babying. She just smacked his head and told him to behave. Besides, he'd slept through his birthday, and he *was* thirty-years-old.

It was another two weeks before the doctor thought it safe enough to remove the cast from his leg. He worked hard on his upper body, and got his arms and back into shape. Once he was free of the cast, it was all the nurses could do to keep him in one place. They insisted he use crutches, which he was more than practiced with from his time at the manor. He remembered vividly the splint he'd worn there and at times thought he still smelled the odor of the rotting wood. He'd shiver and then remember Emma as she cleaned his leg after helping to remove the thing and the warmth would return to him.

* * * * *

Michael got settled back into his hospital bed. After a long morning of exercise, he felt hungry and exhausted. When he heard the door open, he looked up and saw a tall man poking his bald head into the room.

141

"Jack! Hey man, get your ass in here," Michael said, and sat up straighter on the bed.

"Hey, you look a million times better than the last time I saw you." Jack was on crutches. Neil told him what happened to Jack: when the crane operator swung the drywall toward the building they were working on, the whole pallet came apart. Several pieces of the chalky wall hit Jack, and he'd gone over backwards, sitting on a tool-box in such a way that it shattered his hip and the top part of his thigh.

"Neil told me what happened. Are you doing the rehab thing, too?" Michael watched his friend gingerly sit in the chair by his bed.

"Yeah, I started about two months ago. I'm sick to death of crutches." He looked up at Michael. "Your mom was really worried you weren't ever going to come around. I just figured you were being lazy as shit and would come back when you got bored enough. Has the doctor said when you're getting sprung?"

"No, and I tell you, if I never see Jell-O again, it will be the happiest I've ever been in my life. That stuff sucks."

"Go home soon; you'll get better quicker on your mom's good cooking. I swear hospital food is a death penalty." He smiled at Michael and shook his head. "Now explain to me how it was you survived the fall, man. Everyone on the team wrote you off."

"That's the big question. I'll never be able to get it worked out. Neil said I landed on the sidewalk in such a way, I didn't hit my head. The way I came down on my leg must have cushioned the rest of my body, or something like that. You know my brother; he's all scientific about it. I can't understand the words that come out of his mouth."

"What was it like? I mean, did you know you were in a coma?"

Michael looked at Jack and wasn't sure he should say anything about where he'd been. His friend would probably think he'd lost his mind in the fall. "No. When I woke up, I thought it April and maybe the day after the accident."

Jack shook his head. "Weird."

They went silent for a few minutes. "So how's Rachel taking all this?" Michael asked.

"She left me. She got sick of coming to the hospital, and I found out later she had someone else on her play station. It's for the best."

"Yeah, she had backed you into the marriage corner, if I remember it right," Michael said.

"Damn straight, man. At least she didn't bring up kids. I'm way too young to be thinking of family, right?"

"Right. You'd be out in the sandbox playing with the kids, instead of doing your husbandly duties." Michael grinned.

"Asshole."

"Thank you, I haven't been called that in a while."

"You're welcome."

"So, have you been sitting here watching me a lot?"

"Oh, a bit, now and then. It's been great fun watching you snooze." Jack grinned.

"Jerk, you could have woken me up." Michael adjusted the pillow behind his shoulders.

"And miss all the drool? No way, dude." Jack frowned. "Welcome back, man. You've been missed."

"Yeah, my mom's told me several times how worried sick she's been. How's it going for you? Neil said you'd broken your hip."

"It's not bad. I'm going to try to get back to work soon. When your harness broke, man, that idiot up in the crane didn't know which part of his ass to scratch and ran the siding into the building. Because I watched you head down, I didn't see the pallet come at me. I just got the stitches out last week."

"Stitches? Neil didn't mention stitches."

Jack grinned again. "I got a whole new hip. The pallet hit me hard and I landed the wrong way on one of those steel toolboxes. It cracked my hip to pieces."

"Yeah, he mentioned that but didn't say you'd had surgery. Wow, that's a drag. You're up and around though," Michael said.

Jack leaned over the arm of the chair. "Want to see my scar?" He laughed. "I'll show you mine, if you show me yours." He and Michael laughed together. "No, it's crazy. The day after the surgery they got me up and walking around. It hurt like shit, but I guess it's the way they handle these things. The physical therapist said I could switch to a cane next week. It will be great. I hate crutches."

"Have you been back to the site at all since the accident?"

"No. I heard the guy driving the crane was a newbie. He's on restriction now."

144

"A lot of good that will do. He should go back through training."

Jack smirked and nodded. "The crew just started back to work about four weeks ago. It took the inspectors a month to finish their report. On a lighter note, the doctor originally said I'd be out three to six months. I'm bored, so I'm voting for three months."

"Don't push it, man. You should use as much of the disability as possible."

Jack adjusted in his seat. "So, what is it you aren't telling me? You sure you don't remember anything from your down time?"

"You wouldn't believe me."

"Try me."

Michael looked at his friend. "You might think I've gone off my meds."

"Stalling, dude."

"Right. It's really weird though. I woke up in 1815 England." Michael saw a new look on Jack's face. He looked a little surprised. "See, I knew people would think I was nuts."

"Mike, come on. 1815 England? Could you have been dreaming?"

"That's one of the things that makes it even weirder. It seemed so real. I could have dreamt it, I suppose, but I'm not sure what to think."

Jack propped his elbow on the arm of the chair and put his chin in his hand. "What was 1815 like? I bet there were no sports bars with hot chicks."

Michael laughed. "You've got that right. No TV or electric razors either. When I woke up, I thought I'd been sent to some rehab place run by a religious group out in Darrington, but no, that wasn't the case and there was a beautiful woman."

Jack sat back and grinned. "A woman. This is going to be good."

Michael spent the next hour telling Jack about his travel to the past. They also spent some time talking about plans for their work future. Jack told Michael all about the disability insurance and how they'd be covered for a while. Hopefully, both would be able to get back to work before their six months were up. If they didn't, they'd be supported by the state, which neither wanted to consider.

Jack didn't say much about his story, except that Michael should think hard about speaking to his doctor about those meds.

After Jack left for the day, Michael's mom came into the room. He sat in the chair next to the window, stared out and watched rain run down the glass. He felt tired and thought he might cry, but couldn't say why. When he told Jack his story, it left him feeling alone.

"Michael, what's the matter? Are you feeling all right?" his mom asked, as she stepped into the room.

He looked at her, and tried to smile. "It's nothing, Mom. I'm okay."

She moved a chair next to him, sat down and took his hand. "Michael James Drury don't you fib to me now. I'm your mother, and I know when something is wrong." She looked at him, and waited patiently for a reasonable response.

He sat back in his chair and knew she would look at him like that until he said something. "I'm just feeling sorry for myself and having a pity party."

"That's completely understandable, son. This place isn't very mood elevating." She looked around the room. "You'd think they could paint the walls a brighter color than boring gray. Now, I spoke to the doctor this morning. He said, depending how the rehab goes, you could be driving again in about ten days. He wants you to build up more strength in your legs, but gradually. Don't go all gangbusters. He said the bone still needs to heal, and you should pace yourself."

"A goal. That's a good thing. Did he really say gangbusters?" he asked, and rubbed his forehead.

"Well no. I added that, but I got his meaning. He said the rehab technician reported you were overdoing it, which I'm well aware you are capable of. Please, Michael, don't push yourself too hard." Mrs. Drury sat back in her chair, and clasped her hands in her lap. "Now there is something we need to talk about. After the accident, I didn't know how long you would be in here. A month ago, Neil and I packed up your apartment and moved everything into storage. I just didn't have the money to keep paying rent on the place. It doesn't mean you won't have a place to go. I got your old room at the house cleaned out, and you know you can stay with us as long as you need to," she said as he nodded his head and turned to look back out the window. "Honey, I'm sorry about the apartment."

"That's not it, Mom. The apartment is a rental. Those are a dime a dozen," Michael said, trying to smile.

"Then what's bothering you, son? Tell me."

Michael took a breath and looked back at her. "Mom, please don't think I've lost my mind," he said, truly smiling. "When I was unconscious, I was in a different place and in a whole different time."

"I don't understand what you mean by 'a different time'?"

"I travelled to a place called Darlington, England. I was found in a field behind this manor house and cared for there. It's called Delancy Manor, and the people were very kind," he said quietly. "It was 1815."

She sat forward, and took his hand again. "Do you mean you dreamt about that time?" she asked. "I can't grasp what you're telling me."

"I mean I time-travelled there, broken leg and all. I think."

"Michael, have you and your brother come up with some plan to tease me?" she asked, quite seriously.

"No."

"I don't see how it's possible you were anywhere but here. Michael, you've been lying in that bed," she pointed over her shoulder, "since April. I watched you. Neil sat with you. We would have noticed if you weren't there."

"I know, but it seemed real, Mom. I met a really wonderful woman and ..." He stopped when his throat tightened. He looked back out at the rain, as it streaked the window. "I let her go and didn't say goodbye."

"Michael, I'm certain that once you get your strength back and find your routine again, you'll realize it was all just a nice dream."

"Maybe ... I don't know. I feel so guilty for not saying goodbye to her," his voice faded, and finally he shook his head. "Is Neil going to come by this week?"

"I'm not sure. He's taking some pre-college course this summer. I can see that he does though," she said.

Michael laughed. "Will there ever be a time when he isn't taking some course or another?"

"You know your brother, it's doubtful."

"Could you ask him to bring his lap-top with him? I need for him to look up some stuff."

Chapter Sixteen

At the end of the week, Michael had more X-rays taken of his leg. They came back looking good with the rod and screws in place. The doctor said he could probably release him in a couple of days.

Neil came in on Friday afternoon, carrying his lap-top case. "Mom told me you'd cracked your head on something and you thought you weren't here."

"It's about time you showed up, geek," Michael snarled from the bed. He itched to get out of the hospital. He didn't think he'd ever experienced such exquisite boredom in his life.

"Excuse me, loser. Some of us go to school and have work to do. Unlike some who slack in bed all day." Neil unzipped the bag and pulled out a cord. He plugged it into a socket and got his laptop started. "You are such a loser." He looked at his computer and typed in a password. "What are we looking up?"

"See what you can find on Delancy Manor in Darlington, England," Michael said, and watched his brother write the names on a note-pad. "Look up Emma Wallace, too."

"Who's she?" Neil looked at Michael with his eyebrows raised.

"A very beautiful woman," Michael said.

Neil nodded his head and started typing. "A hottie. Interesting." Michael frowned from the bed. "I'm just saying ..." He quieted down and started checking sites as they came up.

Michael realized Neil seemed to be lost in the information. "Geek, if you grunt one more time I'm going to think mom switched you at birth for an orangutan. Speak, please," Michael said, impatient.

Neil grinned. "Sorry, it says Delancy Hall was once owned by Lord Clarence Delancy. He had sheep and a farm but mostly was known for his business savvy. He was admired ... Blah, blah, blah. He never married, and the estate passed to a cousin when Delancy died from a heart attack at fifty-six-years-old. The manor went to ruin after that. It was bought in the 1970s by a family named Billington. They've done some restoration and remodeling, and it's open for tours six days a week." Neil moved to another web-site. "Here it says Lord Delancy cared for many wards over the years that he helped get started on a good path. Oh ..." Neil looked at Michael.

"What?"

"This is really sad. It says Emma Wallace was Mr. Delancy's ward from 1807 to 1818. She gained access to a trust her parents left to her when she turned twenty-five. She remained at Delancy all her life and never married." Neil looked at him again. "That's all it says about her."

"It really says she never married?" Michael looked away from his brother.

"Yep."

"Damn, that woman." Michael hissed under his breath. "I met her. I never thought ..."

"Wait, here's something ... this is weird. I don't see how it's related to the stuff about Delancy and Emma Wallace, but it says a meteor hit in a field just above Delancy Manor. It was reported in the Darlington newspaper. Only two lines were written in April 1815."

Michael sat up in the bed, and looked at his brother. "Here's something else for you to research. I was there at Delancy Manor in 1815. I'd been there since the accident. I think my arrival might be the meteor. There was a gypsy seer who said it created a doorway and I got pulled into 1815. Neil, I don't know how to explain it." Michael ran his hands through his hair. "Don't tell Mom about this. She'll really think I've gone nuts."

"Great. I have a whacked out brother. Just what every average Joe needs. So you think you time traveled or something?" Neil asked. "Which really makes no sense. You've been lying there," he pointed at the bed, "this whole time."

"I like the 'or something' part of that, yeah." Michael felt he'd stepped into hell.

"Did you have, or do you have feelings for this hottie?"

Michael frowned at his brother again. "Hottie? God, Neil. She's a lady, and I don't deserve her. Yes, I do have feelings for her."

"Why didn't you bring her with you?" Neil asked.

"Bailey said the doorway was only for me," Michael answered.

"Who's Bailey?"

"He is the foreman at Delancy Manor."

"Loser, do you think a ranch hand knows the first thing about time travel?

"It wasn't a ranch, geek. It's an estate, and Bailey knows. He was born in 1965 in California. Believe me, he knows. He said it's my pathway, and I was the only one who could use it."

"That's bullshit, man," Neil said, and sat back in his chair. "There's no such thing as a personal pathway. You could have brought her through with you. The only real problem would be where she might end up. You came back to your natural point, where you were supposed to be. It's hard to tell where this Emma would show up."

"You understand all of this?" Michael asked.

"Sure. I took an advanced gravitational time dilation course at the university. I got college credit for it," Neil answered, puffing out his chest a little.

"Damn, you really are turning into a science geek, aren't you?" Michael asked and smiled at his younger brother. "So, in the simplest terms, using words with ten letters or less, can you explain to me what happened?"

"Yeah, but it's all theory," Neil said, and set his laptop aside. "You know, there's something else that's weird. The day you woke up, I went out to the vending machines and an older version of you showed up."

"What?" Michael frowned at his brother.

"I didn't tell Mom about it because she'd think I'd hit my head, too. You told me to tell you to hang on tight."

"I don't think you hit your head. I think you might be taking drugs. I wonder what it meant about 'holding on tight'? How is it possible I was in Darlington, but here in this bed, and then I show up to you out by the vending machines? How does that work?"

"I don't know. I thought you'd died and I was seeing your ghost. I'm going to have to ask one of the professors about it and see if they know anything. It was really weird."

Neil then spent the next hour explaining cosmic string theory, worm-holes, and traveling faster than the speed of light to Michael.

He started out simply enough, and Michael understood the concepts. As the hour wore on, though, Neil's language got more complicated, and Michael developed a headache. He put his hand up for Neil to stop.

"You lost me somewhere with traversable wormholes and negative energy," Michael said, and lay his head back on his pillows.

Neil pointed at him. "Loser."

"Shut up. I think you've been taken over by space aliens."

"You wish." He turned off the computer and packed it back into its case. "What are you going to do?"

"I'm not sure there's much I *can* do. Bailey got me back here by taking me to the place I originally arrived. He said if I wanted to return I had to repeat the process and since I don't really want to jump off a building again -- wait a minute. No, he said to go back I would have to come back here, since I arrived here. I don't feel the same electrical pull I felt on the hillside."

"You lost me on that one. I know mom will appreciate you not jumping off buildings again." Neil smiled. "The really weird part of this ... Michael you've been here. I mean your body has been in that bed the whole time."

"So I'm mentally there, but physically here? I don't get it. The gypsy seer said the doorway would remain open until the autumnal equinox and then close up. Bailey stayed in 1815; he liked it better." Michael shook his head. "Maybe I did have a dream."

"Well, dream or not, one thing to keep in mind, loser, is that if you go there and stay, or Emma comes here permanently, it could change the whole time-line," Neil said.

"Please don't give me the Star Trek space-time continuum crap," Michael replied.

"Man, you really are lost. Get your ass out of the '60s," Neil laughed. "Tell me you've heard of the grandfather paradox?"

Michael frowned. Neil rolled his eyes and they spoke science for the next couple of hours.

Chapter Seventeen

Michael worked in rehab hard to get his body back in shape, and by the first week of August, he'd switched from crutches to a cane, and his doctor finally agreed to let him go home.

After many conversations with Neil, he felt about 50/50 with what happened to him as being a dream. Sometimes Michael didn't know what to think. Being at the manor, being with Emma, all of it felt so real.

His mom brought some clothes, and when he slid on the jeans, he found them a bit baggy. He'd lost some weight but knew that once he got back to work and ate normal food that didn't come from a hospital kitchen, he'd gain it back.

At the appointed time, Mrs. Drury showed up to take her son home. There was a hang-up with the paperwork at the nurses' station and they scrambled to find his doctor to get the release forms signed.

While Michael waited a nurse's aide walked into his room, and carried a large mailing envelope.

"Hi, Mr. Drury. This is the stuff that we found in your pockets when you were brought in from the accident. Your nurse asked me to give it to you." The girl smiled and left the room.

Michael opened the envelope and took out his wallet. He looked inside and shook his head. "Interesting. I haven't thought of this thing once," he said to his mom.

"You should make sure everything's in there. Do you carry your wallet when you work?" she asked.

"I was going to a sports bar that night to watch a Mariners game with Jack. It looks as though nothing's missing." He raised his eyebrows as he put it in his back pocket. He looked in the envelope again and found some change and a couple of pens. Turning it upside down to pour the coins into his hand, Michael saw something gold fall out. He separated it from the quarters and dimes, and pulled up a gold chain with a cross. Michael sat down hard on the edge of the bed, then bounced back up and the change fell out of his hand and rolled onto the floor.

"Michael, are you all right?" his mom asked, standing up from her chair.

"It wasn't a dream," he whispered.

"What did you say? I couldn't hear you. When did you start wearing a cross?"

"It belongs to the woman I met. It's Emma's cross. I noticed she'd stopped wearing it, but she wouldn't say what she had done with it," Michael said, and continued to stare at the necklace.

"Michael, are you seeing someone?"

He looked at her, and saw excitement in her eyes. "Mom, remember awhile back we had a discussion about me being somewhere else while I was unconscious?"

"Yes, I remember."

"This cross belonged to the woman I met in 1815. She is real and I didn't dream any of it. Damn, I've got to talk to Neil."

* * * * *

Once he arrived home, Michael paced around the house, waiting for his brother to come home from his afternoon classes. He'd gone into Neil's room to see if he could find something on the computer but ended up getting angry at himself for not being able to figure out how to turn the stupid thing on.

When Neil turned up at 4:00, Michael told him about his new discovery. Finding the gold necklace was another sign and more proof of Michael's experience -- that it was real. After he showed the cross to Neil, Michael put it around his neck.

"Great. Now I have a girlie loser brother," Neil smirked.

"Smartass. I don't want to lose it," Michael said, and tucked it under the collar of his shirt.

"I called one of the professors I took a class from, and told him what the gypsy lady said about the portal being open until the fall," Neil said. "The professor said it sounded possible and I won't bore you with the scientific details, but if you decided to go back, you'll have to jump off the forty-eighth floor of the building again, which we knew, or find a carrier." Neil turned on his computer. "He sort of knew about the point of origin stuff, but didn't think it would work."

Michael watched as Neil pushed a button and wanted to kick himself. The computer hummed to life. "What's a carrier?"

"It's someone going through their own portal. They would carry you with them. The only problem is finding someone who's going back to Darlington, England, in 1815, or thereabouts. You don't want to know the odds on finding one, and you wouldn't want to wind up some place bad like Pompeii before the volcano blew or France during the revolution. That would be bad." He sat down and typed his password into his computer and then looked at Michael. "I have homework. Speaking of which, when do you go back to work?"

"Probably in a week or a month. The doctor will decide after my physical therapy this week." Michael moved to the door, but turned back before he left. "I don't know why I thought the necklace would be more help." He shook his head.

"Hey, it was. It gives us more proof you were there and not losing your mind." Neil grinned. "I still think you bought it on the street somewhere."

Michael frowned. "Geek."

"Later, loser."

* * * * *

The next couple of weeks dragged for Michael. The doctor delayed his release to go back to work, and he was still trying to build up his stamina. He got back into a routine and felt glad to be around his friends again. He found Bailey had been right though. The present time was noisy and never seemed to shut off.

A couple of times, he'd thought about being at the top of a building or walking a steel girder, and in his mind he'd look over the side and think about just stepping off. The images of his mom and brother would invade his mind and he'd get back to his rehab workout.

Most nights he woke up from a nightmare about being pulled away from Emma or they were in the midst of making love and he'd wake up hard and out of breath.

His mom often came in when he was stretched out on the couch in the family room watching TV.

He remembered what Bailey had said about feeling unsettled. He was having a hard time dealing with everyday realities. Sitting in Seattle traffic wore him out. He missed the quiet of the countryside around Delancy Manor. He didn't remember ever feeling such peace.

On a rainy Sunday afternoon, Michael stood by a kitchen window and watched the rain pour water from above. He heard a light switch flick on and turned to see his Mom. He didn't want to talk about anything. He was tired and empty. He felt her come up behind him, put her arm around his waist and lean on his shoulder.

"What's the matter, Michael?" she asked gently.

He continued to stare out the window. "There's nothing wrong. I'm okay."

"I've told you more than a million times not to lie to me," she scolded him.

"I know. I'm just mulling some things over."

"Your brother tried to explain to me about this time travel business." She turned him around to face her and shook her head. "It didn't make much sense, but when he said you wanted to go back ... well, I guess that made some sense."

Michael didn't say anything. He didn't want to hurt his mother by telling her about the need he felt to return to the peace and warmth he'd experienced with Emma.

"This woman, Emma Wallace ... you think you're in love with her?" Mrs. Drury asked.

He turned his head, and looked her straight in the eye. "Mom, it's not something I *think*. I *know* it. Not being able to hear her voice or touch her makes me feel as though a part of me is missing. It's all I can do ... never mind," Michael said, and looked back out the window.

There was a sudden loud bang upstairs and footsteps began to pound above their heads.

"Your brother ..." Mrs. Drury started.

"Michael? Michael where are you?" Neil's voice carried throughout the house.

Both Michael and his mother turned from the window. "I'm in the kitchen," Michael yelled back.

Hurried steps thudded down the stairs, and when Neil turned into the room, he was breathing hard and his face looked white as a ghost.

"Neil, are you okay? What's going on?" Their mom rushed to him.

"Yeah, fine," Neil said, and turned to Michael. "You are not going to believe this. Remember when you were in rehab, and we looked up information on the manor and Emma?"

"Yeah."

"It's changed. I came home that day and printed everything I could find, but it's different now," Neil said.

"What you printed from that website changed?" Michael frowned.

"No, that's the same. The website says something different, but the last time anything was updated on the site was three years ago. I'm not sure what happened. Come on, you've got to see this."

All three went up to Neil's room. Michael sat at the desk and looked at the screen. Neil flipped through the pages about Delancy Manor. Michael read as quickly as he could and couldn't believe what he read. It said Emma Wallace was one of Clarence Delancy's wards that committed suicide in 1815.

"Michael, it says she threw herself off a cliff at Robin Hood's Bay in North Yorkshire. They never found her body."

Michael tried to understand what Neil said, but felt he'd heard a different language. He felt stunned by this latest development.

"Why are you looking so weird?" Neil asked.

Michael shook his head, and tried to get the images of Emma falling off a cliff out of his brain. Guilt wrapped itself around his heart and squeezed, and made it difficult to breathe. He couldn't reply to Neil's question.

"Okay, there's another entry here," Neil said, and clicked onto another screen. "It says she went mad after a brief involvement with a stranger in Darlington. The man was never identified, but they thought he treated her bad. Mr. Delancy did all he could to help her, but in the end ... well, you get the picture. This was in 1815." Neil handed Michael a stack of papers. "This is what I printed off a couple of weeks ago. Look at the date; it's the one that said she never married and so on."

"I'm not sure I'm getting the point Neil," his mom said.

"I do." Michael looked at them both. "Something changed. It's what you said about messing with the time line. It caused things for Emma to go from bad to worse."

Neil nodded his head. "Something else you need to know. I talked to one of the professors I study with at the university. He's stumped by your being here, there and everywhere."

Michael looked at Neil, and nodded his head. They hadn't said anything to their mother about the older Michael appearing by the vending machines.

"Neil, would you stop being so cryptic? What are you talking about?" Mrs. Drury asked.

"We've been trying to figure out how Michael could be here and there while he was in the coma. My professor doesn't have any idea how it all happened."

They were all quiet for a few minutes. Michael could tell his mother tried to understand what had transpired, but seemed to have a hard time. The shrill ring of the telephone in the hallway caused all three to jump. Mrs. Drury went out of the room and answered it.

Neil leaned against his desk. "What are you going to do?"

Michael rested back in the chair, and stared at the computer screen. He was willing it to change to better news about Emma. "I don't have the first clue, brother."

"Michael," his mom said from the doorway. Both of her sons looked at her. She pointed to the phone, and looked a bit surprised. "You have a phone call."

"Who is it?" he asked, and pushed himself out of the chair. Mrs. Drury only mumbled and backed into the hall. She looked as pale as Neil did when he'd raced into the kitchen. "Mom, I think you need to sit down," Michael said.

"No, just take the call."

Michael went to the telephone stand at the end of the hallway. He lifted the receiver to his ear. "Hello?"

A woman's voice came through the phone. "Yes, is this Michael Drury?" He answered yes and waited. "Mr. Drury, my name is Gretchen Hargrove. I'm a patient coordinator here at Grey's Harbor Hospital in Aberdeen."

Michael's eyebrows came together. For a split second he thought it was someone from the hospital where he'd been a patient, but then remembered he'd been in Seattle, not Aberdeen. He continued to wait.

"Sir, a woman was found washed up on the beach just north of Ocean Shores. She had no identification on her, and all she would say is your name and told us to find you. We think she might be from England because of her accent."

Michael's neck snapped as he looked up at his mom. She had her hands up to her cheeks and was anxious. "She's alive?" was all he could get out.

"Oh, yes, sir."

"Miss Hargrove, did she say why me?" Michael asked.

"No, but she said to tell you Emma Wallace needs your help. Sir, she's being very difficult to treat. We believe she's very dehydrated, but she keeps pulling the IV's out of her arm. At this point, we can't get near her without causing her to erupt in panic. We thought about transferring her to Western State Mental Hospital, but they haven't any spare beds at this time. Is there anything you can tell us to help her?"

"I'm on my way. I'll be there in a couple of hours. Let her know you found me, and I'm coming," he said and watched as Mrs. Drury went into the master bedroom. Michael heard a closet door open.

"Thank you, Mr. Drury. We'll look forward to seeing you." The woman on the other end disconnected the call, and all Michael heard was the dial tone.

He looked at Neil who stood in his doorway. Michael grinned. "She's alive," he whispered.

"Can I come with you?" Neil asked.

"No," Michael said, and heard his mom say the same thing. He walked to the master bedroom door, and saw his mom rummaging through her closet. "Mom, what are you doing?"

"She'll need clothes and a hair brush." Mrs. Drury went into the bathroom. "I've got some extra shampoo and lotion you can take to her. She'll need that, Michael." Mrs. Drury came out of the bathroom, holding a brush. "Are we close in size?"

"No, you're taller than Emma," he said, still grinning.

"Well, if the jeans are too long you can roll the legs up," she said, and put some other things into a travel bag she'd set on the bed.

Michael shook his head. "I'll go put on my sneakers."

Chapter Eighteen

Emma opened her eyes and felt water rush in around her head. She tried to see where she had fallen and was hit in the face when a wave washed over her. It pressed her down into the darkness, and she realized she couldn't feel the bottom below her feet.

She tried to remember all Mrs. Tharp had taught her about swimming, she kicked her feet hard to get back to the surface. She had to find dry land soon or the frigid water would freeze her solid. The weight of her dress pulled her down, but she continued to kick as hard as she could. Finally, she found her way back to the surface and kicked her feet while turning. She saw the shoreline as she made her turn and paddled in that direction.

The harder she tried to get to the shore, the more the current pulled her back. The heavy dress tugged on her shoulders, and she found herself more and more exhausted. She stopped paddling for a moment and kicked her feet just to stay afloat. The water was so cold, she knew if she didn't get out of it soon she would surely catch her death.

Emma gave it one more try, kicking hard and paddling with all the might. A sudden wave came up behind her and seemed to pick her up and push her forward. She couldn't tell how long it took, but she could feel sand under her feet. She struggled with her dress and pushed forward to the beach. She collapsed in a pile, and shivered as her teeth chattered.

The next time she opened her eyes, she saw a man standing over her. He unfolded something and smiled at her when he saw she was awake. The man tried to wrap something around her and spoke in a strange language.

Fear overwhelmed her, and she tried to fight the man. She looked around and saw several other men standing around her. They were all dressed in the same clothes, wearing strange hats. She screamed and fought as the man jabbed something sharp into her arm and then attached something to the instrument that seemed to put fluid into her arm. She began to feel warm and very sleepy, which she knew wasn't right. Several of the men picked her up and put her on a strange carrier. They began to move, and she tried to watch the sky above her slide by, but her eyes wouldn't stay open.

When Emma could actually think a bit clearly, she heard a beeping sound which came from somewhere. She was in a room that smelled of human excrement and alcohol but worse -- much worse. She opened her eyes slightly and tried to look around. The walls were made of brick and painted a grayish green. The smell made her nose burn.

A woman stood over her who must have noticed Emma's eyes open, because she smiled and said, "Hi, honey."

Emma wanted to ask where she was, but her throat felt dry and it was hard to form words.

"You just rest. The doctor is taking good care of you," the woman said.

Emma thought she might be in some sort of monastery. The woman's head was covered by a cap made of a green material that matched the clothes she wore. She knew nun's wore such caps and thought she should trust the woman, but didn't. She felt overwhelmed with fear.

"Can you tell me your name?" the woman asked.

Emma whispered her name and tried to swallow. The beeping nose was very disturbing and she glanced around, trying to see where it came from.

"Emma, my name is Beverly. If you need anything, just call for me. I'll be right here," she said, still smiling down at Emma. "You've had quite an adventure. What were you doing out in the ocean?"

She tried to make sense of what the woman said. She remembered the walk to the edge of the cliff and when she stepped off, just as Mr. Bailey told her to do. She could still see the blackness and then the lights flashing. She didn't know what the woman meant by 'adventure'. It certainly hadn't been that. She had a reason for being here and had to keep that in focus.

"Where is Michael?" Emma asked.

"Who is that, dear? Is he someone we need to contact for you? Do you have his phone number?"

"Yes, please contact him. His name is Michael Drury. He lives in Seattle. Is it very far from here?"

"Far? Well, he could be here in a couple of hours, I guess. I'll let the secretary know and see if she can find him. I'll be just outside the door." The woman moved away.

Emma dozed off and then felt herself float. She opened her eyes and saw several people around her. They had the sheet under her in their hands and were moving her off of one table to what seemed to be a very narrow bed. Emma became frightened and started to cry. She moved her arm and saw the instrument which poked into her vein. It burned. She reached with her other hand and pulled it out. Blood spurted from the vein and one of the people shouted something.

All of the movement scared Emma very much and caused her to fight again. Someone held her shoulders down and another grabbed onto her arm, wrapped a leather band around her wrist and tied it to a rail. A man took hold of her other arm and held it down. Then he put another sharp object into that vein while another man got a bandage on her bleeding arm. The fluid began to pump into her again, and she felt drowsy again, being pulled into sleep. It was the last thing she remembered.

* * * * *

Michael pulled his truck into the Grey's Harbor Hospital parking lot. It was practically empty, and although it was Sunday, he hoped it didn't mean he'd have to wait until the next day to get Emma discharged. The trip from Seattle took about three hours. He'd tried to keep the speed within legal limits.

He quickly made his way into the front part of the hospital, carrying the duffle bag packed by his mother, and was directed to the third floor by a volunteer at the information desk. He found the nurses' station. An aide said she'd find Miss Hargrove and disappeared for a few minutes.

Michael paced back and forth in front of the counter, and tried to be patient. He gripped the handle on the duffle bag tightly, wanting to venture out on his own and find Emma.

A woman with dark hair, wearing an aqua blue scrub outfit, walked up to him. Her white sneakers squeaked on the tile floor.

"Mr. Drury?" she asked, smiling. He nodded his head. "I'm Gretchen Hargrove. Come this way, please."

Michael followed her down a hallway to an office. She turned, and offered him a seat.

"Miss Hargrove, I don't want to be pushy, but where is Emma?" Michael said, refusing to sit down.

"Mr. Drury, we're trying to sort out what's happened to Miss Wallace. It will help us to treat whatever might be wrong with her." She offered him the seat again.

Michael set the bag on the floor and sat down, sighing.

Miss Hargrove sat at her desk and opened a file. "Would you have any idea why Miss Wallace went for a swim out in the ocean?"

"She likes to swim," he answered.

The woman raised her eyebrows. "In an old-fashioned dress and lace-up boots?"

"Hmm ... that one I can't explain. She does like to wear old-style clothing." Michael leaned forward in the chair. "Miss Hargrove, Emma and I had a terrible argument. We've been separated for a time. She may have thought I broke up with her," he said.

"Ah, you two had a lovers' quarrel." She nodded, and made a note in the file.

"Yeah, something like that."

"What can you tell me about her health history? Is there any heart disease, high blood pressure, or diabetes?"

"No, she's very healthy."

"Is there any history of mental illness or drug use?"

"No, why do you ask that?" He stared at the woman, and felt anger tighten the back of his neck.

"She was wild when she first came into the emergency room. She had to be sedated just to get an IV started, even though we had her tied down; she somehow managed to pull it out. She's very dehydrated and when anyone tries to get near her, the panic starts all over again. Since we were able to reach you, we decided to leave her be for now. There's an aide in the room, but no one can reach her at all," Miss Hargrove said, her own anger bubbling up.

Michael reeled in his temper. "Ma'am, imagine if you woke up in a strange place with people poking at you. She's probably in shock from the cold water and scared to death. I'm sure she tried to protect herself. Please take me to her." Michael stood up.

The patient coordinator looked at him with a sour face, but closed the folder. "Fine, follow me."

They walked back down the hallway to a room with a closed door. Miss Hargrove walked in with Michael behind her. The aide looked up from a magazine and pointed at the corner. There was a lump with a blanket pulled over it folded up in the corner of the room.

Michael put the bag on the bed, pushed past Miss Hargrove and went to the corner. He began to worry about Emma sitting on the cold hard tile floor. He squatted down, and felt his thigh tighten. He rearranged himself onto his knees, and rested back on his heels.

He thought for a minute the best way to approach her. "Emma," he said quietly. The lump jerked and tried to move closer to the wall. "Baby, it's me, Michael." He put his hand on the blanket, and felt what he thought was her shin.

"Michael?" she asked in a whisper.

"Yep, I'm right here," he answered and smiled.

The blanket moved, and he saw her head come up. Her blue eyes peeked out at him and blinked.

"Are you real?" she asked.

He found her hand under the blanket and pulled it onto his chest. "I think so. Can you feel my heartbeat?"

She focused on his chest and nodded her head slightly. Her bottom lip started to tremble. "You left without saying goodbye," she said as a tear dropped onto her cheek.

"I know, and I'm going kick myself for a very long time."

She continued to feel his heartbeat. "I missed you," she said, and pushed away from the wall, into his arms.

Michael wrapped her up, and held her. He could feel her shake and knew she was crying. He rocked her slowly and put his fingers through her hair. "Babe, shush now. Everything's going to be all right. I'll never leave you again. Never, never," he whispered in her ear.

Emma took in a deep breath and looked up at him. "I do not want you to think I am chasing after you. There is a reason I came here to find you." She glanced over his shoulder and saw Miss Hargrove and the aide watching them. Emma frowned. "Michael, they took my clothes and hairpins," she whispered.

He looked quickly at the women behind them and then back at Emma. "It's okay. Mom sent some stuff for you, and I prefer your hair down. It's much prettier and softer when you wear it down." Michael turned back to the other women. "If you wouldn't mind giving us a few minutes, I promise we'll answer your questions shortly."

"Mr. Drury ..." Miss Hargrove started.

"Ma'am, please," he said evenly.

The dark-haired woman huffed and turned to leave the room, with the aide behind her.

Michael smoothed Emma's hair back from her forehead and kissed her. "Let's get you off the cold floor before you catch pneumonia." He stood away from her and helped her up.

The blanket fell away from her body, and revealed the cotton hospital gown. Emma scooped up the blanket and wrapped it around her lower body.

"I have not a stitch on under this flimsy night wear. It is atrocious. Do people really wear these things?" she asked as he helped her to the bed.

"Yeah, they do. It is standard wear for patients in the hospital. I had to wear one for a couple of weeks after I woke up. My butt hung out and everything."

She sat on the side of the bed, with her feet dangling. "This place smells foul, too."

Michael poured her a glass of water from a plastic pitcher. "Yeah, hospital smells are pretty nasty. Honey, we need to get some water into you. Drink this." He handed her the cup.

She looked at it, took a sip, and then drank it all down. She held the cup out, and waited for Michael to pour more. She thanked him and drank again.

"Babe, go slow. You don't want to make yourself sick," he said firmly. He sat next to her on the bed. "You don't need to chase after me Emma. You've caught me -- hook, line and sinker."

"I am not exactly sure what you mean by that phrase, but it seems good," she said, and looked at the empty cup. "This is one of the strangest things I have seen, and so far, I have seen a lot of strange things."

"The phrase means I'm yours. Now, why did you jump off the cliff at Robin Hood's Bay?" He wanted to get to the bottom of her time travel experience first thing.

"How did you know about that?" She looked at him with eyes wide.

"It's a long story, which we'll go into later. What's the reason?"

She adjusted herself so she could look directly at him. "The afternoon when you left ... well, that evening I decided to tell you how very much I admired you, but you were gone, and I did not get the chance," she said, her voice very low.

"You were going to tell me you love me?" He tried not to grin too much.

"Yes."

"I see," he said, and nodded. "Why didn't you tell me on the picnic? It was a beautiful day, and we were alone. Why not then?"

"I did not feel prepared. My mind was filled with only the thought of you leaving. It was not until I got ready for dinner that I realized my thoughts were unclear. Are you laughing at me, Mr. Drury?" She looked at him, and scowled.

"No, no sweetheart. I'm not laughing at you. I'm just thinking about everything that's happened and the fact you still want me, makes me feel blessed. I guess I'm getting a little silly." He saw the look on her face and straightened his back. He tried to get his laughter under control. "Tell me how you got here? I want all the details."

"I do not believe we have enough time for that right now. That woman will come back. She is very cross with me." She looked up at Michael. "I have been a very poor guest, I am afraid."

"Don't worry about it, sweetheart. We'll get you out of here, and then I want the full explanation. Emma, my love, do you still admire me very much?"

She put the cup of water on the stand and looked at him. "Yes." She folded her hands around his, and laced his fingers with hers. "Yes, very much."

"Say it," he said, and leaned over to kiss the corner of her mouth.

"I love you," she said, closing her eyes.

Michael smiled. "I'm in heaven," he said, kissing her cheek and nose. "I love you, too, Miss Wallace, very much. The last several weeks were hell without you, but now I'm in heaven. You will marry me, right?"

Emma's eyes opened wide. "Yes, but ... " She stopped and frowned slightly.

"But?"

She looked up at Michael. "Mr. Delancy is still my guardian. We need to ask his permission. I do not believe he would say no."

Michael frowned. "Emma, he's not here. How am I supposed to ask his permission?"

She looked startled. Opening her mouth to answer, she snapped it shut, unable to find any words. She turned away from him. "I am sorry. I guess I am still rather confused," she said quietly.

Michael put his arms around her shoulders and let her rest her head on his chest. "That's okay. We don't have to know the answers right now. We've got all our lives to work on things," he said into her ear. "I love you. Now, we need to get you dressed and out of this place."

"Michael, I have no clothes. They took my dress," she said, and looked at him.

"My mom sent some stuff and then we have to convince Miss Dragon Queen out there to discharge you." He stood up and grabbed the duffel bag. Unzipping the top, he looked in and took out the jeans and a peach-colored fleece sweater.

Emma looked with curiosity at some Jockey under-wear. Michael watched as she pulled up a bra and examined it. He felt his face heat up and realized he was blushing.

"Honey, those are undergarments."

She looked at him as if he spoke another language. "They look as flimsy as this night-wear. Do women really wear these?"

"Yes, let me help you get them on." He took the panties and slid them over her feet and up to her knees. "You-you will need to pull them all the way up," he stuttered. Then he stood behind her and helped hook up the bra. He slid the sweater over her head and handed her the jeans.

"These are a man's pair of slacks." She looked at him confused.

Michael smiled. "No, they were my mom's. Women wear pants a lot now."

She got them on and zipped up. "This sweater is so soft and warm," she said, and felt parts of her body, moving her hands along her arms.

Michael watched, and held a pair of socks. His mouth turned dry, and he felt warm again. "Miss Wallace, I find your movements very distracting and have to tell you I want to touch you much the same way."

She blushed, and put her hands on her cheeks. "I never felt anything so soft. I did not intend to distract you."

Michael put his hands on her waist and lifted her onto the bed. He put the socks into her hand. "Put these on your feet, ma'am."

Emma held them up and looked at the footwear, trying to figure them out. She leaned over and put one on her foot. It stretched up to her ankle. "Women wear the strangest clothing in this time," she said, and shook her head. She put the other one on and held her feet out, looking at them.

He could see the jeans were a bit long on Emma, but once she put the shoes on, they'd be just fine. He held up a tennis shoe. "I hope these aren't too big." He helped her put one on. She pushed his hands away, and said she knew how to do laces.

When she was fully dressed, Michael stood up and smiled. "You look wonderful. How does it feel?"

"Strange, I have never worn slacks before," she said, picking at the jeans.

He went to the door and looked out in the hallway. He saw Miss Hargrove at the nurses' station. He waved at her, went back into the room and sat down by Emma on the bed, who still moved her feet around in the sneakers.

"Baby, let me talk to her. You just keep looking gorgeous. You are so beautiful, and it just occurred to me that I haven't kissed you once. How can you tolerate such a slight?" Michael said, feeling guilty. He moved in close to her and brought his lips down. He'd forgotten how soft and warm her mouth felt. He held back from getting too carried away. Miss Hargrove would be coming, and he needed a clear mind. He kissed Emma's nose.

"Mr. Drury, I do not want to be make too many demands, but I will require at least ten kisses like this daily -- if not more." She smiled up at him.

"I'll do my best to comply with your wishes, Miss Wallace. You know I want to keep you happy." Michael put his forehead on hers as the door opened.

Miss Hargrove came in, and carried Emma's chart. She acted surprised to see the patient up and completely dressed.

"Ah, Miss Hargrove, thank you for coming so quickly. I've made arrangements with my mother's doctor in Seattle to see Emma this evening. Would you please arrange for her discharge? We have to be north of here by seven," he said, and looked at his watch. "We do need to leave fairly soon, too."

"What is the name of the doctor?" the woman asked incredulous.

"Dr. Jeff Winter, he is an internist at the university and a friend of the family. If you'd like I could get him on the phone." Michael held out his cell phone.

"That won't be necessary. Miss Wallace, how do you feel?"

Emma looked up with surprise. "Fine," she answered meekly.

"She's been drinking water, and I think the dehydration caused her to be confused. She felt very frightened. We'll stop on the road and get some bottles to take with us," Michael said.

"Yes, I drank the water." Emma nodded.

The patient coordinator shook her head. "I don't think it's a good idea to move her at this time. We need to make sure she doesn't regress into her prior state. I'd prefer we keep her here one more night. Just to be sure," Miss Hargrove said.

"I don't believe there's anything to worry about. We are willing to sign papers releasing you from any blame if something does go wrong. Isn't there something about being released against medical advice?" Michael asked.

The woman stared at him for a moment and then got an unhappy look on her face. "Fine, I'll get the discharge papers together. Please give me a moment," she said between clenched teeth and left the room.

"Mr. Drury, you are very smart," Emma said.

"Honey, I knew there would be good reason to watch the learning network." He hugged her.

It took only about thirty minutes, to get the proper forms, because Michael acted impatient. He paced by the nurses' station, making the attendants uncomfortable until they received the papers to sign.

Then, he threw the duffle bag over his shoulder, and took Emma by the hand. Bowing slightly to her, he said, "My lady, your carriage awaits." She looked at him as though confused. He grinned. "Never mind, let's get you out of here."

Chapter Nineteen

As they approached Michael's truck, Emma looked in every direction at once, and took in the new world around her. She saw cars moving on the main road in Aberdeen and many different types of buildings. She looked down the hill and couldn't believe her eyes.

Michael opened the truck, and let her see the inside compartment. He put the duffle bag behind the seat.

"What do you think, Miss Wallace? Are you ready to give it a try?" Michael asked, and ran his hand over her hair.

"You ride in this?" She looked up at him as he nodded his head. "Where are the horses?"

"They're in there, but it's a different kind of horse." He offered his hand and helped her get into the cab. He walked around to the driver's side, and seated himself.

He showed her how to hook and release the safety belt and explained locking and unlocking the door. When he started the engine, Emma jumped and looked anxiously at the dashboard.

"It's okay, babe, I promise everything is as it should be. We're going to move now."

He moved a stick in front of him and the truck went backwards. She nodded her head, and gripped the seat until her knuckles turned white.

They headed east out of Aberdeen on the main highway; Emma looked out the side window and saw strange buildings move by. When they turned a corner, she felt her stomach turn, too.

"Hon, it would be best for you to look straight out the front window. If you look out the side, things move too fast," he said, reaching out his fingers to touch her cheek.

"Michael, the way it is moving has made me nauseous. Must we travel so fast?" she asked in a shaky voice.

"See those signs along the road? They tell us how fast to go. We have to follow the signs," he said, and held her hand.

"It seems too fast," she said, her eyes filled with tears.

"I'll try to go a little slower and stay in the right lane. Hey, I've got a coat in here. Why don't you roll it up and put your head down?" She watched him pat his thigh. "It might help with the motion if you don't look out the window."

"Okay," she answered, and tried very hard not to panic. "Where is the coat?"

"Behind your seat."

Emma turned slightly and felt behind her seat. She found the coat and rolled it up. After she adjusted the seat belt she leaned over sideways, put the coat on Michael's lap and rested her head there. She closed her eyes and focused on breathing. She felt his hand smooth her hair and rub her neck, which helped her relax.

* * * * *

While he drove, he glanced down to make sure she was all right. His heart broke for her. He wanted to think of a way to make the trip back to Seattle easier for Emma. She'd been through so much. "Sweetheart, when did you arrive in Aberdeen at the hospital?" he asked.

"I am not sure. I think two days ago," she answered.

He felt her hand on his thigh and touched her forehead lightly. "I'm sorry you were in that awful place for so long."

"Those people kept trying to put sharp pins in my arm. One time there were three of them that held me down. They stabbed my arm, and I could not stay awake anymore. It made my head hurt." She moved her hand over her face.

"They must have given you something to help you relax," he said.

"It made my stomach very upset."

Michael let her cry, but wanted to hold her and give her comfort. "So, tell me how you got here -- every detail."

"Well, the day you left, Bailey came to me and explained that you returned to your own time. He also told me he came from the twentieth century, too. I was very surprised, but so upset about your departure that I could not think about his words." She adjusted the coat under her head. "Two days later, when my thoughts cleared, I went to Bailey and asked if he knew of a way I could travel through the doorway. He did not know, but thought Helga could help me. Bailey took me over to the Martinov's camp and found her. She said she might know of a way to find my opening in space, but she could not guarantee where I would end up. I think it was very lucky I found my way to you."

Michael glanced down at her and squeezed her arm. "I think it was incredibly lucky. I'll be thankful forever."

"At the end of that week, I wrote a note to Mr. Delancy, and told him that I needed to search for you and I would return home as soon as possible. The Martinov's, Helga, Bailey and I set out for the coast, and it took the better part of a week to find the right spot."

"The Martinov's and Bailey went with you?"

"Yes, we rode in Mr. Martinov's wagon. It is quite comfortable, but a little monotonous. When we found the cliffs, Helga felt certain it was the right spot. I hope to tell her she was correct. I have never done anything so strange, and I became quite frightened. When I arrived, I was in the water and swam to the shoreline. It was rather difficult, given I wore my dress and undergarments. I think I have been gone from the cliffs for about three days, but I am not sure."

"Emma, you were so brave. To jump from a cliff must have felt so scary. I admire you even more now that I know what you did. So, tell me what happened with Lord Reggie."

He heard her giggle. "That name is so humorous. I was in no frame of mind to deal with him after you left. One morning, I heard quite a commotion at the front of the manor. Lord Simonton's staff hurried to pack up his wagons, and I found out he departed earlier that day. Later, Mrs. Tharp told me that he and Mr. Delancy had quite a heated discussion the night before. She did not say what the conversation was about but thought Mr.

Delancy supported my decision not to become involved with Reggie." She giggled again. "To be very honest, I was not sorry that he left and I did not get to bid him farewell."

Michael saw an advertising sign posted along the highway and thought he had a good idea. "Sweetheart, we're about an hour out of Aberdeen. There's a Holiday Inn in about a mile. I'm going to stop," he said, and slowed the truck down to take the exit.

She sniffled. "An inn would be good. I am very tired."

He pulled into the parking lot and stopped the truck. "You stay here a minute, babe. I'll be right back." He moved his leg and carefully lowered her head onto the seat.

He went into the main lobby and got a room for the night. He parked the truck and helped Emma get out. Locking the truck, he put his arm around her waist and they walked into the inn.

"Let's get some food and then you can rest. Things will look better in the morning," he said, leading her through the lobby and up some stairs.

They found the room on the second floor. Michael flipped a light switch and everything brightened in the room. He watched Emma look around her and figured she saw some things she couldn't identify. To him the furniture looked big and even the television appeared huge. He saw her examine the pole which emitted light and contained a laugh when it seemed very interesting to her.

"I got two beds because I didn't think you'd want ..."
He stopped when she looked up at him.

She walked to him and wrapped her arms around his waist. She put her head against his chest. He did likewise around her shoulders. They held each other for several minutes.

"Michael, do not ever let me go," she whispered.

"Never, never again."

She looked up at him. "Is it difficult to get warm water up here for a bath? I would like to wash that hospital off of me."

"Easy as pie, my dear." He smiled down at her and kissed her cheek.

"Pie? Hmm ... this is the first time I have felt calm in days. Thank you." She put her arms around his neck. He leaned down and found her lips waited for his. She opened to him and ran her tongue over his lips and teeth. He teased her and she teased him back. They had their first truly passionate kiss since they'd parted at the manor. Michael put his hands on either side of her head, and kissed her eyes, nose, and chin.

"Okay, sit on the bed. I'll be right back." He felt her arms tighten around his neck. "It's all right; I'm not leaving the room. Sit." He steered her to the bed and got her to sit down. He went into the bathroom and filled the tub for a bath. On the counter he found a small sample bottle of bubble bath and smiled.

* * * * *

She saw the light come on and wondered what he was doing. She lay back on the bed, and put her arm over her eyes. She wished her head would stop aching and spinning. She felt afraid she might be sick. She found Michael, and she should be happy, but her body seemed very upset. She heard a strange noise in the room where Michael had gone. The bed depressed beside her, and she moved her arm. Michael smiled down at her.

"What is that noise?" she asked.

"You'll see. I want you to strip down to your nothing theres. I brought you a towel to wrap yourself in. Let me know when you're ready." He leaned over to kiss her, and then stood up.

"Michael, does 'nothing theres' mean naked and without clothes?"

"Yes ma'am and no peaking in the other room. It's a surprise, okay?"

"Yes, okay." She sat up and nodded. She took off everything she wore, and she wrapped the towel around her body. It felt very soft and smelled heavenly. "Okay, I am ready," she called to him.

Michael came back into the room, put his hand over her eyes, and led her to the bath. They turned a corner, and Emma felt the floor under her feet change to a hard, cold surface.

"Okay, babe. Open your eyes," he said in her ear.

It took a couple of seconds to understand what she saw. Water poured from the wall into a tub. The room smelled wonderful and foam floated on the water.

"Oh my. Where is the water coming from?" she asked, almost out of breath.

"There are pipes in the walls that bring it in from the outside. There's a machine that warms the water, and you can adjust the temperature," he explained to her. Then he showed her the other things in the bath that she might like to use.

She felt so tired and found the information he gave too confusing. "Amazing," she said smiling. "Thank you, Michael. It looks wonderful." She watched him lean over the tub and turn off the water.

"My lady, your bath is ready." He kissed the back of her hand and moved out of the room.

She smiled at him as the door closed.

Once down into the water and bubbles, Emma began to feel better. She tried to not get her long hair too wet; it would take forever to dry. She leaned back into the water and felt the warmth seep into her bones. It was wonderful. She splashed her face several times and relaxed back again. Looking around the room, she thought it had been tastefully decorated with subtle colors of cream and pink. She closed her eyes, smiling.

When she opened them again, she found Michael knelt by the side of the tub, and felt him tickle her forehead with his fingers.

"Hi there, babe. You fell asleep," he said softly.

Emma looked down and saw the bubbles had disappeared and the water was cooling. She looked up at him.

He stood, and held out a towel. "Let's get you out of there before you prune up."

She stood and let him help her dry off. His hands gently moved over her body, and he kissed her shoulder.

"Your hair is wet. Shoot, I would have loved to wash it for you," he said, and folded another towel over the wet ends.

"It takes forever and a day to dry," she said, yawning.

"Here is another easy thing."

She watched him pull something from the wall. He flipped a button and it made a buzzing noise. Then he pointed it at her and warm air blew in her face.

"This is called a hair dryer. We'll have it dried in no time now. Mom over packed as usual, but I'm glad she did. She threw in a pair of sweats that I think you'll be comfortable wearing for tonight."

"Sweats? Am I going to do work tonight?" she asked, and frowned.

"No, sweetheart, it's just what they're called."

After he'd dried her hair, Michael helped her put on the sweats. He then led her into the main room, which smelled of something cooked. Emma saw the table set up for dinner and food covered the top. She put her hands up to her cheeks.

"Michael, where did all this come from?"

"Some hotels or inns have a thing called room service and they deliver meals to rooms. I wasn't sure what to order and tried not to get carried away. I want you to have a good dinner." He offered her a chair and then she watched him settle across the table. "Do you like beer?"

"I have never tasted beer, I do not think," she said as he poured brown liquid in a glass. "It looks like ale."

"Yes, that's it. We call it beer. The only difference is we drink it cold." She saw him watch her as she took a sip.

"This is very good," she said as her stomach rumbled.

"You must be hungry." He offered her a plate. "Your stomach is yelling."

"Yes, I am. Everything smells so good." She smiled.

He'd ordered a couple of appetizers, fried chicken, mash potatoes and a couple of salads.

He explained everything to her and she happily cleaned her plate and went back for seconds.

"Would you like some dessert and a cup of tea?" he asked.

"No, I could not put anything else in me. I am very satisfied."

"Good. You've got some color back in your cheeks," he said, and stood to clear off the table and get the remains out of the room. She watched as he moved what he called a food cart into the hallway. He came back in, and locked the door behind him. He went over to a black box with glass in the front and pointed at it. "Emma, this is called a television. It's also referred to as the squawk box or boob tube."

She walked up next to him and grinned. "What does it do?"

Michael hit a button on the remote control and it started to light up. As Emma watched, people appeared on the glass. Her mouth dropped open, and she backed up into the bed, sitting down fast.

"Where are these people?" she asked.

"It's too complicated to explain. My brother, Neil, could probably tell you better than me. People watch these things for entertainment and sometimes they watch it too much. Let's see if we can find something interesting," he said and sat next to her, switching the channels.

"What about the learning show you mentioned? The one that made you so smart," she said, not taking her eyes from the TV.

"That would be very boring, I'm afraid," he answered.

As Emma watched the screen changed to several different things. There was one that looked like drawings come to life, and Michael called it a cartoon. Then another showed people presenting dogs in some sort of a contest. Michael said it was reality television and a big dog show back in the eastern United States.

Michael turned out the lights, sat on the bed, and leaned against the head-board. Emma turned and saw he held out his hand. She slid up next to him, and held his hand, resting against his shoulder.

It wasn't a half hour before she realized she couldn't keep her eyes open. She maneuvered herself under the covers and got comfortable.

"Emma, we never discussed the sleeping arrangement. Do you mind if I crawl in there with you?" he asked.

She opened her eyes and smiled. "Yes, darling," she said and patted the bed. "There is enough room for you, too."

Chapter Twenty

Emma woke in the middle of the night. It took a few minutes to figure out where she was. Her head rested against Michael's shoulder and her arm lay across his chest. For a moment, she felt very wicked. They were unmarried and sinning in the eyes of God, but she couldn't think of any other place she'd rather be now or in the past. She loved Michael so much, and the fact that she made it to the right time, gave her a sense that destiny required them to be together.

Through the curtains at the window, she could see something that looked like a star. She carefully pushed herself up and went to the window. Parting the drapes, she looked out and saw long, silver poles with lights on the ends. She could see Michael's truck parked below. The highway seemed deserted. There were brightly lit numbers that flashed on the building across the street. After a few moments, Emma realized it told the time. It was 2:47.

"Emma," Michael called out.

She moved from behind the curtains. "I am here," she said, and moved back to the bed. Michael sat up, and he watched her. "It is 2:50 in the morning." She moved under the sheets and got closer to him.

Michael hugged her tight. "How do you know what time it is?"

"There is a clock across the highway from here. It lights up. There were other numbers, but I am not sure what they meant."

"My incredibly smart woman." He leaned toward her, and kissed her cheek.

"Thank you, sir," she giggled. Her fingers touched the chain around his neck. "I do not remember you wearing a necklace."

"I'd completely forgotten about it. It's your cross," Michael said. She grinned in the darkness. "When I fell off the building, the hospital had to cut my pants off. They found it in the pocket. I wonder how it got there." She could see him arch his eyebrow.

"I put it in the pants you wore several days before you left. I knew you would not stay and wanted you to remember me."

"Do you want it back?"

"No, I gave it to you," she said, watching him. She touched his lips and let her fingers trace over his chin and neck. Emma realized he'd shed all of his clothes as he usually did at night. She smiled up at him and moved under the sheets. She pushed the sweat pants down and took them off; then pulled them out from under the sheet and threw them aside.

"What are you doing, my love?" he asked.

She sat up, and slipped the sweatshirt over her head. "You seem to enjoy being in your nothing there's in bed. I want to know what is so wonderful about it," she said, and looked at him over her shoulder. She felt his fingers trace along her spine. "Mmm ... very nice fingers, Michael. If I did not wear a night dress, would you touch me like this often?"

"Every night I would. Even if you wore a night dress," Michael said. He sat up behind her and kissed her shoulder.

She felt his hands move under her arms, and caress the curve of her breasts. He cupped them gently and she sighed when her hardened nipples slipped between his fingers.

Emma leaned back into his chest, closing her eyes. His hands were so warm, and it spread throughout her body. "Michael, we are not stopping like before, right? I am not afraid of you anymore. I want you and no one else," she said quietly as his hands worked magic on her breasts. "You have never touched me this way."

He turned her around and put his lips on hers. He kissed her long and hard, and she felt her breathing start to speed up.

"I'm laying claim to you, right here, right now. You're mine, Emma Wallace, and no one else gets to have you ever," he said between kisses.

Emma's hand moved down his chest and under the sheet, touching his thigh. She pulled back, frowned and looked down. "That was not there before. What is it?" She looked up at him.

Michael reached behind him and turned on the lamp. Emma could see the scar on his thigh.

"When I fell off the building here, in this time, they took me to surgery to fix the broken bone. I have a metal rod and screws in there," he said, and touched her hand as she traced over the mark.

"Does it hurt?" She continued to lightly rub the jagged line.

"Only when I try to squat down."

She realized her eyes weren't focused on the scar any longer. "Mr. Drury, are you trying to make me blush?" Her fingers moved over his member, which caused it to twitch. She heard Michael take a breath and sigh. She put the palm of her hand over his penis and wrapped her fingers around it for a snug fit. "Michael, you know I have never done this before. Please tell me if I am doing something wrong." She tightened her hand slightly.

Michael smiled at her, and his breath caught in his lungs. "I'll try to remember. However, since I don't believe there is a wrong or a right way of making love, I don't think I'll have to tell you much. So far your hand is doing just fine."

He let her explore his body for a while. Her fingers lightly touched parts of him, and she felt relaxed and excited all at the same time. She loved when he sighed heavily, which he did several times. She kissed his legs and stomach, and her mouth teased his member, causing it to harden and grow thick.

* * * * *

He'd finally reached his limit. He sat half-way up, and kicked the sheet off his legs. He put Emma on her back and moved her hands over her head. He kissed her face, and said to hold onto the headboard. He moved her legs apart and adjusted his body over her, letting his shaft rest in the junction between her legs. He felt her wet warmth rub against him and almost spilled completely.

"My turn, babe. Close your eyes," he said as he moved down her body. He kissed and licked her breasts, finding her nipples hard little pebbles. He lightly bit around the sides before he took one between his lips.

He heard Emma squeak and a warm ache swelled in his chest. While he suckled one side, his fingers teased the other. He lifted up on his elbows, moved his hands over her nipples, and smiled up at her. "I'll be back here in a few minutes."

Michael kissed down her stomach to her junction. He heard Emma's breathing deepen and puff out. He kissed and licked the inside of her thighs and found her wet and warm spot with his fingers. When he touched her, Emma jerked slightly. He looked up at her quickly.

"Are you okay, Emma?" he asked softly.

"Yes, I ache where you touched just now," she said, and arched her back.

He saw her hands grab at the headboard and smiled. "I'm not hurting you?"

"No, oh my heavens, no," she sighed, letting her back down.

He slid a finger into her tight sheath, and held steady, not wanting to rush her. He wanted her first time to have incredible memories. He moved his finger in and out slowly, pressing his thumb against her spot several times, which caused her to moan. He continued to kiss her thighs, and slid a second finger, then a third, into her warmth to stretch her sheath as much as possible. He was large and didn't want the first penetration to cause her too much discomfort. He kept the pace going. He then moved his hand away, and placed his lips and tongue on the warm swollen folds. He found her core with his tongue and pressed down hard, circling around her spot.

He heard Emma suck in her breath and she arched her back again. "Oh, Michael, oh, oh, do not stop, oh." She climaxed, and released puffs of air and small squeaks. She fell back onto the bed and opened her eyes. "I am okay, Michael. That was wonderful, thank you." He saw her reach down to his shoulder and try to pull him back up to her. "I want to kiss your lips and your wonderful tongue. Please come back up here."

Michael moved up and brushed her lips with his. "You taste so good, Emma. I love you so much."

"I love you, too," she said as he covered her mouth.

He sucked her lips and tongue, and grazed her chin with his teeth. She put her hands through his hair, and kissed him back.

Michael lifted his hips, and brought the head of his shaft to her opening. "Babe, I'm going to enter slowly to give you time to get used to me, okay?" Emma nodded. He pushed his head into her and felt her walls tighten. "Easy now, you need to stay relaxed," he coached calmly.

"Michael, are you sure I am not too small for you?"

"I'm sure. We'll fit together just fine," he said. He continued to push into her channel and came to the tight membrane and stopped. "Emma, this is going to hurt a little. Take in a deep breath and then blow it out. Good, good, now do it again." When she blew out the air he pushed past the membrane and entered her completely.

"Oh Michael," she moaned.

He could feel her nails dig into his back. He hoped the sting would hurt for only a few seconds and then begin to ease. He felt her adjust her legs and her walls tightened again. He wanted to feel every inch of her warm sheath.

"Michael, I love the way you feel. It is so good."

"You're sure? Has the stinging gone away?"

"Yes." She looked up into his eyes. "It hurt at first, but it is all right now."

Michael moved his hips, easing out of her and back in smoothly. He did it several times to get her used the way it felt. He then picked up the pace, and pushed up onto his hands and looked down at her to be certain she felt no pain or fear. She moved her hands up his arms, and caressed his tight and hard muscles.

He watched her closely, and her warm blue eyes crinkled periodically as he pushed into her. Michael wanted to swallow her up whole, but was afraid he'd overwhelm her. They both began to perspire, and he dripped onto her chest. He pushed in and lowered down on top of her. He put his elbows on either side of her head, and kissed her face and lips. She returned the kisses.

"How am I doing, my darling?" he whispered.

"Wonderful, absolutely," she whispered back. "I love you, Michael."

"I'm very close to coming. Are you ready?"

"I think so. Is coming when you expel your seed?" She looked at him innocently.

Michael kicked himself for not remembering there were phrases she didn't know. "Yeah, that's what I meant."

"Is that what I did when your fingers danced in me? And your tongue sent lightening through my body?"

"Yes, that was it."

"Then I am ready again. A strange pressure has built in me like before."

Picking up the pace again, he didn't want to go too hard into her but lost himself. She put her legs around his waist, which sent him over the edge. His body released an explosion and he felt Emma's legs tightened around him; she moaned in his ear. The walls of her tight channel grabbed him as jets poured from his shaft. She milked every last drop from him. He kissed her cheek and lowered his head next to hers. He felt a total lack of energy. They both spent some time catching their breath.

Michael dozed, but the sensation of Emma's arms move from around his ribs, and she brushed her hair from her face, woke him. She kissed his neck and shoulder.

He moved back up on his elbow, and looked down at her and smiling. "I could stay here in this bed with you forever." He kissed her lips lightly. "We'll just order room service for food and never dress. We'll stay here and wake up every morning in each other's arms." He moved off of her and curled up to her side with his arm wrapped around her waist.

"I like the sound of your plan very much," she whispered. "I will take baths three times a day, and you will dry my hair with the contraption from the wall."

Michael laughed. "How are you doing?"

"Wonderful. How are you?"

"Excellent, I can hardly keep my eyes open," he yawned.

"Me, too."

* * * * * *

When they woke in the morning, Michael ordered breakfast to the room. While waiting, they lay together, and kissed and talked more nonsense about staying in bed forever. When the breakfast arrived, Michael introduced her to coffee. She thought she might have tasted it but couldn't remember. She liked the orange juice very much. After breakfast, he showed Emma the shower, which caused her to laugh. They climbed in together and Michael washed Emma's hair. They made love under the hot water, which surprised Emma more than anything so far. He dried her hair with the contraption, and they finally got dressed.

Before they left the room, Michael sat her down on the end of the bed. He took her hands between his, he kissed the tips of her fingers. "Sweetheart, I want to make sure you're going to be all right in the truck. I don't want you to be scared," he said concerned.

"I am not as nervous as I was yesterday." She shook her head. "I had very little to eat or drink. I felt frightened from that place and their sharp pins."

"The hospital?"

"Yes." She smiled down at him. "My love, I trust you will get us to Seattle safely."

"My love? You called me an endearment." He smiled back at her.

"Yes, that one I have figured out and darling. I called you that last evening. I love to say your name though."

She leaned forward and kissed his nose. "Michael," she whispered. "See, it flows so nicely off my tongue."

Michael parted her legs with his hands and scooted closer to her. He nipped at her lips causing her to grin. They kissed passionately for several minutes.

He finally pulled back. "If we don't stop now I'll never be able to drive. I love you so much Emma." He stood up and held out a hand.

She took his hand and stood up next to him. As they made their way out, Michael grabbed the duffle bag and shut the hotel room door.

Chapter Twenty-One

The ride to Seattle was uneventful. Emma turned sideways in her seat and watched Michael drive. They talked about things she would need to know. He explained about his mother who raised the two boys when their father passed away. She was amazed that Mrs. Drury held a job, kept a home and provided for her sons. Emma told him that she already liked his mother -- she seemed so strong.

During the drive up interstate 5, Emma sat up straight and stared out the driver's side window. Michael asked what had caught her attention.

"What are those giant white things?" She pointed out the window.

She saw Michael glance to his left, as they passed a huge field. "Those are called airplanes. People get into them and fly to different cities around the world. We could be back in England in just a few hours -- well, maybe more than a few -- but we could get there."

"They fly? Up in the air with people in them?"

"Yes."

"This time is very amazing." Emma put her head on the back of the seat and closed her eyes. She felt Michael's hand on her leg.

"Emma, are you going to fall asleep?" he asked.

Her eyes popped open and she saw his smile. "No, I am awake."

"Have you thought about where you'd like to live?"

"No, not really. I guess it does not really matter as long as I am with you," she said. She glanced briefly out the window. "I will have to learn how to ride in this truck if we stay here."

"You'll get used to it. If we stay here, you'll have a lot of things to learn," he said.

Emma picked at the sleeve on his shirt. "It moves so fast and is a little overwhelming, but I believe I will learn to understand. I did with the hair dryer." She smiled. "I think you could teach me everything."

"I would be more than happy to try, babe. However, there are some lady things I'll have to let my mom teach you about." He looked at her and crossed his eyes.

She laughed. "Lady things? What could that possibly mean?"

"You know, those monthly things," Michael said, and she thought he became slightly uncomfortable.

"Ah, yes, I understand." She nodded. "You know, Helga told me I could come back. She said you would be able to come, too."

"Would you rather go back to the manor?" Michael asked seriously.

It suddenly occurred to her that they truly needed to think about which option would be better, but she knew he didn't want to leave his mom and brother behind. She needed to give this some thought. Plus, the idea of jumping off a cliff again didn't make her stomach feel well. "I do not know. I like the warm water that comes out of the wall. It is very comforting." She undid the seat belt and moved over to his side. She put her head on his shoulder. "I do not like being so far away from my time. It is so very different here." She saw him smile, again and he patted her thigh.

"We have plenty of time before the equinox. We don't have to make any decisions yet."

"Good. However, the Martinov's and Bailey will only wait a week or two. They have to return to Delancy Manor. I am not sure how Bailey will explain his absence."

"We're almost to my mom's house; just another ten minutes or so. We'll discuss it more once we're settled. How are you holding up?"

"I am good. When I do not look out the windows it helps." She put her hand on his thigh, and tested the waters. "Michael, if I touch you while you drive this truck does it distract you too much?" she asked.

"It's a little distracting, but I'll make it."

"It is very wicked to have my hands on you. Our activities in the middle of the night were sinful, too." She looked up at him, and smiled. "I do so love being wicked."

Michael laughed. "I can't wait to see how wicked you're going to be once we're married."

She watched as he moved the smaller stick on the wheel. It made a light start to blink and she felt the truck slow down. When they came to a stop, she looked around a little.

"We'll be going slower now," he said.

Emma straightened up and looked out the front window. There were other carriages on the highway around them; all were stopped.

"Why are they not moving?" she asked.

"See those lights up there?" Michael pointed. "When the light is red, cars going this direction must stop. When it turns green, we get to go."

The light changed to green and the carriages moved again. Emma watched as buildings passed by. Michael made a right turn and followed another road through what he called a 'neighborhood'.

"The houses are so close together and small," she said.

"The manor is a bit large for so few people, and it's on a lot of property," Michael replied.

They drove to the end of a street and turned left onto a long drive. Coming to a carriage house, Michael stopped the truck.

"We're here. What's the matter Emma?" He asked and she heard concern in his voice.

"What if your mother does not approve of me?" She looked up at him.

"Oh honey, my mom's always wanted a daughter, and I think you will fit perfectly." Michael hugged her.

* * * * *

He looked out the window and saw his mom come out of the house. She stopped at the front of the truck with her hands on her hips.

"Is she your mother?" Emma whispered as Michael nodded. "Michael, she is so beautiful."

He squeezed her once more, opened the truck door, and slid out. He walked up to his mom. "Hi there. She's very nervous, be nice," he whispered in passing.

"Michael, I'm always nice," she hissed at him.

He went up to the passenger side and helped Emma get down. When he closed the door, he put his hand on the small of her back.

"Mom, this is my fiancée, Emma Wallace," he introduced.

Mrs. Drury's mouth dropped open. "You're engaged? That's wonderful."

Michael watched Emma smile at his mom. "It is a pleasure to meet you, Mrs. Drury. Thank you very much for the clothes, and the other things, you sent with Michael."

"Please, Emma, call me Mom or Liz. I'll answer to either one and you're welcome. That sweater looks better on you than it ever did on me."

"It is very comfortable and soft," Emma said, and smoothed the sweater down.

"Yeah, fleece is wonderful stuff," Mrs. Drury answered.

"Fleece? Do you mean this is from sheep?"

"Oh no. That's just what it's called. It's a fake material called a synthetic."

Michael leaned on the truck. "So, are we going to stand in the driveway all day, and discuss fabrics?" he said, and scratched his chin.

"Smart aleck." She hooked Emma's elbow and led her toward the house.

Michael shook his head and followed the ladies. They moved to the kitchen. Michael took the duffle bag up to his bedroom, emptied his pockets and went back down the stairs to join them. As he entered he heard Emma say "Oh yes, Michael was a perfect gentleman last evening." He found them sitting at the kitchen table. His mom smiled up at him.

"See Mom, I know how to behave." He walked up to the refrigerator and opened the door.

"Michael, don't snack. I've got a casserole warming in the oven. I've also got water boiling for tea," Mrs. Drury said.

He pulled out a wedge of cheese. "I'm just going to eat a couple of slices. I'm starving." He found a knife in a drawer and sat next to Emma. He sliced off a couple of wedges, and offered one to her and one to his mom.

"So, Emma, my other son, Neil, tried to explain to me about all of this time-traveling business, but I'm afraid I don't get any of it. What year were you born?" Mrs. Drury got up when the teapot whistled, poured water into cups and carried them to the table.

"I was born in 1793 in Darlington," Emma answered. Michael watched her lift the tea bag up and stare at it. "This is tea?"

"Yep, companies package it in bags. I'll show you. Let it steep for a minute," Michael said gently. He looked at his mom who had tears in her eyes. "Mom, what's wrong?"

"You remind me of your Dad so much sometimes. I'm just being sentimental. Now," she dried her eyes, "have you two thought about where you'd like to live?"

"There's plenty of time to decide on that, Mom. We don't need to rush." Michael polished off the cheese. "Unless you'd rather we didn't stay here?"

"Michael, that's not what I meant and you know it. Emma, are your parents still alive? -- where you come from, I mean?"

"No ma'am. They died from a fever when I was young," Emma said.

Michael took the tea bag out of her cup and pressed it between his fingers. "Mr. Delancy took Emma in and became her guardian," Michael said, and smiled at Emma who still watched him.

"Are you related to this Mr. Delancy?"

"No, he and my father were very good friends and business associates." She smiled back at him. "It is tea now?" He nodded once and moved the cup to her. She took a sip of the brown liquid. "Thank you. It is good."

Mrs. Drury got the casserole out of the oven and pulled a salad out of the refrigerator. Michael saw Emma watch his mother's every move. It surprised him when she found the cold salad and hot casserole very impressive.

They sat at the table for most of the afternoon. Mrs. Drury asked many questions and Emma answered as best she could. Michael noticed that she began to look pale and raised his hand when his mom started to ask another question.

He moved his hand to Emma's hair and ran it down to her neck. "Babe, are you feeling okay?" he asked quietly.

Emma looked up at him. "My head hurts a little and it seems overly-warm in this room."

Michael put his hand on her forehead and cheek. "Sweetheart, you're warm," he said, and frowned. He looked at his mom.

Mrs. Drury stood, leaned over the table, and touched Emma's forehead. "You have a fever. Let me get the thermometer." She moved away from the table and disappeared through a door. Michael could hear her footfalls on the stairs.

"Why didn't you say you weren't feeling well, Emma? We could have stopped much earlier," he said.

"Your mother seemed to be enjoying herself so; I did not have the heart to interrupt her." Michael saw her try to smile. He stood up, and pulled her chair back. He leaned over, and picked her up into his arms.

"Michael, what are you doing?" she whispered.

"You're going to bed, my love. I can't have you sick," he said, and carried her to the stairs.

Michael met his mother half-way on the stairs. She was on her way down, and stopped. He told her follow them into Michael's bedroom. He watched as Mrs. Drury put the thermometer into Emma's mouth and leave the room. He sat on the edge of the bed and heard his mother on the stairs, as she returned. She carried a pitcher of ice water and a glass. He turned and looked at her as she stood in the doorway.

"What?" he asked.

"I'm so proud of you; I could almost cry." She smiled at him with obvious pride.

She came all the way into the room, and put the pitcher and glass down on the night- stand. She took the thermometer out of Emma's mouth and looked at it. "102 degrees. Sweetie, do you feel achy or sick to your stomach?"

"My stomach is all right. I do feel a bit achy, though."

Michael saw his mother pull a bottle out of her pocket and pour two pills into her hand. "This will make you feel better."

Michael helped Emma sit up and watched her swallow the pills. She looked at them both.

"Thank you. I do not believe I have ever gotten sick quite so quickly." She lay back down, and put her hand on her forehead.

Michael got up and went to the hall closet, and pulled out a quilt. He brought it into the room and covered Emma. "We need to keep you warm, right Mom?" he asked.

"Right. I'll just excuse myself. I think I have some chicken soup in the freezer. I'll see about getting it warmed up," she said, and left the room once more.

Michael lay down beside Emma, and pulled her and the quilt into his arms. She fell asleep and he held her for a time. He thought about getting up, but decided against this idea. If she woke up alone, she might be frightened, and he couldn't let that happen.

Chapter Twenty-Two

Mrs. Drury stirred the pot of chicken soup. She hoped Emma would feel up to eating after a while. She smiled to herself while the pot boiled. She liked this woman very much even though they'd just met. Mrs. Drury was so happy that Michael finally found a woman he could settle down with. He'd been at such loose ends the last few years and wasn't getting any younger.

She heard footsteps come up the back steps and turned when the door flew open. Her other son, Neil, stepped into the kitchen and dropped his book bag on the kitchen table.

"Hey, Mom. Where are they?" he asked.

"Hi back at you. Try to keep your voice down. They're up in Michael's room. His young lady, Emma, doesn't feel well and is resting. Please, pick up your book bag and take it to your room." She turned back to the stove.

"Yeah, she's got to be overwhelmed by all she's seen," Neil said in a lower tone. He bent over and retrieved the bag.

"It isn't being overwhelmed. I think she's got the flu. She had a pretty high temperature and headache."

"What?" Neil gasped. "Shit, it's already happening."

211

"Neil, watch your language, please," she said, and turned to look at him angrily.

"Sorry, Mom."

"What do you mean 'it's already happening'?"

"This isn't good," he said, and left the kitchen.

"What isn't good? Neil, slow down." She followed him up the stairs.

"I've got to talk to Michael."

* * * * *

Neil dropped his books in the hallway and opened the door to Michael's room. When he stepped in, he saw Michael lift his head off a pillow and frown.

"I need to talk to you, loser," Neil whispered.

"It is all right, I am awake." Neil heard a female voice and saw a head of blonde hair turn to look at him. "Hello."

He watched his brother help Emma sit up. "How are you feeling?"

"Better," she yawned. "I think the pill your mother gave me helped a lot."

Michael put his hand on her forehead. "You're much cooler."

"It does not hurt to move as much either."

"Emma would you like me to get you some tea or juice?" Mrs. Drury asked from the doorway.

"Thank you, but no. I am going to drink some more water." She smiled. Neil stood at the foot of the bed and admired her. His brother had caught a beautiful woman.

"Babe, in case you haven't figured it out, this is my geek brother Neil," Michael said glowering at him.

Neil lost his ability to form words and continued to stand and stare at her.

"My brother seems to be suffering from brain damage at the moment. Hello, geek. Earth to Neil," Michael said, and threw a pillow at him.

Neil took it on the chest and slowly looked at his older brother. "Loser, when did you get so lucky? She's gorgeous." He moved to sit on the edge of the bed and took Emma's hand. "I am so pleased to meet you, Em."

She blushed and smiled. "I, too, am pleased to meet you, Neil."

"He says there's a problem he needs to discuss with you, Michael. I want to hear it, too," Mrs. Drury said, and grabbed a chair.

"What's the problem, geek?" Michael said, and put his arm around Emma's shoulders. Neil was still at a loss for words. He smiled at Emma and held her hand.

"The floor's all yours, dude. Speak. What's going on?" Michael pushed at his brother.

"Oh right. I spoke with one of my professors this morning about Emma being here from the past. See, there's a theory that traveling past to present is impossible. She shouldn't be here. It's called point of reference, and it's not scientifically proven, but basically, since Emma doesn't have a bloodline now, she shouldn't be able to exist here."

"You have completely lost me, brother," Michael said.

"When you traveled to the past, Michael, it worked because of our family's bloodline. Great-grand-parents or cousins, whatever, they existed back in 1815. It gave you a point of reference. Everything we've seen about Emma on the Internet says she had no children. There's no point of reference here for her. It would be the thing that held her to this time. Since there's no point, she has nothing to hold. I don't know if I can explain it any simpler," Neil said frowning.

"How do you know I did not have children?" Emma asked quietly.

"It's in the history of Delancy Manor," Neil answered, and then looked at Michael. "There's another problem we need to think about. Since Emma's not from this time, she hasn't gotten inoculated for the current diseases."

"Now what are you saying?" Michael sat up.

"Remember when we were in school and got all those shots for mumps, German measles, etcetera. They didn't do that in 1815, which means she's got no immunity built up. Basically, a cold or the flu could kill her, and it could happen pretty easily." Neil looked at Emma and tried to smile. "I don't want to scare you."

"That one I think I understand," Mrs. Drury said, putting her hand to her cheek. "She could catch anything just walking down the street."

"Mom, I know you like to think we're a bacteria-free zone here at Drury Estates because of the amount of bleach you use, but anything could get her," Neil said.

"Emma probably got the flu from one of the people who found her at the beach or from the hospital," Michael mumbled.

"I'm sorry, Emma. We're talking like you're not even in the room," Neil said, and squeezed her hand.

"It sounds a bit like I should not be here to begin with," she said.

"Don't think that, sweetheart. There's got to be a reason you're here. Mom, Neil, can you disappear for a while? Emma and I need to talk," Michael said.

"Yeah, I have homework." Neil stood and walked to the door. He saw his mom look at him then back at Michael and Emma.

"Dinner will be ready after a bit. I'll call." She stood, joined Neil at the door and he closed it behind them.

* * * * *

Emma looked at Michael. "This is not a good thing, yes?"

His hand came up and tucked a loose hair behind her ear. He touched her cheek. "Babe, it could be bad and we'd have to get you back to the manor. I think if we're really careful, though, you should be all right. I'm going to discuss it some more with Neil. Maybe there's a way we can make it safe for you."

"I will not leave here without you, Michael." She watched him, seeing a frown slowly move over his lips. "I know you came back for your family, and they do need you. I do not have anything to return to ..." Her voice faded and she leaned against him. "I will not lose you, my love," she whispered. She felt his arms tighten around her.

"Emma, listen to me." He pulled her up, and put his hands on either side of her face. "There are diseases in this time that your body just isn't used to. They can cause me a runny nose, but they can kill you. I can't let that happen, babe. There are shots they give us when we're kids that help our bodies develop immunities to bad things. Maybe Neil can find out a way we could get you those shots, so we won't have to worry about going back right away. There's so much here in Washington I'd love to show you."

"If I have to go back, you will come with me?" Emma looked deep into his eyes and saw his pause. "Michael, you will come back to the manor, will you not?"

"I'd want to go back with you, but I can't. I know you understood some of what Neil talked about, and you'll have to go back to your own time, eventually."

Emma pushed away from his hands, the frown on her face deepening. She got off the bed and continued to stare at him. "I am not going to give up so easily. There has to be a way I can stay here with you."

"Sweetheart, you're already sick. Unless we can figure something out you might get even worse than you are now."

She continued to back away from him and hit the closet door. "You do not want me anymore," she said quietly. She saw Michael frown, as he got off the bed.

"I don't know where that came from, but you couldn't be more wrong."

"So, I gave myself to you and you were not satisfied?"
"Emma!"

"Then why do you say I will have to go back alone? We have to at least try to find a way that I can stay here with you." As he came toward her, Emma moved into a corner. "You said I had to return to the manor."

* * * * *

216

Michael caught her in his arms as she tried to push him away. When he touched her cheek, he realized she was getting warm again.

He watched her eyes cross and she slid down the wall. He saw she was faint and grabbed her before she crumpled completely. He carried her back to the bed and laid her gently down. Holding her hand, he kissed her palm and closed his eyes. His heart ached and tears welled in his eyes. He didn't think he'd be able to speak.

When Michael opened his eyes, Emma looked up at him again. She breathed normally, but she red spots appeared on her cheeks.

"Babe," he choked and cleared his throat. "Emma, I feel like an idiot. I don't know what to do," he said softly. "My area of expertise is building. I don't know the first thing about time travel or viruses. That's all Neil's area of expertise." He put the palm of her hand on his cheek. "I've let you down and made you feel as if I don't want us." He moved her hand to his heart. "I want us together. Please, don't think anything else."

He helped her sit up, and she wrapped her arms around his neck. "I am very frightened Michael and ..." She pulled back from him a little and seemed to shrug. "Sweetheart, you have not let me down. I panicked and caused myself to go faint."

Michael watched her as a tear rolled down her cheek. He traced it with his finger. "You're getting warm again. I'll get my mom. She'll know what to do. I'll be right back."

He raced down the stairs finding his mom in the kitchen with her pot of soup. She gave Michael another

ibuprofen for Emma and he got a glass of orange juice
for her to drink.

* * * * *

Mrs. Drury shooed Michael out of the room, and
told him to go talk to his brother. She sat on the edge of
the bed and smiled at her patient.

"My son is very taken with you, Emma. I've never
seen him act so protective over the years. He's had other
girlfriends, but never one like you," Mrs. Drury said.

"What do you mean one like me? Is there something
wrong with me?" Emma asked, looking seriously at the
older woman.

"Oh no, there's nothing wrong with you, dear. I think
if you asked Michael to jump, he'd ask how high, and
then do it until he got it right. He's never acted this way.
Before he got the call about you being in the hospital,
he'd been moping around for weeks." Mrs. Drury saw a
crease form between Emma's eyebrows and confusion on
her face. "Moping means he was really sad. I'd find him
staring out the window. When he finally told me about
you being in a different time, I didn't believe him. I
thought he'd dreamt it all. Now I feel like a bad mom for
not having faith in my son."

"When Michael was in my time, he spoke of you and
his brother very lovingly. He wanted to come back to you
so very much. I suppose if I were a stronger woman, I
would have ignored my feelings for him and tried to do
everything possible to get him back to the right place. I
was selfish, and I still am. I guess it makes me a very bad
lady to be so self-serving, but I love him very much, Mrs.
Drury," Emma's voice faded.

"Emma, when you're in love, nothing else matters."
Mrs. Drury patted her hand.

"You loved your husband very much?"

"Oh, yes." The older woman smiled. "He was the
best. We were high school sweet- hearts. We went to
school together and fell in love when we were seventeen.
We were together up until the day his heart gave out."

"Does Michael look like Mr. Drury? I can see your
eyes, but ..." Emma said.

Mrs. Drury stood up, and held out her hand. "Come
with me. I've always wanted to do this. Come."

Emma crawled out from under the quilt and they
walked together to the master bedroom. Mrs. Drury
pointed at a large chair in the corner and told Emma to
sit.

"That bed is very large, ma'am. Do you ever get lost
in it?"

Mrs. Drury opened a closet and pulled out a small
chest. She put the lid up, took out two books, and carried
them to Emma. "That bed is called a California King. My
husband felt we needed something big. I can't seem to
bring myself to get rid of it." She put the books on a table
and pulled a stool from her vanity next to the chair and
sat down.

"These are photograph albums. It just occurred to me
that they didn't have cameras in your day." She pulled one
of the books off the table and handed it to Emma, who
sat it on her lap.

When she opened the cover and looked at the first
page, Mrs. Drury heard her suck in her breath.

"Oh my, they are so clear and detailed. Who are these people?" Emma asked.

"That's my husband and me the day we brought Michael home from the hospital. He was born around 7:00 in the evening."

She saw Emma frown, as she looked from the picture to her. "That is you?"

"Just wait until you see Michael as he grew up. He was so sweet," Mrs. Drury grinned.

* * * * *

Michael stared at his brother and couldn't believe what he heard. There were times when he wished his mother had given Neil up for adoption. He could give Michael instant headaches.

"No really, loser, you should go. Live your life with Emma. It would change the time- line, but how often are you likely to find such a beautiful woman who can tolerate you? And, go figure, she's crazy about you," Neil said.

Michael flattened out on Neil's bed. "You're just trying to get rid of me."

"Now you're just being an asshole and into a serious pity party." Neil turned back to his computer.

"Don't let Mom hear you talk like that," Michael said with his eyes closed. He ran his hands through his hair. "I can't go back, idiot. Who will take care of you and Mom?"

"Man, get over yourself and stop thinking so high and mighty. In case you didn't notice, Mom's done just fine keeping the roof over our heads," Neil said, and typed something on the keyboard.

"That's not the point, geek," Michael said flatly. "It might come as a surprise to you, but I happen to love you and Mom a lot."

"Oh, spare me, loser. Playing the sympathy card doesn't carry any weight with me, and you know it." Neil shook his head, and continued to look at the computer screen. "You're just being a chicken shit about going to a different time. You've never had any sense of adventure."

Michael sat up, and stared at his brother again. "You should talk, seventeen-years-old and all you do is sit in front of your computer. Are you ever going to date?"

"Hey, I'm still in high school and have homework," Neil said, defending himself.

"Twenty-four hours a day, seven days a week, you sit in front of that machine. I can't talk to you," Michael mumbled, and lifted himself off the bed. He went down the stairs, through the kitchen and out to the back yard. He went up to the shed where he and his dad used to do their carpentry work. As he opened the door, he realized it was some time since he'd been in there. Spider webs hung from the corners of the ceiling, and there was dust everywhere. He could also tell his mother had moved things around. There were storage boxes neatly stacked in one corner.

Michael turned on one of the overhead lights and found a broom to sweep up the webs. He spent an hour cleaning things up and swept out the dust. He pulled a set of knives, off a shelf, that he and his dad used for whittling and carving. He sharpened them and put them back into the case in order. He remembered the sound of dad's voice. He would tell Michael stories and give instructions when they worked on one of the many projects they'd shared. He smiled at the memories.

Michael sat at the workbench and cleaned out a toolbox when he felt a hand on his back. He turned around and smiled. Emma stood behind him. "Hey, what are you doing up? You should be resting?"

"I helped your mother get dinner ready, and she sent me out to tell you." She looked up at the ceiling, and he saw her lips move. "I'm trying to remember the exact words she said. Wrap it up out here, wash your hands, and come in for dinner now." She nodded. "I feel all right. Not great, but better."

He put his fingers around her wrist and pulled her to him. She put her hands around his shoulders and rested her head against his chest. He could feel her tremble.

"Hey, you're shaking again. There's no reason to be frightened. We're going to get this worked out," he said quietly. Emma remained silent. "Hey, are you still with me?"

"Yes," she sniffed, and looked up at him. "Michael there is so much ..." She turned and looked out the door of the shed."I feel so stupid. Your mother has a strange thing that opens cans, and she poured water into something that made a strange noise. She offered me a cup of coffee, and I did not understand any of what happened."

He saw tears roll down her cheeks. Michael moved her back into his hold, and tried to sooth her. "It will be all right, I promise, Emma. We'll get it worked out."

She looked up at him and put a finger on his lips. "I am going to have to go back to 1815, Michael. I do not want to leave you, but I do understand your reasons for wanting to stay. Your Mother is kind, and she loves you so much. I could never live with myself knowing I came between you and your family. If you were to come with me, I am sure at some time you would grow to hate me for tearing you away from them." The tears continued down her cheeks.

"Stop, stop, Emma." He put his hands on either side of her face. "I could never hate you. Never. If I make any decision, I'm the one to blame. I love you, babe." He put his lips against hers, and felt his throat tighten.

She kissed him, and held his arms. "I love you, Michael. I do not want to leave, but I understand. At least I think I do," she said against his chin.

"Let's go in and get some dinner. We'll just relax tonight and get a good night's sleep. Tomorrow, things will look much better," he said, and kissed her cheeks. "No more crying, okay?"

"I will try," she said quietly.

Michael turned off the overhead light, closed up the shed, and they walked hand in hand back to the house.

When they entered the kitchen Michael saw his mother pour soup into a large bowl. She put it on the center of the table, and walked into the hall. "Neil Drury, get your butt down here. It's the last time I'm calling," he heard her shout.

Michael and Emma sat at the table next to each other. Michael looked at the kitchen door when he heard a loud thump come down the stairs.

"My son with the lead feet," Mrs. Drury mumbled, and shook her head.

223

The dinner passed quietly. Emma complimented Mrs. Drury on her cooking skills and helped her clean up the kitchen. She was most intrigued by the dishwasher.

Michael poured coffee for everyone and moved Emma into the family room. They sat on the couch, and watched the evening news. Neil went back to his homework.

Then the telephone rang and Mrs. Drury, who was sitting next to it, picked up the receiver.

"Hello?"

Michael looked at his mom, who stared back at him. She had a strange expression on her face.

"I'm sorry, Miss Hargrove, but my son and Emma are out for dinner. Is there something I can help with?"

Michael frowned, and got up from the couch. He went into the kitchen and quietly lifted the extension. Emma followed him. He bent over and put the phone between them so she could hear.

"I'm just doing some follow-up, Mrs. Drury. How is Emma?"

"She's doing just fine."

"Has she been getting enough fluids? She was terribly dehydrated."

"Not any more, she's bounced back very quickly."

"I have some lab results I should forward to her doctor. Your son said it was a doctor of yours. Would you have the name and address handy so I can mail these out?"

Mrs. Drury turned to the kitchen door, where Michael lowered the phone and quietly said "Jeff Winter."

"Oh yes, that's Jeff Winter. Hang on a minute, I have his card." She pulled the phone book out and found the listing for Dr. Winter. She gave the address to Miss Hargrove.

"Emma also left her dress and shoes behind. Would it be all right to mail them to you? Mr. Drury gave us your address and phone number for contact," the woman on the other end said.

"That would be fine," Mrs. Drury answered. "Miss Hargrove, I have another call coming in. I'll let Michael know you called," she said and hung up the phone.

"Way to go, Mom. I think she wanted to ask more questions." Michael walked out of the kitchen with his arm around Emma.

"Questions about what though?" She looked up at her son.

"Mom, Emma has no identification and an accent. First of all, the country's been paranoid since 9/11. Does Emma look like a terrorist?"

"No, of course not. Don't be so silly, Michael."

"Good. Secondly, you'd better call Jeff and give him a heads-up. We were supposed to see him last night, and he should know just in case that nosey, busy-body gets it in her head to call him." He led Emma back to the couch. She looked at him and smiled. He kissed her nose. "What are we watching?"

"I am not sure, but the man with the moustache keeps asking questions. Are those people playing some kind of game?" she asked.

Michael nodded, and recognized the show. "Do you feel strong enough to go for a walk? I would like to show you the neighborhood."

"Yes, I will go put my shoes on." Emma stood up and looked at Mrs. Drury. "Thank you for dinner, ma'am. It was lovely."

"You're welcome, sweetheart." Mrs. Drury watched as she left the family room. "Michael, is everything all right? I mean with you?"

"Yep, we only have a few things to worry about, but I'm okay," he said, and tried to ease his mother's concern.

Chapter Twenty-Three

Michael showed Emma the houses around the neighborhood. She told him how it shocked her that they stood so close together, but she thought if they were like his mother's house they would be cozy and charming.

"The woman from the hospital is going to mail your dress and shoes," Michael told her.

"Mail?" she asked, and looked up at him.

"Ah, sorry. She'll put them into a box and they'll be sent to my mom's."

"Okay." She stopped on the sidewalk as a motorcycle drove by. "Is that a man? His hair is longer than mine, I think."

"Yes, that's a 'dude'."

"Dude?" she giggled.

They watched the motorcycle turn a corner, and then walked again. They returned to the house after dark. Mrs. Drury gave Emma a pair of pajama's to change into and said good night. She told Michael she didn't like the idea of them sleeping in the same bed, but realized he wouldn't sleep on the couch. It would be better if he stayed with Emma and kept watch over her.

Michael helped Emma get changed, gave her another ibuprofen, and got her comfortable in bed. He lay next to her, and held on tight. He noticed she had her hand up in

227

the air and looked at it in the moonlight that came through the window.

He traced a finger down her arm and connected with her fingers. "What are you doing, my love?" he asked.

"I just want to check to make certain I am still here. Neil said I should not be. I do not want to disappear." She moved closer to him.

"He may be smart, but he is only seventeen, and I think he still has a whole lot to learn," Michael said. He felt warmth radiate from her body. Any other time he'd probably be turned on, but knew the fever increased again. "Are you tired?"

"Yes, this was a very big day, with so much to see. Your mom showed me ...oh, what was the word? Photographs. Yes, that is what she called them. They were in a book, and some were of you when you were a baby. They were amazing," she said, remembering. "You look very much like your father."

"Please, tell me she didn't show you the ones of me naked in the bathtub?" He ran his fingers through her hair.

"Yes, but I saw you naked in the bathtub, so I didn't feel shocked," she laughed.

"Ha-ha. Mom loves those pictures, but some of them are a little embarrassing. You're my first girlfriend she's gotten the chance to show them to. She does love to look at those things."

"We have nothing like them in Darlington. You would have to hire an artist to come and paint a portrait, but compared to the photographs, it is not as realistic," she said, and yawned.

228

"I've been thinking ... if you're feeling up to it tomorrow, I'm going to take you to the zoo. It's very peaceful there and we can wander at our own pace."

"I do not believe I know what the word zoo means."

"It's a place where animals from all over the world are kept."

Michael could hear Emma breathing deeply and realized she'd fallen to sleep. He glanced at the clock and saw that it was after midnight. He carefully moved away from her and got up, tucking the sheet and blanket around her. He pulled his jeans on and quietly went down to the kitchen.

He poured himself a glass of milk, and went to the back window. He looked out, and saw shadows move around the ground in the yard. Clouds were moving in, and the moon kept peaking in and out. He felt as though he were too stupid to figure things out. He wanted to keep Emma here with him but didn't want to turn her into a pincushion. If she stayed, she'd have to get every current inoculation for diseases in this time.

The overhead light came on, blinding him for a second, and then he heard his mom.

"Michael, what are you doing up?" she said. She walked in and got a glass of water.

"I couldn't sleep." He turned away from the window, moved to the counter, and leaned against it.

"Are you still having a mulling session?" she asked.

"Yeah, and I'm getting really frustrated with myself. I should be able to figure this out," he grumbled.

"Michael, I think I may have come up with a solution." She looked at him as she sipped her water. He waited patiently. "Neil said it was possible for you to go back with Emma. Why don't you do it?"

"Mom, no. I can't leave you and Neil ..."

"Son," she interrupted him calmly. "I know since your father died, you've felt it necessary to help us out and take care of us."

"Mom..."

"No. Now hush up and listen to me. You've done a great job, but you're thirty now, and I don't want you to waste anymore time worrying about your brother and me. You've put off your own life for too long, and there's a young lady upstairs who is very much in love with you. She told me why you came back. It would make your father very proud." He could see tears in his mother's eyes. "Just think of the adventure you'd experience. You'd have a whole different style of life. Just think of the things you could witness, son."

"And all the things I could invent and make millions of dollars on," Michael chuckled.

"Smarty pants." She put her hand on his arm. "You know I'd miss you very much, but Emma needs you and I think you need her, too."

Michael looked at her. "I think I know where Neil got his smarts from. I wish we could all go."

"You think I'm giving up the beauty salon? Think again, mister."

"And the ice maker in the fridge?" Michael laughed.

"That will never happen. Could you imagine Neil without his computer?"

Michael shivered. "That's too frightening a thought. He'd never make it." He smiled at his mom. "I love you two, and it would be really hard not being around you."

"But you're head over heels in love, and she just can't stay here. Michael, once you get back to 1815, I know you'll find a way to communicate with us. Maybe another doorway will open; Neil can discover it, and you'd come for a visit."

"Maybe," he sighed. He finished his milk and rinsed out the glass. "I'd like to have a family day tomorrow. Keep Neil out of school and we'll take everyone to the zoo. I think Emma would not be so threatened by the zoo, and it isn't too far from here. She has a hard time with the motion in the truck."

"What if it rains? There are clouds moving in," she thought aloud.

Michael stared at her. "Damn, I hadn't thought about the weather. We could do the aquarium. It's inside. We can decide in the morning when everyone is up. Hopefully, we can stay here for a while. The fortune teller said the doorway wouldn't close until the fall, so as long as Emma doesn't get too sick, we should be okay."

"Michael, do you think it's a good idea to take Emma to such a public place? There might be a lot of kids with runny noses," Mrs. Drury said.

"I get your point, Mom. If we steer clear of the crowds, it shouldn't be too bad. Maybe if we went to the arboretum for a picnic; if the weather isn't too wet, it would be nice. Emma and I went out to a field ..." Michael remembered his last afternoon with Emma in 1815.

"Some of the flowering trees would still be out. I should charge the batteries in the camera and take some pictures," she said to herself.

Michael looked at her and realized he wasn't listening. "I'm sorry, what?"

She looked up at her son, moved to him and put a hand on his arm. "Michael, believe me, I don't love the idea of sending you off to another time. I know I'll probably never see you or your children or Emma, but you have a look on your face that tells me you're really struggling with this decision. Whichever way you go, I'll be proud of you. You're a good man and have always been a good son."

"Except the time I put nails in the oak tree out back, so my friends and I could hang our canteens. I thought Dad was going to kill me." Michael hugged his mom.

"I remember that. Wasn't your punishment to clean out the work shed?"

"And he grounded me for a week with no TV privileges. It sucked."

"You know," she let him go and looked up again, "I think it was the worst thing you ever got into trouble for."

Michael crossed his eyes, and frowned. "Then I'm not going to mention the time Gary stole a six-pack of beer from his dad, and we drove your car up to the falls and back."

Mrs. Drury's mouth dropped open. "You didn't?"

"Sorry. True confessions, Mom. Dad said not to tell you. I was a bad boy in high school." He arched his eyebrow and smiled.

"Right, I don't want to know anymore. Go try to get some sleep, Michael. It's been a long day." She kissed his cheek and left the kitchen.

He laughed, turned off the light and followed her up the stairs. He went quietly into the bathroom to brush his teeth. Crawling back into bed beside Emma, he wrapped his arms around her, and felt her move.

"I had a dream you disappeared," she said in a sleepy voice.

"It was just a dream. I'm right here. I had a talk with my mom down in the kitchen." He nuzzled her neck, feeling the heat on his cheek.

"I like your mother very much. She is so kind."

"She likes you, too, sweetheart -- so much so, that she told me I need to get you back to the manor and your own time. She thinks I should stay with you," he said, and propped up on his elbow. She rolled onto her back, and looked up at him. He touched her face, lightly tracing her lips. "Emma, I love you so much. Once we're back in Darlington, will you marry me? I know we haven't really courted for very long, but I refuse to not be with you and couldn't stand it if you married Reggie."

Emma looked up at him and gave him a crooked smile. "I accepted your proposal yesterday, and yes, I would rather be your wife, than his, very much," she said weakly. "You will have to ask Mr. Delancy's permission, of course."

"Right, Delancy. I forgot about him. We'll get that worked out. Now, money will be a little tight as we start out. Hopefully I'll be able to find work right away. Do you think Mr. Delancy would mind very much if we stayed at the manor?"

"I doubt he would turn us out, my love. There is a thing I have not mentioned to you." She looked up at him.

"Not another thing, Emma. We've done this once already," Michael said.

"Yes, and I told you the thing then, did I not? When my parents passed away, I was very young," she started.

"Right." He nodded.

"The estate and properties my father owned were sold, and Mr. Delancy put the money into a trust for my benefit. If I am not married when I turn twenty-five, the trust would be turned over to me. However, it would seem that I will be wed long before that, and you will be in charge of our purse strings." She stopped and touched the frown on his lips. "What is wrong, Michael?"

"How wealthy are you, Emma?"

"I assure you it is a great amount. Fifty thousand pounds at least, and it can keep us comfortable for a lifetime."

"But it's *your* money, babe."

"It will be *our* money. We could purchase a home, and you could begin plans to make water come out of the walls." She smiled and tried to kiss his chin.

Michael laughed. "We'll discuss this some more in time. Tomorrow will be a nice, fun day. Mom and Neil are coming with us, and you will have an experience like you've never had." He put his head down on the pillow and closed his eyes. He wanted to tell Emma that fifty thousand wasn't very much, but then realized that it was probably a fortune in 1815.

Chapter Twenty-Four

Emma stood at the rail, and looked at the vast grassland with her mouth open. There were several long-necked beasts strolling around, pulling leaves from the tops of trees. Michael had said they were called 'giraffes', and she'd never seen anything like it before in her life.

There were other animals roaming out there on what was called the 'African Savanna'. She saw a striped animal that was some sort of a horse. Emma couldn't remember all the names, but she thought she'd never forget the giraffes. When they moved, she thought there might be something wrong with her eyes. Their motion seemed to slow down.

They arrived at the zoo just a few minutes earlier, and her head already spun. The ride was one thing -- they took Mrs. Drury's smaller carriage. It was more comfortable than Michael's big truck. Emma found the ride a little better than the day before and was able to look out the windows as it moved. She wasn't sick to her stomach at all.

They passed a row of trees and there was a loud, roaring noise. It startled Emma, and she tightened her hold on Michael's hand. Neil told her the name, but all Emma heard was something sounding like heavy breathing. When she saw the creatures, her legs shook and she backed up a step.

"What did you call them, Neil?" she whispered.

"Elephants."

She listened closely and pronounced the word slowly. "Ellie-faints?"

Neil smiled. "You're close. You almost have it. Elephants."

Emma moved to the rail and put a hand on the cold steel. "They are enormous." She could still see the long-necked beast moving slowly to her left. "This is amazing. They are real? Not like those animals we watched last night on the glittering box?" She looked up at Michael.

"Yep, they're real. They breathe and eat and everything," he said.

"Everything," she whispered as she watched the huge animals move slowly around the grassland.

When Emma woke up this morning, it took a couple of seconds to remember where she was. It was just like the inn, with Michael lying behind her with his arms wrapped around her stomach and Emma felt safe and warm. In the small room, they arose, and Michael asked how she felt. She'd thought for a second and realized she felt pretty good. The plan for coming to what Michael called the 'zoo' had set into motion pretty quickly.

What appeared before her was something else entirely. As they walked along a path, she felt as excited as a child, with the wonders all around. This place felt a little overwhelming, as though it was too big and she had a hard time taking it all in.

As they walked along a gravel path, they saw the most amazing animals. There were large cats and very strangely-built dogs. They had a cackling bark that sounded like a laugh. Emma couldn't say the name properly.

The four spent most of the morning wandering through the park. Emma found herself so turned around, she couldn't say which way to go. She turned one way and Michael would grab her hand and point her in a different direction.

"All right, children. I need a break. My feet are tired, and I want something to eat," Mrs. Drury said.

They followed her to something called a 'food pavilion'. The aromas were strange and enticing. Emma let Michael choose a meal for her, which turned out to be 'fish fingers', 'French fries', and 'coleslaw'. She found dipping the fish and French fries in the red sauce made them taste better. The coleslaw also tasted very good, but after eating the meal her stomach felt heavy. Neil said he was stuffed and when Emma thought about it, she felt stuffed, too.

After they ate, they sat in the sun, and talked quietly for a time. It was very warm and relaxing. She thought her head seemed to be clearer, but wasn't certain. She watched the people walking to and fro, and it seemed strange. They moved too fast.

Mrs. Drury talked about how excited she was to have another woman in the house and that she felt pleased that Michael's new girlfriend was so amenable.

Emma found it difficult to pay close attention to the conversation. The people walking by wore the most fabulous, colorful clothing. She found their choices rather remarkable. She saw men with long hair and short and some of the women were wearing strange flat shoes that made a funny flopping noise. The dazzling colors and different fabrics made her dizzy.

"Would you like to do that, sweetheart?" she heard Michael ask.

Emma turned her head to look at him and was going to ask him to repeat his question, but her vision went fuzzy. She tried to clear her eyes, and look at this man she loved, but the world around their table began to spin.

"Michael, why are you sitting sideways?" she asked, before she fell backwards off her seat. The last she remembered was hearing Mrs. Drury say she was hot.

* * * * *

When she lifted her head the room spun around. "Oh Michael, something does not feel right."

He sat up and put his hand on her forehead. "Babe, you're burning up. That came on quick," he said, and reached across her to turn on the bedside lamp.

"I took the pill a couple of hours ago. Should it not last longer?" She grabbed his hand as he moved over her to stand. "Where are we? Do not leave me, please." She felt frantic and tried to sit up.

"I'm right here." He sat on the edge of the bed. "We're back home. You gave us quite a scare at the zoo. We got you back here as quickly as we could."

When she sat up halfway, her eyes crossed and she flopped back down on the pillow. "Oh Michael. Every time I try to lift my head, the room goes round."

"Emma, I 'm going to get my mom. She'll have something to help." He kissed her forehead. "I'll be right back."

* * * * *

Mrs. Drury took care of Emma with Michael's help. She gave her a stronger anti-inflammatory drug, which was Mrs. Drury's own prescription. Michael raced to and from the kitchen. He got water and at one point ginger ale, which Emma had never tasted and liked very much.

The noise of Michael going up and down the stairs caused Neil to cover his ears. He stood in the doorway, and held his head. When Michael headed back down to the kitchen, he followed.

"Your pounding on the stairs is going to give me a headache, and I can't concentrate on anything," he said.

"Shut up," Michael said, and filled a plastic bag full of ice.

"Yeah, right. Listen loser. Something came to mind," Neil said. "We have to get Emma well before you go back," he said, pushing himself up on the kitchen counter. "Remember, anything is possible. If Emma goes back with some weird flu, it would be the same as when she came here. The people in her time won't have immunity to our bugs. She could cause an epidemic, which might kill a lot of people."

Michael leaned against the refrigerator door, and registered what his brother had just told him. "It seems as though the fever is coming faster and hotter now. What are we going to do?"

"If she's sick when you go back, she should be isolated for a couple of weeks and get better. She should stay away from those gypsies you mentioned. They could carry it all over Europe."

"It could kill her, right?" Michael didn't want to know the answer. Neil didn't answer but had a grim look on his face. "Shit, I was glad she came here, but now I'm asking myself if it was worth it." Michael looked away, and his eyes burned. "What can we do to get her well, Neil?"

His brother jumped off the counter. "I'm going to call my professor."

"Geek, are you sure that's a good idea? What if you tell him where she's from and he thinks you've lost it?" Michael put his hand up to stop Neil.

"I already told him about you time-jumping." Neil looked at him with patience. "He's smart and has heard weird theories in his life as a teacher. He's probably on his computer right now."

"Of course, then yes, contact him. We need all the help we can get."

They went back upstairs, and Neil peeled off to his room. Michael found his mom and Emma talking.

"Where's the ginger ale?" his mom asked.

Michael nodded. "Right. Neil side-tracked me. I'll get it." He handed her the ice bag and started to turn around.

"Michael, it is all right. I do not want any more to drink right now," Emma said, and sat up on her own. "Since your mother gave me another miracle pill, I am feeling better."

He turned back around and saw her smiling.

Mrs. Drury stood up and passed her son. "I'll be right back. This is a little uncomfortable," she said.

Michael sat on the edge of the bed and held her hands in his. "Don't ever scare me like that again.

"Yes, sir."

"I'm serious. I don't mean to be bossy, but no more of this, okay?" He kissed the palm of her hand.

"Yes, you do mean to be boss me around, but it is all right. I need to get used to it, I think." She smiled and put her fingers on his cheek. "I love you."

Michael put his lips against hers. He'd meant to be gentle but found he wanted more of her mouth and all of her tongue. He framed her face with his hands and pulled back. "I think I need to get you back to Darlington. I hoped to show you Seattle, but I'm afraid you'd just get sicker."

Emma frowned. "I want to stay longer and become better acquainted with your mother."

"We can't, babe. You might get better, but there are other illnesses you could catch. I don't think you'd want to be sick in bed all the time. We'll head to the beach as soon as the sun comes up tomorrow."

"Are you very certain, Michael?"

"Yes." He hugged her to his chest. "We'll get married right away in Darlington. There's no way Mr. Delancy will allow us in the same bed, and I'll be damned if I'll be separated from you."

"Bailey and the Martinov's are waiting on the cliff. I told Bailey if I was not back in ten days, he should return to the manor and announce my death. It has been only four or five days, they should still be waiting."

"Good, we'll probably need a witness ..."

"Hey, Michael." Neil came into the room and saw them holding each other. "My professor found some penicillin, and will bring it here. It should knock out whatever Emma's got, but if she stays..."

"We're not staying, brother." Michael turned to face him.

"Does Mom know?"

"Yes, she said I should go and enjoy the adventure. I'm giving you my truck, geek," Michael said.

"Why would I want that piece of loser crap? I'm saving for a BMW," Neil snorted, shaking his head.

"My geek has turned into a preppy. I'm very disappointed and, Lord, please don't let him marry someone named Buffy." Michael grinned.

"You are such a loser." Neil grinned back. "Don't guess I'm getting any work done today. I better go see what Mom's up to."

* * * * *

Emma got out of bed and cleaned herself in the room with the bath. She washed her face and got her hair brushed out. Mrs. Drury gave her the most fascinating hair wrap. She called it a 'scrunchy' and told Emma how to tie her own locks up. She'd lost her hairpins at that hospital place where she had first been kept and wished she could get them back, but Michael seemed to like her to wear her hair down. She supposed she could get used to wearing it with the scrunchy thing.

She looked at herself in the mirror and smiled. The journey home scared her, but other than wanting more time with Mrs. Drury and Neil, she could only think of a couple of things she might have liked. She ran a hand up

243

her arm feeling the night-shirt she wore. It was soft and warm. She wished she could have stayed longer at the zoo.

* * * * *

Mrs. Drury came into the bedroom, carrying a backpack. "Michael, I've put some things in here to take with you. Pictures of us, and I put in three cameras with several memory cards. I'm not sure how long the batteries will last, but you'll be able to take some pictures."

"Mom, I won't be able to send them on to you," Michael said, and looked into the pack.

"You're smart, son. I know you'll figure out a way. I know you will," she answered. "I also put a couple of fleece sweaters in there for Emma. I know she likes them." She looked up at Michael. "Son, I want to give you something. I haven't worn it for sometime because I've been afraid I'd wreck it, but," she handed him a small box and watched him open it. "It's my engagement ring."

"Are you sure you want to give this up?" he asked, looking at the ring.

"I never wear the thing. I have my wedding band and that ring sits in my drawer. Do you think Emma would like it? I mean she should choose her own ring, but I thought if it was a pass down it would mean more." She smiled.

"I think Emma will love it. Mom, it's beautiful," he said as Emma walked into the room. Michael and Mrs. Drury both turned to her.

* * * * *

Emma clasped her hands in front of her, and felt slightly uncomfortable. She wasn't sure what they were grinning about.

"Have at it, Michael," Mrs. Drury said, and left the room.

"What is happening?" Emma asked.

Michael looked from the box to Emma and smiled again. "Mom gave me something to make our engagement official." She watched him lower his long frame down to one knee. He turned the box around, and looked up at her. "Sweetheart, for the last time...will you marry me?"

She walked up to him and gazed at the ring. "Oh, it is beautiful. Where did she get it from so fast?"

"It was her engagement ring from my dad."

Emma put her palms around his hand and the box. "Michael, I could not take her ring."

"Yes, you could, Emma," they heard from the hallway.

"Mrs. Drury, the sentiment you must feel about it..."

Michael's Mom walked back into the bedroom as he stood back up. "Listen, I don't have a daughter to give it to. If I gave it to Neil, he'd probably figure out a way to shoot a laser through it and Michael... well, Lord only knows what he'd do with it."

"You mean like put it in a drawer and forget it's there?" Michael grinned and chuckled.

"Hush up and put it on her finger. I want to make sure it fits." Mrs. Drury put her hands on her hips.

The ring was a little big. Mrs. Drury got a roll of cloth tape and wound it around to make the fit a little snugger. Emma found herself continually looking at her finger.

"There. Now you shouldn't have to worry about it falling off. I'll be downstairs. Dinner will be ready in about ten minutes."

Michael and Emma sat next to each other on the bed. She saw him glance around the room and he explained he wanted to memorize every detail.

"It seems very weird to think I'll never see this house again," he said, and put his arm around Emma's shoulders.

"Are you terribly upset about leaving?"

He looked at her and put his head against hers. "I'm not so sad about the house."

"The people in it you will miss. I think I can understand that feeling," she said, leaning into him.

Michael put his forehead on her shoulder. "It's going to be hard leaving my mom and Neil."

"Michael," Emma said, bringing his head up with her hand, to make eye contact, "I want you with me always, but I cannot be selfish and take you away from your family." She took off the ring and tried to give it back to him.

"Emma, sweetheart, let me make myself clear," he said, and slipped the ring back onto her finger. "When I left you the first time, it was absolute hell. I'm not losing you again. I'll miss my mom and Neil, yes, but I want you. It doesn't mean you're selfish, and I don't want you to feel guilty. It's a really strange situation. You are in my heart, and it would kill me if you were taken away and we were separated again. Am I making myself very clear to you?"

"Yes." She looked at him and felt a tear roll down her cheek. "I love you so much," she whispered.

Michael pulled her into a tight hug. She never wanted to let go.

* * * * *

While they ate dinner, Neil's professor showed up with an antibiotic for Emma. He wouldn't say where he got the pills. Neil speculated later that he may have broken into the Student Health Department on campus and stolen them. He gave them the instructions and left. Emma took one of the pills and put the bottle into the backpack.

They spent a quiet evening, listening to music and watching TV. They talked about a lot of subjects that night. Emma told them all she could about her background and life at Delancy Manor. She described Mr. Delancy as a gentleman and quite well-educated. Michael got to laughing and had to excuse himself. He had to think about what he'd be dealing with when he asked Mr. Delancy's permission to marry his ward.

At three in the morning, they decided to try to get some sleep. None of them could really relax, and Emma felt nervous about what they were going to attempt. Michael held her tight until the sun came up.

Chapter Twenty-Five

"Okay. Everyone hit the bathroom one more time and we'll head out," Mrs. Drury said, washing the breakfast plates.

"Mom, you and Neil don't need to come with us," Michael said, and finished his coffee.

"Yes we do," Neil said. He stood up and put his dish in the sink. "How else are we going to get the loser truck back to Seattle?"

"Geek, you will learn to love that truck, trust me," Michael snarled.

"Yeah, when pigs fly." Neil laughed his way out of the kitchen.

Michael picked out a few pieces of clothing to take back with him, most particularly wool socks. He thought the manor house would probably be cold and drafty in the winter, and he hated to have cold feet. He'd have to work on underdrawers once they were back. He wasn't sure how Jockey briefs would go over. He insisted on taking his work boots -- he'd paid a lot of money for them and wasn't about to give them up -- the duffle bag they packed was full and hard to get closed. He asked his mom if it would be all right for him take the sets of carving knives that he and his dad had used. She agreed, and he put the two heavy sets into another duffle bag. He hoped they could figure out a way to get them back. He might be able to use them for work once he and Emma settled.

As the sun began to rise, Michael and Emma got into the truck. Neil and Mrs. Drury would follow them in her car. Traffic through Seattle was slow due to people racing to work. The slow pace meant Emma could sit up and look out the window. She wondered at the tall buildings and saw a large cargo ship in Elliott Bay. She was amazed at how huge it all was.

She, again, marveled at the planes lined up on Boeing Field and found them of great interest, but the thought of people flying in the air was more than she could understand. Passing by slowly in the lane of cars, she saw one of the planes take off and couldn't believe what she was witnessing.

Michael seemed to enjoy telling her about this time and answered her questions while he kept his eyes on the road ahead.

When the congestion on the freeway lightened, the truck moved faster. Emma put her head down on Michael's thigh and tried to ignore the motion.

"Michael, how many children would you like to have?" she asked, and tried to think of ways to keep her mind focused.

"Hmm... I'd say at least six; maybe eight or nine. If we had nine children, we'd be able to put together a baseball team." He grinned down at her.

"I see we will have a lot of work to do," she sighed. "What is baseball?"

"And you know I'll hate every minute of that work as I'm sure you will, too." He explained that baseball was a little like cricket and talked about the differences.

After they got off the freeway in Olympia and headed west, Emma became quiet for a time. Michael tickled her ear. "What are you thinking about, Miss Wallace?"

"Nothing really," she answered. She felt herself tense and felt Michael squeeze her shoulder.

"What's wrong, babe?"

"My stomach is upset. Michael, could we stop somewhere for just a moment?"

"Of course. There's a rest area in a few miles. We'll stop there," he said.

She watched as he pulled the thing he called a cell phone out of his pocket. He pressed a button on it and began to talk to Neil about the stop.

Mrs. Drury assisted Emma in the restroom. Michael and Neil waited by the cars.

* * * * *

"It could be the penicillin that's made her sick. Em's not used to it," Neil said, and leaned on the truck. "Did she eat this morning?"

Michael paced back and forth on the sidewalk, and didn't take his eyes off the restroom door. "Yeah, she ate Mom's four-star breakfast." Michael stopped and looked at his brother. "You were there. You ate."

"Yeah, at five in the morning. I'm not real alert at that time of day, particularly when we'd just gone to bed.

250

I'm too young to be an insomniac. Besides, who watches other people eat?"

Michael shook his head and paced again.

* * * * *

In the restroom, Emma's stomach burned. They'd made it just in time for her to lose the lovely breakfast Mrs. Drury had prepared. She opened the stall door and moved to a sink.

Mrs. Drury smiled and seemed sympathetic. "I'm sorry, sweetheart. Do you feel some better?"

Emma couldn't figure out how to turn on the water faucet and began to cry.

"Oh, Emma, don't cry." Mrs. Drury patted her on the back. "I'll hold the water on for you. I hope it's at least warm."

"Thank you." Emma said. She put her hands in the water and cupped them to drink and rinse her mouth. She tried to get her crying under control. "I am sorry for being so silly, but I do not feel very smart in this time. I could not even make the water come on," she croaked. "And there are no towels to dry my hands."

Mrs. Drury showed her how to make the contraption on the wall work and after three tries, Emma got herself straightened out. "The water at your home tasted better," she said and half smiled.

"Oh goodness, you must be thirsty. There are some machines outside; we'll get you a bottle of water to take in the truck," Mrs. Drury said, and moved to the door.

"Mrs. Drury, please wait a moment," Emma said, stopping her. The older woman turned back. "I have considered all that occurred in the last days and..." Her voice faded.

Mrs. Drury walked back to Emma and took her hand. "What's troubling you, dear?"

"I have thought about it quite seriously, and I do not think Michael should return to Darlington with me." She looked at the older woman with tears pooling in her eyes.

"No, Emma. He loves you very much. I've never seen Michael act this way before. He'll be all right in your time. He's very smart when he needs to find work, and I just know you two will make it just fine." Mrs. Drury squeezed her hand.

"Ma'am, you are so kind," Emma whispered. "I know he loves me, but he cares very much for you and Neil. I find it very difficult, and believe I will be the cause of separation between him and those he loves most dearly. You really need him more than I do." Emma felt Mrs. Drury pull her arm and found herself in the woman's embrace.

"Sweetheart, it is very difficult knowing my son will leave and be in a whole different time and place. I'm not the type of mother who needs her children to watch over her. I love my boys very much and am very proud of them, but they deserve their freedom to choose what they want their lives to be. Michael has chosen you and your time. We will miss him very much, but I'll know he's happy with you." Mrs. Drury pulled back from Emma. "Now listen to me, I don't want you to feel guilty about any of this. I'm excited about the adventure he's going to have. With you by his side, I'm sure he'll have a wonderful life."

"I do not understand why you are so kind to me?" Emma said. They moved out of the restroom and stood on the walkway.

"Well I suppose it's a mother thing. I told you earlier, I never had a daughter, but the more I know you, the more I would have liked one exactly like you. Now don't start crying again. Let's get you some water."

She watched Mrs. Drury step off the sidewalk and head across the grass toward Michael and Neil. Emma walked up beside Michael and tried to smile at him.

"Why was Emma crying?" Michael asked.

"Nothing is wrong, Michael. Go get a bottle of water. She needs some fluids." His Mom pointed to the machines.

Emma leaned against the truck and felt the cool metal through her sweater. She wiped at her eyes and watched Michael go to where water would miraculously appear.

"Is the fever starting up again? You have rosy cheeks," Neil asked.

Emma put her hands up to her cheeks. "I do not know. My eyes burn, but I was crying."

Mrs. Drury put her hand on Emma's forehead. "You don't feel warm."

"It could be a reaction to the penicillin. Your body isn't used to it," Michael said, as he opened the bottle of water and handed it to her.

"Excuse me, loser, but that was my thought you just stole." Neil looked at him, and crossed his arms.

"Shut up, geek. When did you get your medical degree? It doesn't matter who thought of it." Michael put his arm around Emma's shoulders, and she snuggled against his chest.

She smiled up at him. "My heroes," she sighed.

"Boys, behave." Their mother frowned.

"Sorry Mom," Michael said. "How do you feel, sweetheart?"

"The water helps. I do not understand about reactions. Is it the sickness I have or the cure for the sickness that is making me feel ill?" Emma asked.

"It's probably a little of both," Neil answered, looking smug.

"Dr. Drury makes his educated guess," Michael said.

"Shut up, Michael," Neil snarled. "You can be such a jerk at times." He shook his head and a grin appeared on his lips. "Loser. Drink the water Emma. It might have been better if we'd gotten something bubbly to settle your stomach, but the water is good, too."

"Thank you," Emma said, still leaning against Michael.

They piled back into the cars and headed west again. Michael said he was concerned about finding the place where Emma arrived at the beach. She remembered her experience and shivered a little when she thought about the cold water. Michael spoke about when he'd gone back to the location on the hillside above Delancy Manor, and something had pulled at him.

Emma wondered if she would feel the same pull.

Chapter Twenty-Six

They followed the road out of Ocean Shores toward the beach. After arriving, they walked around a little to see if Emma could sense a doorway. It was cloudy and cool, and the waves rolled one over another, washing the shoreline.

Emma stopped, and put her hand up to her cheek. "When they took me on the cart, I remember the ground was hard and black. There were white lines striping it." She looked up at Michael.

He nodded his head and looked back at the land. "It probably was a parking lot. Where is there beach access with a paved parking lot?"

"If we drive farther north up the highway, I'm sure we'd see lots of different beaches and campgrounds," Mrs. Drury said.

They returned to the cars and checked parking lots along the highway. The first couple were too dense with trees and bushes. Emma remembered it being more open.

Following the road, they passed a wooden building painted green. Emma turned in the seat, and looked out the back window.

"Michael, I saw that sign by the doorway. We are very close." She turned back around and looked out the front windshield. Rounding a corner, Emma leaned toward the dashboard. "There," she said, and pointed to the left.

Michael put the blinker on and turned onto a two-lane road heading toward the water. They arrived at a large parking lot. It was worn, but you could see the white vertical lines painted for parking spaces.

Emma got out of the truck and looked around. Michael slid across the seat, and put his hands on her shoulders.

"What do you think? Does this feel right?" He pulled her back into the doorway of the truck and rested his chin on her shoulder.

"Yes, I think this is it. I have a strange sensation in my stomach and it is not like the sickness."

She turned, and put her hands on his arms. He saw her eyes had tears ready to roll. "Michael, you cannot go with me. You must stay here and watch over your mother."

His hands pulled her closer. "Listen to me. I'm sorry, but you're stuck with me."

"Your mother needs you here. Neil needs a man in his life to teach him the ways of the world. If you leave, he will have no one to help show him the right paths to choose," Emma said.

"Ah, pardon me, Em, but my brother is the last person I'd want to teach me anything," Neil said, as he approached the truck..

Michael looked up and saw Mrs. Drury and Neil stare at them. He smiled at his brother and shook his head. "And you call me a 'loser'."

"I love Michael dearly, but give me a break. He fell off a building and broke his leg."

"Thanks bro. Love you, too," Michael said sarcastically.

"That's enough, boys. Is this the correct place?" Mrs. Drury asked.

"It looks right."

Michael felt Emma begin to move away and tightened his hold on her arm. She looked up at him and he saw her frown. He waved his hand at his mother and Neil. "We'll meet you at the beach in a minute," he said.

They walked toward the sand and when they'd gone a distance from the truck Michael put his finger under Emma's chin, and turned her face to him.

"Now, tell me what's going on in that beautiful brain of yours," he said.

"I have already said it. I am taking you away from your family, Michael. It is not fair to you or them to be so far away. I do not know if I can live with coming between you and them," she said softly.

"I've talked to Mom and Neil about this. They understand what's at stake and that it's doubtful I'll ever be back." He pressed the palm of her hand to his lips and kissed it. "Honey, think about the way it is in your time when people leave England to go to the America's or somewhere else around the world. They're usually never seen again. What we're doing is the same sort of thing. Don't you see that?"

"Yes, I suppose so. I wish they could come, too. Mrs. Tharp has always tried to be a mother to me, but in the end, she is only a servant to Mr. Delancy."

"I think Mrs. Tharp cares for you very much and considers you to be a part of her family," Michael said.

"Oh, yes, and I her, but a real mother is different." She looked up at him. "Michael, are you sure you want to do this?"

"I don't think I've ever been so sure of anything before. There is no way I ever want to be without you, my love. You've got my heart wrapped around yours now, and there's no way I know of to untangle it. So, what do you say we blow this Popsicle stand and get moving back to Delancy?" He saw confusion cross her face. Michael stood, moved out of the truck, and picked Emma up around the waist. "Let's go home, babe." He smiled and kissed her lips lightly.

She nodded, as he let her back down gently. He pulled the duffle bags out of the bed of the truck, and swung the two lighter ones over his shoulder. He grabbed the one with the case of knives and they walked hand in hand to the beach.

Catching up with Mrs. Drury and Neil, they found Michael's brother held out some sort of electronic device, and walked slowly around the sand.

"What's Neil up to?" Michael asked, as they approached his mother.

"Beats me. He mumbled something about electric fields and away he went," Mrs. Drury answered.

"I can feel something. It makes my skin tingle," Emma said, holding out a hand. "Can you feel it, Michael?"

"Probably not," Neil said, and walked toward them. He kept his gizmo held out in front of him. "This is your portal, Emma."

"That's right. Bailey said I needed to return to the point where I entered 1815. When he took me back to the hillside, I could feel a strange energy pull at me," Michael commented as his brother walked up to them.

They all looked around, but only silence greeted them, except for the waves as they rolled to the shore.

Neil continued to look at his meter. "There's a tough part coming for you both."

"What are you talking about now, Neil?" Mrs. Drury asked.

"Emma will be able to go through the port with no problem. Michael, you'll have to hang onto her tightly and don't let go. If you get separated, Em will go back to her own time, but Lord only knows where and when you'll end up." Neil's eyebrows came together and he glanced at his brother. "Sound familiar?"

"Yes, it does. Okay. Hang on for dear life. Got it. What else do we need to know?" Michael asked.

Neil shrugged his shoulders. "This is all theory, right now. I don't have anything else to add, but hang on."

"Great, just great," Michael said, and looked around. "Well? Ready to give it a try?" He looked down at Emma.

She nodded once and turned to Mrs. Drury. Michael could see both women had tears in their eyes.

"I wish we could stay longer. I would have liked to understand this time better and get to know you." Emma moved toward his mom.

Mrs. Drury wrapped Emma in her arms, and they hugged tight. "Listen to me. Michael is a stubborn mule sometimes, but he has a good heart and will take good care of you. If nothing else trust in that."

"Thank you. I will," Emma said.

Michael watched his mother turn to him. "If you don't take care of this one, Michael James Drury, I'll find a way to get to you and kick your butt," she said, matter-of-fact.

"I know, Mom." Michael handed the bag with the knives to Emma. He pulled his mom into a hug. "Keep an eye on the geek. Make sure he doesn't blow something up. I'll find a way to let you know we made it." Michael looked at his brother. "Keep checking the website from Delancy, okay?" Neil nodded and shook his brother's hand. Michael laughed at Neil, and pulled him into a tight bear-hug. "A hand shake won't cut it today, bro."

"Good luck and be careful," Neil said, and backed away.

They helped Michael adjust the pack on his shoulders. He handed Neil the keys to his truck.

"Michael, what should we do with all your things in the storage locker and your accounts?" Mrs. Drury asked.

"What you don't want to keep, sell or give away I guess. I'm not sure what to do about the bank. There isn't much in there anyway. My last paycheck was deposited months ago. Would you mind contacting my boss and Jack?" Michael asked.

"What should I tell them?" She looked startled.

"Just say I've left the country, which is basically true. Tell them you're not sure when I'll return. Tell Jack...I don't know. Tell him to watch English cricket. Maybe he'll understand." Michael laughed. "You are my next of kin. I don't know what to tell you, Mom."

"Don't worry about it, loser. I think I know of some things we can do," Neil said.

"Mom, strike that about him blowing up something. I think he's turned into a thief and will work on dominating the world," Michael said seriously, but grinned. He turned to Emma who held tight to the duffle with the knives. "Ready, sweetheart?"

She nodded and turned to face the spot on the beach which pulled at her.

"Michael, remember to hold on tight," Neil said as they moved away.

Michael wrapped his arms around Emma's waist and lifted her off her feet. "Tell me if I go in the wrong direction."

She laughed. "I will not let you go, my love."

They moved in the direction she pointed. The air around them became heavy and out of focus. The next thing they knew it was black.

* * * * *

Mrs. Drury and Neil watched as the two dear ones disappeared. They both stood and stared for several minutes, unsure what to do next.

"Mom, that was too cool. I think I may have to do some research and write a paper," Neil said. He put his electrical device into his pocket.

"I almost didn't believe it. I thought for a few minutes maybe Emma and Michael were crazy, but what do you know? It really works."

Mrs. Drury and Neil watched the waves move up on the beach. A part of them didn't want to leave, just in case they returned.

Chapter Twenty-Seven

Neil finished his homework. He reviewed his figures and sat back in his chair, stretching. He started to switch his computer off and then stopped and leaned forward.

It had been a week since Michael and Emma had disappeared from the beach north of Ocean Shores. He hadn't looked at the Delancy website, feeling he should wait. He toyed with the mouse, and tried to make up his mind. He finally decided to pull it up.

Neil found the home page and immediately saw something wrong. His brows came together as he looked at the picture of the manor house.

"Shit, Mom!" he shouted, twisted out of his chair and walked into the hallway. He continued shouting for his mother. He'd gone to the top of the stairs and heard her come out of her room behind him.

"Neil, stop shouting. I'm right here," she said, and moved toward him.

"Sorry, I thought you were downstairs," he explained.

He stared at her for so long Mrs. Drury finally put her hands out. "What is it, son?"

He took her hand and led her into his room. "The website changed Mom. Michael and Emma changed the past." He sat at the computer, and pointed at the screen. He held up a picture he printed out over a week ago of the manor house and compared it to the one on the screen.

263

Mrs. Drury leaned over his shoulder. "What is that?" she asked, pointing.

"I'm not sure, but I didn't want to find out without you here." He looked up at his mom who smiled. "Let's see what the loser managed to pull off." Neil moved the mouse and went to a page labeled photos. They found a picture of the structure behind the manor house.

Across a small field from the main house was another home built of stones and wood. The caption underneath read 'Drury Cottage'.

"Neil, is there anything in there about that house?"

"All it says is the cottage was built by Michael Drury for his wife Emma and their five children. Wait a minute." Neil backed up and went to the search engine. He typed in his brother's name. A site appeared, about historical figures. "It says Michael Drury was a carpenter and mason... geez, he learned how to lay bricks. It also says he built furniture for many illustrious clients around Darlington, including several lords, dukes, and knights of the realm. Drury Cottage was the first home in the area to have running water."

Neil went back to the site, and they looked at the pictures of the cottage. There were several that showed the front and back of the dwelling taken from different angles.

"Neil, can you get that travel website?" Mrs. Drury asked.

"Sure."

"Good. Look for flights to England. I'll go get my credit card," she said.

* * * * *

By the beginning of the next week, Mrs. Drury and Neil had landed at Manchester Airport, rented a car, and checked into a hotel in Darlington. It was early in the morning when they arrived and both felt the jet lag. They were tired from the flight, but both wanted to go out to Delancy and have a look around. After a quick breakfast, they piled into the car and followed the directions Neil printed off the computer.

Upon their arrival at the manor house, they discovered that for a couple of pounds, they could tour the house. Listening to a guide tell the story of Mr. Delancy's good works for the community, they strolled around the rooms and looked for anything that might tie in with Michael and Emma. The guide said Mr. Delancy left some of his massive property holdings to a group of gypsies. Called Travelers, they started a small community of their own, which became East Darlington.

"When Mr. Delancy passed away in 1831, he left the manor and the rest of the property to Michael Drury and his wife Emma Wallace-Drury. Mrs. Wallace-Drury lived with Mr. Delancy as a child after her parents passed away from a fever. She was Mr. Delancy's ward until she married Mr. Drury in 1815. The Drury's built their own home in one of the back fields and didn't move into the manor. It remained empty for many years. In 1860, Mr. Drury helped his son, Neil, upgrade the house and put on a new roof. Mr. Neil Drury and his wife Catherine moved into the manor, and it has since been our home," the tour guide said, and showed a library area.

Both Neil and his mom stopped in their tracks upon hearing the last. Mrs. Drury raised her hand.

"Yes, ma'am?" the tour guide asked, smiling.

"Are you related to the Drury's?"

"Yes, Mr. Michael Drury was a great-grandfather four times over."

Mrs. Drury looked at her son and took his arm. He saw the shocked expression on her face.

"Are you all right, Mom?" he asked.

She nodded. "I think my knees are about to give out. This is incredible."

"Would it be possible to tour the cottage?" Neil asked the tour guide.

"You'll be able to walk around the grounds outside, but I'm sorry, no one is allowed inside the cottage at this time. If you would follow me, I'll show you the upstairs rooms." The guide smiled and led them up the stairs.

Neil's mind spun. In a very odd way, he and his mom were related to the woman giving the tour. As they went through the rest of the house, he felt in a daze and hardly saw the rest of the dwelling.

He tried to figure out which room Michael had been brought to when he first came to Delancy Manor, but he was stumped.

They went through the kitchen and out a back door to a patio where tables and chairs were set up. The tour guide said the group could enjoy a cup of traditional English tea and take in the gardens, if they desired.

Through the trees, Neil could see the cottage. He tapped his mother's arm and pointed. He squeezed her hand, moved away and left her behind on the patio.

* * * * *

She watched him walk to the cottage and look around the building.

The guide came up next to her. "That young man seems very interested in the cottage."

Mrs. Drury nodded. "Yes, he is." She turned to look at the woman. "My name is Elizabeth Drury. My family is... was related to Michael Drury."

"Are your Drury's from Cardiff?"

"The Drury's were actually my husband's side of the family. All he ever said about the Drury's was that he thought they came over to America from Europe, but he felt they originated in Germany. He wasn't very interested in family heritage." She glanced at the woman. "Our relationship to Michael Drury is rather complicated."

The woman went quiet for a moment and smiled. "I'm Eugenia Drury. I was born in Darlington and raised here at the manor. Excuse me, but you're from America?"

"Yes."

The two women walked toward the cottage. Mrs. Drury crossed her arms, and wondered about the tour guide's curiosity.

"Where in America?" Eugenia asked.

"The west coast. Seattle, Washington," Mrs. Drury answered as her son Neil shouted at her to come and look at something. "Sorry. My son's been jumping up and down for a week."

Neil stood at the bottom of the front steps of the cottage, and looked at a pillar. The two ladies joined him.

He grinned at his mom. "He made it."

She looked at where Neil was pointing. "Oh my Lord," she whispered.

The pillar at the bottom of the stairs was made of brick. One of the red squares near the bottom had the word 'Geek' carved neatly into its hard surface.

"Excuse me, but do you know what that means?" Eugenia asked Neil.

"My brother used to call me geek, and I called him loser," Neil said.

"What is your name?"

"Neil Drury."

Eugenia stared at him, and then slowly a grin formed on her lips. "I never believed it. You two need to come with me," she said, and started up the front steps of the cottage.

"I thought you said we couldn't go into the cottage?" Mrs. Drury asked, when they reached the front door.

"My family lives here. I don't like strangers lurking around inside," Eugenia said, showing them into a hallway.

Mrs. Drury watched Neil look in every direction at once. She glanced, too, and could see doorways and a stairwell heading up. There was woodwork everywhere, and although it wasn't signed, she knew Michael had done the work.

Eugenia showed them into a family room. Mrs. Drury and Neil both looked at a portrait above the fireplace. Mrs. Drury put her hands over her mouth and tears welled up in her eyes. The painting was Michael and Emma with three of their five children.

"If you'll excuse me a moment, I'll just be a tick," Eugenia said, and left the room.

They stood together and looked at the portrait. In it, both Michael and Emma smiled. Neil hooked his mother's arm but stayed quiet.

"This is so weird, Neil. I can't get my head to accept it all," she whispered.

"I know. Thinking about Michael living another life in a different time is really strange." He glanced around the room. "This was their home, Mom."

In another room, they could hear voices. They grew louder, and came toward the family room. Eugenia returned with a man at her side. Mrs. Drury felt her knees start to tremble as she looked at the man. He was tall with dark hair, and the spitting image of her son.

"This is my brother, Michael James Drury the fifth. He's the eldest of my siblings," Eugenia said.

"Eugenia says you're Drury's from America?" he asked, and then frowned. "Ma'am, do you feel all right?" He moved forward to Mrs. Drury and helped her sit on a couch.

"I'm sorry, I just... it must be the jet lag," she said, breathing in deeply. "Yes, we're from Seattle, Washington."

He nodded and smiled. "Well then, catch your breath. Eugenia, why don't you get them some tea and I'll go get the crate."

"The crate? What..." Mrs. Drury started, but held her voice when this Michael Drury put up his hand.

"We'll explain everything in a minute. Go," he said to his sister, and pushed her to the door.

"Please don't act like a prig," she mumbled as she went out with him behind her.

269

Mrs. Drury sat and stared at the portrait. "Neil, you do know this means Michael and Emma are both gone."

"In a way, yes, they're gone, but think of it Mom. He had a really incredible life. They had five kids..." he stopped and swallowed, "which means I'm an uncle or something," he finished, half to himself. He looked at his mom. "You're a grandmother. I would be a granduncle to these people... I think."

This caused them both to go silent for a moment. They looked at each other and laughed.

"Oh, my goodness. This is so strange," Mrs. Drury said, and put her hand on her cheek.

The other Michael came in, pushing a hand truck. On it was a very old wooden chest with a folder on top. He set the crate down and picked up the folder. He sat in a chair across from Mrs. Drury and Neil, and smiled again. "You've come a long way."

Eugenia came in, and carried a tray with cups of tea. She handed one to Mrs. Drury.

"We had to see the cottage. Thank you for allowing us to invade your home," Mrs. Drury said, sipping the tea.

"When did you arrive?" Michael asked.

"Just this morning."

"You did need to see the cottage. Are you staying in Darlington?"

"Yes, at the Cross Bow Inn."

"Ah, yes, the Martin's. They'll take good care of you." Michael sat back in his chair. "The reason..." He started to chuckle."Let me start at the beginning. Last year, we had a pretty harsh winter and spring. It rained like nothing I've ever seen before. In the back of the cottage," he pointed toward a wall. "The roof leaked, and when we discovered it, we found more damage than we initially thought we'd have."

"Michael, you're dragging the story out. In the master suite, one of the walls in a closet had begun to grow black with mold. We tore it down and were going to put in a new one," Eugenia continued, and got a frown from her brother. "In that closet, we found a small, hidden room."

"Yes, and in there we found some furniture, clothing, and this crate." Michael put his palm on the wooden box. "There was a note on top, which explained that it was put in there by Michael and Emma Drury, our great, great, great, great grandparents. When we opened it, there were two letters." He picked an envelope out of the folder, opened it, and took out the note. "This one says, 'These items were put here by Michael and Emma Drury in 1850. They should not be disturbed. Others from Seattle, Washington, in the Americas will arrive in 2009 or 2010 to gather them'. There's a little more, but you get the gist. Since it's only 2008, I guess you're a wee bit early, but who can figure out time?"

Mrs. Drury and Neil looked at each other.

Michael reached again into the folder, and pulled out a thicker envelope. "I believe this one is for you," he said, stood up and handed the packet to Neil.

The young man looked at the envelope. Mrs. Drury leaned toward him looking, too, and saw Neil's name and home address written neatly.

"Emma must have written this. I could never read Michael's handwriting," Neil said, and glanced at his mom.

"Open it, sweetheart," she said, smiling.

Neil did as she asked and pulled out several pages of folded notes. He opened them, and smoothed out the crease. He began to read silently.

"Read it aloud, Neil," Mrs. Drury said, and sat back on the couch.

"Oh right. Okay, it starts off, 'Dearest Mom and Neil'... I think Emma did write this. Sorry... 'It must be quite a surprise for you to see the cottage. I don't remember if it showed up on Neil's computer, and I've always wondered if it did eventually turn up on the Delancy web-site'," Neil looked across at Eugenia who smiled. "'Emma and I returned safely through the doorway, although we were spit out not on the beach at Robin Hoods Bay, but were about one hundred yards out in the water. Bailey and the Martinov's were on the bluff above the beach and somehow managed to see our return. There was another flash of light, Bailey said, and a very loud booming sound. I was so relieved I hadn't broken my leg again'." Neil looked at his mom. "Michael must have dictated this to Emma or he learned how to write well."

"Neil, let it go about the writing and keep reading," Mrs. Drury said.

"'So, the Martinov's got us into dry clothes, and we were able to get warm by the camp fire. It took a day and a half to ride to Darlington, and on the third day, Emma and I were married at the Church of England. The Martinov's and Bailey were our witnesses. We returned to Delancy Manor and Emma explained to Clarence as best she could about what she had been through to find me.

She was honest with him and told him of traveling to the future. I think he believed some of it, but for the most part, acted as though Emma had gone off her nut and would need time and patience to heal.'" Neil shook his head. He turned over the pages and frowned.

"What's wrong, Neil?" his mother asked.

"Nothing, I wanted to see if it was dated. I wonder when he wrote this," he said, and continued to read. "'Several weeks after our return to the manor, we learned that Emma was pregnant, and we both believe he was conceived in 2008 but born in 1816. There's one for the science books, Neil. The following summer, Neil Edward Drury was born. Emma has since given me four more; three sons and one daughter. They are quite fit, except for one and have their mother's wonderful looks and charm. Emma would tell you they all look like me. The debate rages on.

"'Clarence Delancy continued managing Emma's trust at our request. In 1818, when she turned twenty-five, the funds were turned over to her. My lovely wife asked the Lord of the Manor if he would sell us a piece of property in a back field so we could build a home of our own. Clarence was very giving and hence our cottage was built, and we have lived here, very happily, since. Home building was so much cheaper in the 1800s. I'm sure the men I dealt with in getting the materials thought I was quite daft when they gave me price quotes, and I laughed my head off.

Emma turned seventy-two this year, which makes me a spry eighty years of age. My leg bothers me sometimes during the winter months, and I've wished more than once we had ibuprofen. I wonder at times what the doctors of this day and age would think if they discovered the steel rod in my thigh. Perhaps it would become a story about a mechanical man.

Emma and I discussed it several times over the years, and we have both put in the effort to write down daily happenings in journals. In the crate...'" Neil stopped reading and looked at the wooden box. "'In the crate, you'll find our journals. Emma's are the ones with legible handwriting. We've thrown in some other items you might find of interest. Mother, the cameras you sent along, we used sparingly. We took a few pictures of the cottage as it was built, but mostly they're photos of our first three boys who were born quite close together. After the fourth or fifth year, the batteries died and the cameras were no longer useful. I hope you'll be able to get the pictures downloaded from them. Neil, you'll be proud of me. I took the batteries out of the cameras so they wouldn't corrode.

I've thought of you often over the years and miss you both terribly. I wish you were able to watch your grandchildren grow, Mom. My oldest boy, Neil, followed in my footsteps and has become an excellent cabinet maker. Some of the richer families in England have seen his work, and he's bombarded with orders. He's done very well. Neil has three children of his own now and several grandchildren.

The next two boys, Edward and Jacob, went off to college and became teachers. They are both nearby and visit as often as they can, with their families.

Our youngest boy, Jonathan, we lost early on to the flu. It was very frustrating being unable to do anything for him. He was only five years old. Emma had a difficult winter that year and did very little around the house. She was so sad and depressed. It broke my heart.

In the spring, we discovered Emma once again pregnant. Her spirits picked up, and in the fall she gave birth to the most beautiful little girl. She is Elizabeth Rachel, and I thanked the Lord above for a very long time for bringing her to us. If Emma hadn't gotten pregnant, I fear what the depression would have done to her.

So there you have a little bit of the history. The journals are probably very dull, but you'll learn more. Remember, always, how much we love you and wish this time travel thing were different. Wouldn't it be great if we could just pop back and forth? Enjoy the stuff in the crate and rest assured we'll meet again in the great hereafter.'" Neil finished, and looked at the words.

Mrs. Drury cried some, but dried her eyes and wanted to look through the box. She noticed the other Michael across from her, smile and he held a crowbar.

"I guess in some weird way, this makes you my great-gran." He continued to smile.

Mrs. Drury thought about it and slowly nodded her head. "You look so much like my son, you could have been twins. I'm not sure how many greats I am, but, please, call me Elizabeth." She looked at Michael again. "Do you know if the Travelers are still in this area?"

"Emma and Michael left some of the estate land to them along with what Clarence Delancy left. That's why there are neighborhoods built around the manor now," he said and laughed. "I don't know how you did it, but the Cross Bow Inn is run by descendants of the Martinov's."

"I know this is probably silly, but do you really believe a fortune teller can see these things?" she asked.

"Elizabeth, let me ask you a question first. Do you believe your son time-traveled back to the early 1800s?"

"When my Michael woke up in the hospital, several months after he fell forty-eight floors off a building, I thought all his ramblings were dreams he'd had while unconscious. Then Emma showed up, and I realized what he'd been saying was true. The hardest thing to wrap my brain around is..." she looked at Neil, "...we only said goodbye to them a week ago, and they've had a life and a couple of generations have been born," she stopped, and confusion took over her brain.

Neil took his mom's hand. "That's okay, Mom. I think I get it."

She scowled at him. "I know I'm not the brightest fish in the pond, but I don't understand any of this."

"Mrs. Drury," Michael said and smiled. "Elizabeth, there is another fortune teller in Darlington. I'm not usually one to believe in prognosticating, but she said some things that were correct, and I have no explanation for it. I saw her in the local market one morning a week ago, and she said that distant family members would show up on my doorstep soon."

"Mitch, you can be such a dolt at times," his sister Eugenia said, and stood up. "Open the bloody box would you?" She turned to their visitors. "The seer's name is

Martha. She's from the Martinov's tribe and is incredibly accurate. Did you want to meet with her?"

"If it's possible, yes, that would be wonderful. If we were going to try to get to the 1800s would we have to jump off of something?" Mrs. Drury said, and looked at her son.

"Mom, what are you thinking?" Neil frowned.

"I don't know. Maybe it would be interesting to be a grandmother. I could help Emma with the kids and maybe figure out a way to keep Jonathan from catching the flu."

"Mom, you said you didn't want to give up gadgets? Are you ready to give up your car and the microwave oven?" Neil shook his head.

"Let's discuss it later at the inn," she said, and stood up next to Eugenia as Michael took the lid off the crate.

They all looked in. There were piles of books, and in a smaller box, the cameras were wrapped in a linen pillowcase. Mrs. Drury said she hadn't brought the cables with them to attach to the computer.

"Let's go into the study. I may have a fire wire we could use," Eugenia said.

"Yeah, but will it be adaptable to cameras from the U.S.?" Neil asked, and followed her.

Mrs. Drury pulled out one of the journals and leafed through the pages. "This is so incredible. It will take a lot of time to stop my brain from feeling shocked."

"Elizabeth, why don't you and your son come out here to stay? Other than the house staff in the west wing, the manor house is all but empty. Or we have spare rooms here in the cottage," Michael offered. "Our parents won't be back until the fall. I'm sure they'll want to meet you and Neil."

"That's very kind, but I know our just showing up is surprise enough for you. We don't want to invade. The room at the inn is very lovely," Mrs. Drury said.

"Well, then you must have dinner with us this evening, and don't be shocked when my sister insists you stay. She's very spoiled and usually gets her way. She loves to call me names, too," he said.

"It must run in the family. My Michael and Neil always did."

"It's different with sisters."

"Neil noticed his nickname on your doorstep. Michael always called him geek, because of his love of electronics and computers."

"So, we finally know what that means. It's been the cause of debate in the family for years. He and Eugenia will have a lot to talk about."

Neil reappeared at the door and was out of breath. "Mom, you've got to see this."

* * * * *

They spent the rest of the day looking at the pictures. Michael and Eugenia let the visitors sit in front of the screen to see them better. Mrs. Drury laughed and cried and finally sat back.

"He looks so happy," she said quietly.

Eugenia excused herself to get dinner started, and Michael left the room.

"Mom, you aren't seriously thinking about jumping off a cliff, are you?" Neil asked.

"That fortune teller woman told Michael the doorway would be open until fall. It is a possibility," she said, and stared at the picture on the screen.

"Mom, think. I mean really think. It was a fluke or an act of God that Emma wound up in the right place and time. There are no guarantee's you'd make it to their time, and if you didn't, then what?" Neil said as gently as he could. "Besides, who's going to take care of me? I'm only seventeen-years-old, and I'm not ready to be on my own. I start college in the fall, and I don't want to take a chance on something and miss out on school. I don't want to act like a brat Mom, but I need you more than Michael and Emma."

She sat back in the chair and looked at her younger son. "You and your brother have always been such good sons. Your Dad and I never worried. The differences between you and Michael are so subtle, except for little things. You, Neil, don't do change real well. I'll make you a deal. Once you're into college, we'll make a try?"

Neil thought about this proposal. "After I finish my degree, we'll make a try?"

"That will be ten-odd years, since I'm sure you're going for a doctorate. In five years, we'll make a try?" she said.

"Fine, fine, in five years," he said, shaking his head.

Chapter Twenty-Eight

Sometime earlier at Delancy Manor

Emma finally got Jacob off to sleep. She gazed down at her youngest son, who would turn one-year-old soon. She looked across the room where Michael sat in an overstuffed chair with Neil and Edward curled up with him. He'd been reading a bedtime story to them and still read, although the two boys had nodded off.

Carefully tiptoeing across the wood floor, Emma lowered Jacob into a crib and covered him with blankets. She walked over to the chair. Michael smiled up at her. "Hey, papa, you have lost your audience."

Michael looked down at the two blond boys. "Dang. The big bad wolf was just coming."

"Maybe he can blow the house down tomorrow," Emma said, and slipped the book from his hands.

She helped Michael get the boys into their beds. As she finished tucking Edward in, she felt Michael's hands wrap around her waist. She leaned into his chest, and felt warmth on her back.

"Wife, do you realize how very blessed I am?" He kissed her ear.

"I believe I too am blessed. I have the most handsome and fertile husband in the North Country and three of the most beautiful sons in England," she said. She turned in his arms and put her hands around his neck.

"Hmm, maybe we should get to work on another little Drury. You know, planting seeds," he snickered, and arched his eyebrow.

"Mr. Drury," Emma said blushing. "You are an absolute scallywag."

"Yes, but you love me, right?"

"Always. I will love you always," she smiled, and stood on her toes to brush his lips with hers. When she pulled back from him, she saw a frown. "What is wrong, my love?"

Michael seemed to be listening to something. He let go of Emma's waist and went to the window. He looked out at the front drive.

"There is a coach coming up. Did Clarence say he was going into town?" Michael worked very hard with Bailey, to learn not to use contractions.

Emma walked up next to him. "No, I think he had some work to do tonight. Who could be coming this late?"

Michael held out his hand. "Let us go downstairs and see."

She smiled, and laced her fingers through his. They went down to the ground floor and met up with Mr. Delancy in the front hallway.

"I heard a carriage pull in. It is probably a message from Darlington," Delancy said, and opened a large front door.

The three went out and stood on the top step as the enclosed carriage pulled up. Mrs. Tharp came out of the back of the manor and followed them out to watch the carriage in the drive.

After the driver had the horses secured, he jumped down and opened the side door. He bent and pulled a double step down. A tall, broad-shouldered young man stepped down, adjusted his vest and jacket, and glanced up at the foursome. He had shoulder-length blonde hair, tied in back. He turned back to the carriage doorway, and held out his hand.

Michael grinned and moved forward a step. "No way," he whispered.

"He seems familiar, but I cannot place him. Michael do you know him?" Emma asked.

"Yeah, I do believe we know him."

A woman with graying hair took the proffered hand and stepped down. Her face was covered with netting from a pill box hat.

Michael let go of Emma's hand and went halfway down the steps. "Geek, is that you?"

The man looked up at Michael, quite seriously, and in a very deep voice said, "I present the Duchess of Attlees."

Michael came up short. "I think I've missed something."

The woman lifted the net and her eyes crinkled as she smiled.

"You son of a..." He flew down the rest of the steps."How did you get here? How is it possible? You must still be working word jumbles. Attlees? How stupid do I look?" He got the man in a bear hug.

"Very, very stupid, loser," the man huffed, and patted Michael on the back.

Emma saw the woman and recognized Mrs. Drury immediately. Her mother-in-law smiled up at her. "Oh...oh my goodness, it cannot be." She ran down the stairs, and embraced the older woman. "Please, tell me you did not jump off the forty-eighth floor?"

"No, my brilliant son came up with an alternate way. No falling from heights was necessary," Mrs. Drury said, hugging Emma.

Michael looked at Neil and squeezed his shoulder. "You nut. I suppose you worked your way through college trying to figure out the way to discover doorways."

"It wasn't really very hard. Once I figured out the mathematics, it was a breeze. My professors were stunned." Neil smiled and put his nose up, looking a bit self-centered. "I published a paper in a science journal, as a matter of fact."

They heard a throat clear and turned to the stairs. "Oh, Mr. Delancy," Emma said. "Please, forgive me. Let me introduce you. This is Michael's mother, Mrs. Elizabeth Drury and his younger brother, Neil."

Mr. Delancy came down and when Mrs. Drury put her hand out to shake, he turned it and kissed the back. "Ma'am, it is a pleasure to make your acquaintance. I thought, perhaps, Michael dreamt you up. May I ask where the Attlees are?" he asked.

Mrs. Drury laughed. "It is also very nice to meet you, sir. You'll have to forgive my son. He meant it as a joke. Attlees is a letter jumble for Seattle."

Mr. Delancy nodded. "I see. The Seattle over in the Americas? Yes, I understand now," he said. He turned to the carriage driver. "Please, unload their cases, and if you would like to rest overnight in the barn, I will see to it breakfast is ready for you at sunrise."

"Thank ye kindly, sir. I'll see to it," the driver said, and tipped his hat.

Mrs. Drury looked up the stairs and saw Mrs. Tharp waiting patiently at the top. "You must be Mrs. Tharp." She watched the older woman come down the stairs.

"I am, ma'am. It is a pleasure to meet you." The two women took each other's hands and began a quiet discussion.

"I cannot believe you made it through. I thought the passage closed several years ago," Michael said, and put his arm around his brother's shoulders.

"Dear brother, there are other openings. It's just a matter of finding them and working the science. I'll try to explain it, but doubt it will make much sense to you." Neil gave him a fake punch to the ribs.

Mrs. Drury looked at her sons and Emma. "I wish I'd been here for the wedding," she sniffed.

"Mom, you did not miss much. It was a very small service on our way back from the cliffs," Michael said. "I am sure Emma will be happy to fill in all the details."

284

"Good. Neil says I'll be able to stay a while. I want to spend as much time with my grandson's as possible." Mrs. Drury smiled.

"How do you know about the boys?" Emma looked at her surprised.

"It's a long story. We have plenty of time to tell you about the wonderful connection we've made in Darlington, your grandchildren times four, the Martinov's and a fortune teller named Martha." Mrs. Drury winked at Emma.

"Just remember, Mom, no modern amenities exist here." Neil arched his eyebrows. "There's no Mr. Coffee, and you'll have to air-dry your hair."

"May I escort you, ma'am?" Delancy asked, bowing slightly. "I am having difficulties understanding your son."

"You may, thank you. Don't worry about understanding Neil. I have a difficult time, too," she said. She took his arm and let him lead her up the stairs. Mrs. Tharp followed them.

Emma turned to the two men and crossed her arms. "I think when last we saw you, I was taller. It would seem you have added some height," she said, looking up.

"Hey, that is right. Since when do you look me in the eye?" Michael said, and bumped Neil's shoulder.

"After you left, I had a growth spurt and my voice changed again. When I was in college, I dated a lady who challenged me to go to the gym. Believe it or not." He grinned at them.

"I think you just took a bunch of growth hormones and steroids," Michael said.

"Ha,ha, I forgot how funny you could be," Neil said, and shook his head.

"I think I should go see about introducing your mother to her grandchildren. Excuse me, gentlemen," Emma said, and turned to go up the stairs.

Michael watched her go up, and then turned to his brother. "So tell me, how did you do it?"

"It took a lot of research, some study of magnetic particles, and... do you really want me to give you the complete scientific details?" Neil crossed his arms.

"No, I guess not. I will never understand it."

"Michael, I thought at first you wouldn't fit in, but you sound just like someone from the nineteenth century." He frowned and looked down at his hands. "I think Mom is going to want to stay, like forever. She will have to come back to the present time eventually. If she passes away here it could change the future," Neil said.

"Why would changing the future be a problem?" Michael frowned.

"If she dies here, she might not be born, which could jeopardize you and me, etcetera," Neil said.

"I get the point. Will I have to return eventually?"

"I don't think so. We met your descendants, a brother and sister, who live in the cottage you're building in back. In fact, we've met the whole Drury clan. It's amazing. You wouldn't believe the gossip about you and Emma. None of the Drurys who have ever done family tree tracing could find any records that you were a real person. It's incredible to talk to them and know we're all related."

"How do you know about the cottage?"

"It showed up on the website. We also saw the pictures you took with the cameras. It was so weird." Neil shook his head. "It was smart that you took the batteries out. The corrosion would destroy the memory cards."

"I am not sure how all this works. I have taken a few pictures with the cameras, but we just started the cottage a year ago and we are not even halfway finished. The time thing is not computing."

"So, the batteries are still good?"

Michael answered yes and creased his brows.

"We must have arrived before you thought of it or I gave you the idea. I am pretty smart, aren't I?" Neil laughed and pushed his chest out.

"You are still strange. How long can you stay?" Michael asked.

"I can stay until the beginning of September. My PhD program starts then. Will it be all right with Mr. Delancy if Mom and I crash here?"

"It will be okay. I can put you to work in the cottage for room and board." Michael laughed when he saw the look on his brothers face. "I know you do not do hard labor. Come on, you need to meet your nephews."

"I'll have you know I've been weight-lifting. You would have been very proud of me," he said, walking up the steps with his brother.

"Good, then I will put you to work. We must keep you strong."

They walked through the front doors of Delancy Manor and closed them -- for now.

ABOUT THE AUTHOR

Lauren Marie lives with her four cats in Western Washington State. She is the author of The Men of Haller Lake - Trilogy.

In her other existence, she is an amateur paranormal investigator. She has had many unusual experiences which have put in appearances in some of her stories. She is still trying to find a way to incorporate "Buddy" the ghost dog on State Street into a story.

Although, she has been focusing her current efforts in the paranormal romance and time-travel genres, she has also written general fiction and strictly paranormal.

55625853R00161

Made in the USA
Charleston, SC
03 May 2016